# GAGE LEE

# ECLIPSE CORE

## SCHOOL OF SWORDS AND SERPENTS BOOK 2

# THE RETURN

THE SCHOOL OF SWORDS AND SERPENTS SEEMED smaller when I returned for my second year. Three months of traveling around the world as the School's champion had shown me towering skyscrapers and sprawling neon-lit cities. The Five Dragons Challenge had taken me to the overcities of Kyoto, Ulaanbaatar, Moscow, Dallas, London, and more in all their lavish glory. I'd also visited the undercities of New York, Cairo, and Paris. The world that had seemed so large when I was trapped in my work camp had become a tiny place, its far-flung cities connected by portal networks that let me cross continents with a single step.

It wasn't just the School that had shrunk in my eyes.

Everything seemed smaller now.

"Thank you for your assistance, honored Officer Fezal." I bowed low to the Portal Defense Force escort who'd overseen my speedy jaunt from the Atlantis overcity back to the School. "I am in your debt."

"It was my pleasure, honored Champion," Fezal responded, with a low bow of his own. "It is not every day I provide transport to the undefeated warrior of the Five Dragons Challenge. Twenty-five cities and not a single loss. Most impressive."

My bow went a little lower to hide the flush that rose in my cheeks at Fezal's praise. I still hadn't gotten used to all the changes that had come with my rise to champion. I wasn't sure I'd ever adjust to being treated not as an outcast, but as a treasured member of Empyreal society.

"Be well, Officer Fezal," I said. "And thank you again."

"Be well, Champion Warin." Fezal stepped back through the dark gateway, and his portal vanished.

Relieved to be alone, even if only for a moment, I took a deep breath and cycled sea air through my recently advanced core. I'd gone from a child's foundation-level core to the more advanced initiate-level core during my time on the tour. That had increased my core's ability to store jinsei for later use and further refined my already advanced skills at purifying the sacred energy. I split the salt and water aspects from the sea jinsei, and the purified sacred energy settled easily into my Eclipse core, as secure as water in a bottle.

My eyes burned with unshed tears at this simple miracle. I'd spent my whole life with a hollow core, unable to hold on to even the smallest wisps of sacred energy for longer than a handful of seconds. Then I'd gained an Eclipse core, and everything changed. I'd become stronger than I'd ever imagined, more powerful than most of those who'd ridiculed me when I was weak.

Those memories stirred the coals of old anger, and my fists clenched into white-knuckled knots. I'd already beaten one of my tormentors, Hank Eli, during my first fight as champion. The duel had been a lopsided mess; the old champion had never had a chance against me. Neither would the others who'd stood against me.

Hagar.

Rafael.

Deacon.

Professor Ishigara.

Thoughts of revenge swirled out of my core and filled my head with dark images. This is what the *Manual of the New Moon* had called "the Eclipse nature" and what I hoped to master during my second year at the School of Swords and Serpents. Because if I couldn't control the dark urges that had haunted me throughout the Five Dragons Challenge, I was a terrifying danger to myself and everyone around me.

Serpents of light burst from my core and plunged into the sand at my feet. A patch of scrubby grass at the beach's edge blackened and crumbled to ash. The sea breeze blew the dark remains away, leaving no trace there'd ever been anything there at all.

"Welcome back!" Niddhogg called from beneath the torii that framed the path up to the School. His stubby wings flapped excitedly and lifted him a few feet off the ground. He waved both his front claws at me, and I couldn't help but grin.

I banished my hungry serpents and let the sea breeze wash through my core a final time. When I exhaled, I let go of the bad old memories and the rage they'd ignited. Experience during the tour had taught me the fires of that black rage would only burn me if left unchecked. Better to focus on the future and leave the past behind me.

Because the Eclipse core had already claimed a high price for the power it had granted me. I didn't ever want anyone to pay it again.

"Coming," I called out to Niddhogg, and raced the first rays of dawn's light up the path to meet him.

"How's my favorite dragon doing?" I scratched the ruff of bristly scales between the dragon's nubs of horns.

"Not as good as you, apparently," the black dragon said with a lopsided grin. "I've been stuck in this dump while you've been out showing off for the crowds. I must have watched you beat a hundred contenders."

I blushed so hard I thought my cheeks had caught fire.

"You watched me fight?" I'd done my best to pretend the cameras and castcrystals weren't there while I was in the ring. The only person I'd hoped would see me was my mom, and her only because I'd thought she might come to one of the fights. Niddhogg's admission that he'd seen so many of those fights made me want to crawl into a hole and die.

"Everyone watched you fight." The dragon chuckled and jerked his head toward the School. "Kitchen's open. Let's get you some breakfast before the initiates arrive for their induction. Anyway, after what happened in Singapore, your ratings went through the roof."

Singapore.

My stomach tied itself into a knot at the memory. The contender with the jinsei weapons hidden in the folds of his gi. Those twin blades of pure sacred energy had stabbed straight for my heart.

I'd never been so scared.

Or so furious.

"There were some good contenders." I pivoted the conversation away from that horrible day. "A couple of them almost took me down."

"Bah." The black dragon scoffed at the idea. "A few of them made you chase them around the ring. None of them really had a chance, champ."

Champ.

I had something in my eye again.

"Who else is here?" It was time to talk about literally anyone else. My cheeks would burst into flames if the dragon said anything else nice about me.

"The Disciples of Jade Flame showed up a couple of days ago with their new initiates. Resplendent Suns showed up yesterday morning with the new headmaster. Most of the Shadow Phoenix upperclassmen came in last night," Niddhogg said. "Including Hagar."

That name made my blood run cold. She was the warden who'd nearly killed me, then exposed my misdeeds to the world. If she'd had her way, I'd have been bounced out of the School and straight into prison. She, and the rest of the Shadow Phoenix clan, hated me for refusing to bow down to the people who wanted me to fail.

Thinking about the warden and what she'd done threw me into a foul mood. A hunger took root inside me, and I knew the buffet wouldn't satisfy it.

"Sorry, Nidd," I said to the dragon. My voice was tight and sounded unnatural even to my ears. "I need to take a rain check on breakfast. I'm not feeling great."

"Ah, man," the dragon pouted. "I knew I shouldn't have said anything about Hagar."

"It's okay," I lied. "I never really adapted well to portal travel, and all the jumping around has me off my game."

The miniature black dragon eyed me for a moment, then shrugged.

7

"Suit yourself, kid," he said. "If you change your mind, I'll be in there stuffing my belly with bacon."

"Sure." We'd reached the School. I gave the dragon another scratch on the head, then opened the heavy front doors. "We'll catch up later."

"Take it easy." Niddhogg flapped his wings and floated past me toward the dining room. He glanced over his shoulder as he went, and I gave him a fake smile and a little wave to send him on his way.

I bolted out of the main entryway the instant the dragon turned his attention away from me. My muscles cramped and my molars ground together. Reckless thoughts tumbled through my head, and it was a dark test of my self-control to resist them.

The urges had been coming closer together since Singapore.

Worse, they were getting stronger. I needed space to gather my thoughts and get the urge under control.

I willed myself to find a courtyard, and the School's shifty architecture twisted around me. Instead of leading me outside, the hallway funneled me down a rickety set of stairs and into a narrow stone corridor. The only light came from narrow slits of windows up near the ceiling, and most of that was obscured by thick blades of grass. I was underground, somewhere below the School. I'd never been there before, but there were hundreds, maybe thousands, of other places in the School's sprawling campus that I'd never discovered.

A curious chittering sound plucked at my attention. A black rat, fat and juicy, emerged from a hole in the wall. It perked up on its haunches and stared at me.

My Eclipse nature surged to the fore of my thoughts. Its hunger made my jaws ache and my stomach growl. I knew what it wanted, and I struggled to refuse its demand.

"Go away," I pleaded with the rodent. "Please, just go away."

The creature had other ideas. It sensed something familiar about me and scampered down the tunnel, sniffing the air as it bounded along. The little beast was so excited. It must have been one of the rats I'd bonded with last year. We'd been friends. Now it was coming to play.

I wanted to run away from the little guy before he got too close. My darker nature, however, had other ideas. The ache in my core cemented my feet in place.

When the rat was fifteen feet away, I crouched down and held my hand out to it. The urge was too strong for me to resist.

"Come here," I whispered in a shaky voice.

The rat stopped and reared up on its hind legs as if sensing danger. Its whiskers twitched, and it licked its paws nervously. The black marbles of its eyes were glued to mine.

For a moment, I hoped it saw the Eclipse nature that stirred within me. If the rat ran away, I could resist the urges. I could do that much. If it got any closer, though, I wasn't sure my willpower would hold out against my core.

The rodent dropped back to all fours and rushed toward me. Its bounding steps carried it to me like a puppy eager to beg treats from its master.

My Borrowed Core technique forged a connection to the curious rat in the blink of an eye. Our breaths fused before I was even aware of what had happened. My time in the arenas had honed my instincts and reflexes to a razor's edge. For the first time, I regretted just how fluid my control over my techniques had become.

"I won't hurt you," I whispered to the rat. The promise was a plea to my Eclipse nature to *please, please* behave. A heavy pressure built behind my eyes, and I knew they'd turned as black as a shark's.

Images of Singapore flashed through my mind again, as fresh and raw as if they'd happened just moments past, not two months ago.

The challenger was Thomas N'gaori, a promising young martial artist from the work camps outside the overcity.

It had all happened so fast.

Thomas had lunged forward with a double palm strike aimed at my chest. Twin blades of jinsei had erupted from the simple cord bracelets around his wrists in the same instant he'd thrust a clumsy serpent strike from his palms.

My mind had registered the attack a split second too late to defend against it.

My Eclipse nature, however, was faster than the speed of thought and reacted to protect me before I could stop it. The truth I'd hidden from everyone, even myself when I could, was that I wouldn't have stopped my core even if I'd been fast enough.

The contender came into that ring ready to kill me. And in the moment when he'd revealed that intent, I'd been beyond furious. If he'd only used a different tactic, some trick that would have immobilized or stunned me so he could score a point, it all would have worked out differently.

But that's not what the contender had done. He'd elevated the stakes in a stupid attempt to defeat the School's champion.

In the instant before his death, Thomas had looked at me with the same open, hopeless eyes as the rat crouched at my feet. He'd seen his death coming like a freight train and hadn't been fast or strong enough to avoid it.

"I won't hurt you," I promised the rat.

My aura filled with the rat's feral and animal aspects as our breaths cycled through my core. I licked my lips at the taste of the creature's essence. It would be so easy to pluck out its core. No more than a moment's thought.

Just like Thomas N'gaori.

Alive, vital, one moment.

A dead husk the next.

No.

Killing was too easy. I wouldn't give in to that urge again. I was the master of my core, not the other way around.

I forced my body to obey my command, lowered my hand to my side, and stood up.

The rat squeaked and rushed off, frightened by the exuberant footsteps headed down the old passageway.

"What are you doing down here?" Clem, one of the few people in the School who'd stood by me after I'd been labelled a thief, called out. I was relieved to hear her voice, rather than someone like Hagar. I didn't need any more stress while I was wrestling with my Eclipse nature. "We've been looking all over for you!"

"Could you have found a creepier place to hang out?" Eric, a member of the Resplendent Suns who'd befriended me along with Clem, practically shouted the question at me.

Beams of light fell across my back and cast long, distorted shadows down the hall. I took a deep breath and pushed the urge down deep. That had been far too close. I waited until the pressure behind my eyes had retreated and then turned around.

Clem shifted the glare of her jinsei lantern away from my eyes, then slapped Eric's hand down when he failed to do the same. Abi towered behind them, his face hidden in shadow. Of my three friends, he was the one who'd been most disappointed that I'd stolen from Tycho Reyes. I hoped time had mended that fence, because I didn't think I could go through a year of his disapproval.

"I was looking for Hahen," I said. "I thought the alchemy laboratory was this way, but I guess not."

There was a kernel of truth in that. I wanted to see the ancient rat spirit again to thank him for the training he'd given me. There hadn't been time to hunt him down at the end of last year, and I'd regretted it ever since.

"He's definitely not down here," Eric said. When he wrinkled his nose like that, the diagonal scar he'd earned in last year's final challenge really stood out. "Let's grab some breakfast before the newbs arrive and get all the bacon."

"Buffet's open," I offered as I headed toward my friends.

"We know that, silly," Clem said. "When we didn't find you there, we came looking for you. It's a good thing you stopped moving around, or we'd have never found you."

Clem passed through a shaft of early morning sunlight that highlighted all the ways she'd changed over the summer. She'd chopped her dark hair off short and dyed the remaining spikes neon pink. She still wore the sky-blue robes of the Thunder's Children clan, though this year she'd added bold scrivenings that glowed with shifting white and pink patterns around her waist. Her robe's' style was also far from traditional, with no arms and a skirt slit far up to the hip on both sides. She wore bright pink knee-length bike shorts under the robes and a pair of rugged black jika-tabi with glowing white laces and chunky soles that added an inch to her height.

"You look awesome," I said. She really did. The look suited her more than I would have expected.

"And how do I look?" Abi razzed me. He'd grown over the summer and seemed more like a full-grown man than the tall teenager he'd been the last time I'd seen him. His smile lit up his face when he spoke, even though it didn't reach his probing eyes. His robes were far more utilitarian than Clem's and didn't look anything like the gear of the Titans of Majestic Stone he usually sported.

"You're in the Portal Defense Force?" I asked when I recognized the white and gray uniform as the same style Fezal had worn. "I didn't know they allowed students to sign up for that duty."

"You made things very interesting when you discovered the emissary from the Locust Court," Abi said. "And the anti-Flame protests have everyone on edge. The school staff and the Empyreal Council decided it was best to have a junior force here on campus until we're sure there are no other hungry spirits lurking about."

My Eclipse nature stirred at his words, and I faked a cough to hide the darkness I knew had flickered across my eyes. I'd defeated the Locust Court spirit by pulling a part of it into my core. A part I still battled every day.

I was very close to being one of the hungry spirits they were all worried about.

"Let's eat," I said with a forced smile.

"Finally." Eric let out a long, melodramatic sigh. He spun on his heel and headed for the stairs.

Clem snorted with laughter and followed after the Resplendent Sun, while Abi and I took up the rear of our little group.

The Titan eyed me as we headed back to the dining hall. Finally, I couldn't take it anymore.

"Something bothering you?" I asked, more sharply than intended.

"My friend is unhappy," he said, clapping a hand on my shoulder. "And that bothers me."

"I'm the happiest I've ever been," I said. "Honestly, Abi, I'm doing great."

My friend's dark eyes probed mine as we walked, and I felt the weight of his attention fall across my aura like a damp towel. For a moment, I wondered if his senses had penetrated the veil wrapped around my core.

"Ah, Jace," Abi said. He squeezed my shoulder firmly, offering his support. "No man can be truly happy until he is at peace with himself."

We'd reached the main hall and were suddenly surrounded by other upperclassmen who'd arrived ahead of the new batch of initiates.

"I'm good, man," I said to Abi. "Honest."

"You *are* good," Abi said, a strange emphasis on the middle word. He tapped his finger against my chest. "You are not, however, at peace. Those two things may be related. Tell the others I had to check in with my squad. I'll catch you at lunch."

He winked and backed away from me, swallowed by the crowd.

I was glad that Abi seemed to have forgiven me for what had happened last year. But something about his words chilled me, and I wasn't sure what he meant.

I shook my head and headed to breakfast, glad to be back at the School and unsure of what the year would bring.

# THE HEADMASTER

OOD HELPED KEEP MY ECLIPSE CORE'S URGES AT bay. It was as if a full belly tricked my core into thinking it was full, too. It was a close call between Eric and me to see who loaded up on the most bacon, sausage, eggs, and fluffy waffles.

"You two won't be able to walk if you eat all that," Clem said with a wrinkled nose. "There's a table over there."

We followed her pink hair through the crowd of other upperclassmen. I spotted Rafael across the room and couldn't help but smile when he ducked his head and looked away from me. He'd clearly watched my fights and knew that the next time we crossed swords, there'd be a very different ending from what had happened last time.

"Where'd Abi go?" Eric asked. "I thought he was right behind you."

"Portal Defense Force stuff," I said around a mouthful of bacon. "He'll catch us at lunch."

Several of the other upperclassmen gave me uncertain waves when they passed by. It was hard to get used to all these people who'd shunned me last year being suddenly friendly. On the one hand, I knew they weren't sincere, they were just sucking up to the

School's champion. On the other hand, the attention really was nice.

"The trial's not even going to happen until the end of the school year," Clem said as she took her seat. Her plate was mostly fresh fruits and berries, with a sprinkling of crispy-skinned fried donut holes covered in a sugar glaze. "Grayson's convinced the judiciary he needs more time to prepare his case because he's had so much trouble getting a lawyer to take him on as a client. What with the assassins and the anti-Flame stuff."

Clem rolled her eyes at that last, like it was the most ridiculous thing she'd ever heard.

After he'd been arrested and hauled off to a holding cell awaiting trial, Grayson Bishop had insisted his life was in danger. He blamed me for upsetting the pact he'd made with the Locust Court and insisted the hungry spirits would kill him before they'd let him testify. That had severely limited the number of lawyers willing and able to defend him in court. If there really were spirit assassins coming for the former headmaster, anyone close to him would be in danger.

"The hungry spirits won't kill him," I said. "Though they'd kill me if they got the chance."

My friends looked at me like I'd sprouted a pair of horns.

"Don't talk like that!" Clem said. "You're safe here. They've got all the portals on lockdown. No one can come in or out of the School without security knowing about it."

I shoveled in a forkful of syrup-drenched waffles and chased it with half a sausage patty. I hid my disagreement with Clem's thoughts behind an unnecessarily long drink of orange juice.

Everyone insisted the emissary I'd killed last year was the only member of the Locust Court who'd made it past the Far Horizon portals. Of course, before I'd ripped the core out of that hungry spirit, everyone had insisted there were no members of the Court on this side of the portals at all.

If the headmaster of the most prestigious Empyreal martial arts school had been in contact with renegade spirits, anything was possible. That's part of what had sparked the anti-Flame protests and attacks. We'd been promised we were safe after the Utter War. That didn't seem like much of a guarantee after what I'd uncovered.

A loud chime rang through the dining hall, saving me from any further conversation on the subject.

"Oh, man." Eric groaned and shoved his plate back. "I'm still starving."

"Then keep eating," Clem said as she popped a doughnut hole into her mouth. Sugary crumbs clung to her pink-glossed lips for a moment, and she licked them away with a quick swipe of her tongue. "That wasn't the end-of-meal chime."

We didn't have to wonder about the bell for long, because the dining hall's doors flew open a moment later to reveal a flood of new initiates. They rushed in, eyes wide and mouths hanging open as they tried to take in every detail of their surroundings. They were only a year younger than me, but their rambunctious entrance made them seem like children.

"There are so few of them." Clem grinned at me. "You did your job too well."

Eric laughed, and I grimaced. Beating the School's champion was a sure way to gain admission, or higher ranks if you were an upperclassman, but no one had gotten past me during the whole Five Dragons Challenge. Even Hank, one of the School's most famous former champions, had been beaten, and not just by me.

Of course, he'd also seriously injured dozens of other contenders on Grayson Bishop's orders.

I'd only killed one.

"I was just following the rules," I said to Clem. "Maybe this year's contenders just weren't very good."

"What about that one?" Clem asked and speared her fork over my shoulder.

I twisted in my seat to find an initiate waving at me from across the room. The girl was very short, less than five feet tall, with sharp elfin features and long smooth black hair she wore braided over one shoulder. Her robes marked her as one of the Disciples of Jade Flame, the only clan that wasn't assayed by the school when they arrived. I remembered her from Dallas. She was one of the contenders I'd beaten most easily. I gave her an offhanded wave and turned my attention back to Clem.

"That's Rachel Lu. I'm not sure why she's here," I admitted. "I dropped her in the first ten seconds."

"Doesn't look like she has any hard feelings toward you about it," Clem said and harpooned a raspberry on the tines of her fork. "You really were something out there, Jace."

"I've never seen anything like it," Eric agreed. He washed his pancakes down with a gulp of milk so cold condensation rolled down the glass like beads. "You're going to have to teach me some of those moves."

I chuckled nervously at the request. To those who'd watched me fight, I'd seemed faster, more agile, and stronger than my opponents. From the audience's point of view, they saw flashing serpents, careful blocks, and stunning strikes that dismantled my opponents with skill and ease.

I wondered how they'd feel if they knew the truth.

No, I wouldn't be teaching Eric any of my tricks.

"We'll see," I said. "Remember, most of my fights were against newbies who didn't have any training at all. I probably could have—"

"Greetings, initiates and upperclassmen," a tall, slender woman with a mane of fiery red hair called out as she entered the dining room behind the flood of initiates. "As I'm sure you're all aware, Sage Bishop will not be joining us as headmaster this year."

She paused for a moment to let the Resplendent Suns clan grumble and the Disciples of Jade Flame cheer before she continued.

"I will be stepping into Sage Bishop's shoes for the year." She nodded and smiled easily at the uncertain applause from the rest of us. "As I'm sure you're all aware, the circumstances surrounding the School of Swords and Serpents have not been, to put it mildly, well received. As a result, the adjudicators have assigned me to help restore order to our campus and ensure there are no repeats of last year's unfortunate events."

"So, she's the one," Clem said with a frown. "Mother told me they were sending a disciplinarian to crack down. That explains the Portal Defense Force presence."

"My name is Morgan Cruzal," the woman said. "I will be your new headmistress. In order to avoid any further unfortunate events at the School, we have implemented several new rules this year. You will also find curfews posted for initiates, restrictions on techniques, and other safety codes posted in the common areas. Please review and remember them."

That drew groans from most of the upperclassmen.

"But, first," Headmistress Cruzal said, "I'd like to take a moment to congratulate our champion for his perfect record during the tour of the Five Dragons Challenge."

The headmistress crossed the dining room with flowing steps that carried her to me far more quickly than I would've thought possible. Her long, thin fingers closed warmly over my left shoulder, and I couldn't help but return her beaming smile.

"Initiates, this is Mr. Jace Warin." She gave my shoulder a gentle squeeze and pulled me closer to her side. Her ornate gray robes did nothing to shield me from her warmth. It was like standing too close to a working stove. "Mr. Warin served the School better than any champion in my memory. We would all do well to follow his example this year."

She stepped back from me, and I was struck by just how beautiful she really was. When she smiled at me, I felt the first glimmers of something I'd been searching for since the first day I stepped through the School's front doors.

Acceptance.

She put her hands together with vigorous applause. I basked in the warmth of her praise, then felt my cheeks redden as the other students stood from their tables to join her. Everyone was looking at me with what seemed like real pride.

For the first time in my life, I didn't feel like an outsider.

# THE ROOMS

WHILE THE NEW CLASS OF STUDENTS scrambled to grab their food before they were yanked away to get their clan assignments from Mama Weaver, the rest of us finished our breakfast at a much more leisurely pace. We didn't have classes the first day back, which left my friends and me free to do whatever we wanted.

What Eric and I wanted to do was eat.

"Will you two finish stuffing your faces so we can go look at our rooms?" Clem asked. "I'm so excited to see where we'll be staying this year."

"We saw the dorm towers last year," I said. "They weren't very exciting."

"You saw the initiate dormitory towers," Clem corrected me. "Rooms for upperclassmen are much nicer."

That was news to me. I'd been expecting to return to the same narrow room I'd lived in last school year. Whatever the upperclassmen dorms were like had to be better than that uncomfortable cell.

"Well, now I'm excited," I said and pushed back my empty plate.

"I guess I've had enough." Eric leaned back in his chair and patted his hands on his flat stomach. "Hard to keep my girlish figure eating like a horse."

"More like a bull," Clem teased. She pushed back from the table, and I gathered up the plates.

"You don't have to do that," Eric said.

"It's not a big deal," I said. "The staff has more than enough to worry about with the new initiates and the new security. Dumping our plates into the bus buckets by the door won't kill me."

I headed across the dining room, nodding and waving back at my fellow students. This felt like a dream. For the thousandth time, I wished I could share it with my mother.

Unfortunately, she was still in hiding, worried about what the Disciples would do after I'd defied Tycho Reyes. I was sure that danger was behind us, thanks to Adjudicator Hark, but my mother had no way of knowing that. Even with the School's help, I hadn't been able to get word to her during the Five Dragons Challenge.

I considered asking Clem if her family could help me find mine. As a member of the judiciary, her mother had resources I could only imagine. That seemed a little greedy, though. Her mother had already kept me out of prison and had me named School Champion. Asking for more might be pushing it.

I dumped the plates in the bus buckets next to the door, then turned to follow Clem and Eric out of the dining hall.

And almost ran into Rafael on his way back from the buffet line.

The Disciple dodged around me, eyes averted, and crashed into Rachel Lu, who'd been headed in my direction with a big smile on her face.

"Watch where you're going!" Rafael boomed at the initiate.

The scrawny girl bounced off the Disciple, who gave her a hard shove. Her feet slipped out from under her, sending her crashing toward the floor with her black braid whipping through the air.

I dropped to one knee and caught the girl's shoulders before she could hit the tiled floor. I helped her back to her feet, then lunged after Rafael as he tried to escape into the crowd. My fingers closed around his collar and dragged him back to the girl with me.

"Apologize for that," I demanded of him as I gave the girl a quick glance to make sure she wasn't badly injured. "You should treat members of your own clan better than that."

"I'm not apologizing to her..." Rafael started, but the rest of his sentence died on his lips when he saw my dark glare.

"I'm sorry," he muttered.

"For what?" I said.

"For knocking you over." Rafael forced the words through gritted teeth and glowered at the new student.

"Thank you," I said, and patted him on the shoulder. I leaned in close so only he could hear the rest of my words. "I catch you doing anything like that again, and it's a duel. Understand?"

He nodded, and I squeezed his shoulder to make sure he got the point. I didn't let up until Rafael winced and nodded again.

"Thanks!" the girl I'd saved said as she vanished into the dining hall's crowd.

I waved over my shoulder and hustled to catch up to my friends. I wasn't in the mood to fight Rafael, but I also wasn't going to let him bully younger students. I'd suffered with that enough, and no one else would have to while I was around.

"Oh, there you are," Clem said as I stepped up beside her on the stairs from the main hall. "Like I was telling Eric, the quarters are still divided by clan. We all share a common area, though. They used it for duels a lot, but that's been banned this year. Along with the challenges."

"Seriously?" Eric asked. "No duels or class rankings?"

"Nope," Clem confirmed. "Mom says the sages decided we weren't doing any of that this year. I guess the big focus is on working together in harmony, not competition."

That made sense to me. The clans were all in an uproar after what had happened last year. The anti-Flame protests hadn't helped matters, either. The sages needed to pull the Empyreals back together, not push us further apart with competitions.

"That sucks," Eric said. "This was going to be my year to be the top-ranked student."

"Sure it was," I teased. "Did you forget I was here?"

Clem laughed at that, and Eric snorted.

We walked in silence until the School finally took pity on us and dumped us out into an open chamber the size of our exercise yard. Eight hallways led off it, like spokes from a wheel. Other students had gathered in small knots all over the room, friends renewing their acquaintances, rivals sizing one another up. I didn't recognize most of the students and realized just how many more upperclassmen there were compared to the initiates. We had to outnumber them at least a hundred to one.

My eyes drifted across the students that surrounded me, searching for potential threats. The dark urge wanted me to find Deacon and let him know I hadn't forgotten or forgiven that he'd tried to murder me last year. He needed to know—

"Hey, Warin," a harsh voice called out.

"Oh, no," Clem said.

Hagar stomped across the room toward me. She wore the same tight-fitting black robes as the rest of the Shadow Phoenixes, a stark contrast to her shocking red hair. Hagar had shaved the sides of her scalp down to the skin over the summer, transforming her once long, curly mane into a wavy Mohawk down the center of her skull.

"Yeah, you." She stormed through the room, and I remembered our fight from the year before. I tensed when she reached me and tapped my chest with a red-lacquered nail.

"What do you want, Hagar?" My Eclipse nature urged me to strike first and take the threat out before she could attack. I almost gave in.

"Welcome back," the warden said with a devilish smirk. Before I could react, she threw her arms around my neck and squeezed me into a tight hug. She lowered her voice, her lips only inches from my ear. "We should talk. Later. Alone."

She clicked her teeth next to my ear, a sharp snapping sound that made me jump.

She pushed back from me, her hands on my shoulders, and winked.

"Seeya around, champ."

Clem and Eric watched her go, jaws hanging open.

"Well, that was not what I expected," Eric said.

27

"I thought she was going to kill you," Clem confessed. "You must be pretty popular with your clan to warrant a hug from Hagar."

"I guess so," I said, confused. The last time I'd spoken with any member of the Shadow Phoenix clan, they'd made it clear I was persona non grata. They'd been running a long con on the other clans, pretending to be weak while they built up a hidden power base, and my display during the final challenge of the previous school year had disrupted that plan. I'd assumed that my showing in the Five Dragons Challenge tour would have further cemented their anger at my displays of strength.

Not that I cared what the rest of my clan thought. I'd spent my whole life getting kicked in the teeth by people stronger and richer than me. For once, strength was on my side, and I wouldn't pretend otherwise. It was time for the world to see what a camper could do.

"Come on," Clem said excitedly. "Let's check out our rooms."

I was amazed at the number of scripted items we passed on our way through the common room. Instead of lighting fixtures, there were floating rings of pure jinsei bound in place by scrivened anchor points on the walls and ceiling. A lounge chair lifted itself into position behind a Disciple whose tight green robes made it difficult for her to bend her knees, much less sit. She reclined in the chair, a contented smile on her face.

Complex scripts also surrounded the common area's many windows. When we passed from one side of the room to the other, the scenery changed dramatically depending on which way you looked through the windows. To the north, the terrain was dominated by snowcapped mountains. To the east, enormous sidewinders shimmered as they made their sinuous way over a shifting sandscape of towering dunes. And to the south, a jungle loomed just outside the window. Curious monkeys peered from their perches, and jewel-plumed tropical birds zipped from shadow to shadow, their raucous cries only slightly muted by the glass. The west wall didn't have any windows, but there was a wide passage that led down to a pair of enormous double doors that were also heavily scripted.

"This is unbelievable," I said. "I've seen some nice places on the tour, but nothing like this."

"This is one of the School's best-kept secrets," Eric said with a grin. "After the Portal Defense Force, the tax that most Empyreals complain about is education. The luxuries you see here cost the rest of our society a pretty penny."

As we left the common area and headed down a long hall, I thought about what Eric had said. We were the next generation of Empyreal society. Every citizen had invested their taxes in the School of Swords and Serpents. These luxuries were a constant reminder of that cost and the return the rest of society would want on their investment.

Suddenly, Tycho's machinations seemed much greedier than they had before. He hadn't only stolen my time to make himself rich, he'd also taken away from the time I could've spent perfecting my martial arts and becoming a better member of Empyreal society. He'd hurt everyone, not just me.

I'd always considered attending the School to be a privilege. Now I saw those luxuries for what they really were. A reminder of the debt I owed to those who'd paid for all this.

"The Thunder's Children clan dorms are just ahead," Clem said. "Try to behave yourselves."

"Are we allowed in here?" I asked.

The previous year, the clans had been engaged in cutthroat competition. Going into another clan's dorm hadn't just been forbidden, it had been dangerous.

"Oh, sure," Clem said. "We're not initiates anymore. No one's going to challenge you to a duel or ambush you here."

"Not even the wardens?" I asked.

"There aren't any wardens for upperclassmen," Eric said. "Geeze, you must have missed out on a lot of stuff last year if you didn't know that."

I frowned ruefully at that and tried not to imagine what else I hadn't learned while Hahen had me stripping down aspected jinsei.

The thought of the little rat spirit stung. My frown deepened, and it was a struggle to push the dark thoughts away. The last time I'd seen him, Hahen had seemed unsure of our future together. Maybe I couldn't find him because he disapproved of my becoming an Eclipse Warrior and he didn't want to be found.

I vowed to find the little rat and make it up to him. Somehow.

"Here we are," Clem said, and pushed open the double doors to her clan's dormitory tower.

It was even more lavish than the common area. Tiny, fairy-like creatures flitted up and down the hall, sprinkling the students with glittering powder that sizzled and popped with electric sparks where it touched them.

"Oh, thunder sprites!" Clem cried with glee. She clapped her hands together excitedly. "They say it's very lucky if they dust you."

Just then, a trio of the agile creatures swooped through the air above us and unleashed a storm of fine, glittering particles. Most of it landed on me, and I yelped in surprise as a hundred tiny shocks erupted across my scalp and down the back of my neck. My skin tingled after the surprising pain died down, and threads of jinsei spun down into my core.

Clem and Eric both squealed with surprise, too, and grinned. The sprites gave me another dusting for good measure, then zipped away laughing as I yelped.

The other upperclassmen in the hallway pointed and shouted with delight as the sprites approached them, turning their faces up toward the dust clouds and beaming with pride. Clearly, they thought a little pain was worth a blessing from the tiny creatures.

"I don't recognize any of these people," I pointed out to Clem. "Are they new?"

"New to you!" Clem shouted to be heard over the laughter and surprised yelps from the other students. "Last year, we only saw the other initiates and second-year students. Third years on up through adepts keep their distance from the newbies. Less chance of an accident that way."

It was hard to wrap my mind around what Clem said. Students spent seven years at the School. We'd seen less than a third of our classmates last year. If the other students and professors had a whole other section of the School to themselves, just how big was this place?

As it turned out, the answer to that question was very, very big.

The dormitory hall was fifty yards long, with thick wooden doors spaced evenly down each side. Scripted placards projected the names of the occupants onto the floor in front of each door. I had to resist an urge to take off my soft boots and curl my toes in that thick carpet.

"This is me!" Clem called out. The placard projected "C. Hark" on the carpet.

"It's perfect!" she exclaimed as she threw the door open and burst into her room. She raked her nails through her short pink hair and turned in a slow circle to take in everything. Eric and I shrugged and followed her inside, curious about just how special a dorm room could be.

Everything in the room perfectly matched Clem's personality. The jet-black floor was splattered with pink swirls of light that crisscrossed it like strokes of random graffiti. It wasn't carpeted, but it was soft and had a slight give to it, like a training mat. The walls were covered with moving images of giant thunderheads that flickered with silent flashes of cloud-to-cloud lightning.

A queen-sized bed dominated the far corner of the room. A mountain of fluffy pillows was piled on top of gray sheets pulled so tight you could have bounced an obolus off them. A closet on the room's left side was open to reveal neat wooden hangers that held a variety of clan robes, from formal to the new casual style Clem was wearing. A desk occupied the wall between the closet and the bed. A sleek laptop had been placed in the center of the desk's dark wooden surface.

"Is that one of the quantic models?" Eric asked. He was halfway across the room, his hand reaching for the smooth rectangle of what appeared to be polished copper.

"Don't you touch it," Clem called. "I bet you have one in your room, too."

"Let's go see!" Eric called. His excitement was infectious, and after we spent a few more minutes admiring Clem's room, we took off for the Resplendent Suns' dormitory tower.

The Resplendent Suns' dorm hall lived up to the clan's glorious tradition. Instead of carpet, the hall had dark wooden floors sanded to a satin-smooth finish, varnished with a translucent red lacquer that gave the wood a mysterious inner light. Copper candlesticks mounted on the walls shed artificial flames from scrivened wicks to give the hall a somber, yet somehow cozy atmosphere. The walls were finished with a rustic plastered treatment that had a surprising depth of earthen hues and made the hall feel as if it were an ageless relic from another time. Crouching stone tigers with manes of crimson fire had been placed between the doors, and they watched us with inscrutable granite eyes as we made our way down the hall.

Eric hustled from door to door, his eyes scanning the nameplates. The impressive doors were solid pieces of black metal with heavy ringed handles set into their centers. Unlike Clem's dorm hall, the placards didn't project the names onto the floor, but glowed like a fire above the doorways.

"This one!" Eric called. A lion growled and rose from its crouch as we approached the doorway. It didn't settle back onto its haunches when Eric glanced at it.

"No sprites, but we've got some killer guard dogs," he said with a grin. "Make sure you knock before you try to open the door if you come visit me."

"I'm not coming here without an escort," Clem said. "These lions look too dangerous to have loose in the School."

"More dangerous than open portals to each of the overcities?" Eric asked with a wry grin. "Your clan would shut all those down if they were really worried about security."

"It's not the same thing," Clem protested. "The portals the Children operate are for the good of the School. We couldn't get supplies in or out of here without them. My clan also pays for most of the Portal Defense Force, so I think we've taken more than our share of responsibility for security while the rest of you enjoy the rewards of our risk."

"Settle down," Eric said. "I'm only kidding. Come on, don't spoil the mood."

Eric flung his door open, and for a moment I had to double-check to make sure we were still in the School. The square bedroom bore little resemblance to the traditional and almost primitive hallway. The floor was a smooth stone tile etched with the clan symbol of a white circle surrounded by a fiery corona. A thick layer of resin covered the floor as smooth and even as a freshly groomed ice-skating rink. The bed against the wall opposite the door was flanked by a pair of chests of drawers secured with what looked like a digital lock complete with a thumbprint scanner.

A sleek black floating desk was attached to the right-hand wall. As Clem had predicted, it was topped by an exquisite laptop. Eric ran to it as soon as his eyes landed on the machine.

"I've wanted one of these puppies forever." He took a seat in the task chair in front of the desk and pressed his hand to the top of the slender laptop. The copper slab shifted and shimmered under Eric's hand, individual keys emerging under his fingertips. A vivid green glow shone from between the keys, and my friend started tapping away with a wide grin across his face.

"Where's the monitor?" I asked.

"In Eric's core," Clem said. "I'm not sure why they keep including the keyboards on these, honestly. We don't need them. Once the laptop is attuned to you, everything happens in your core."

I'd never seen anything like the quantic laptop. Almost nobody in the labor camps had been able to afford any kind of computer. The few I'd seen around the undercity now seemed hopelessly archaic next to the device Eric tapped on.

"You think he cares about seeing my room?" I asked. "Or should we just leave him here with his new girlfriend?"

Clem giggled and shrugged.

"Let's go see what you ended up with." She hooked her arm through mine and led me out into the hall.

We closed the door behind us and strode down the empty hallway arm in arm. I felt a sudden rush of emotion when I realized this was the first time she and I had been alone since last year. Before I could stop myself, a jumble of words poured out of my mouth.

"I missed you," I said. "While I was on the road, I mean. I was so busy, though. Every time I thought of reaching out to you, we were already on our way to the next city."

"I saw you," Clem blurted out. "In Kyoto, I mean. My mom wanted to make sure you were okay after... everything. We tried to get passes to come backstage, but security was too tight. There'd been another anti-Flame attack in the overcity, and they weren't letting anyone near you."

The stone lions watched us move down the hallway, eyes half-lidded, yawning and swiping lazily at the floor beside our feet. The weight of the constructs' awareness was heavy against my aura, and I knew they were far more prepared for a fight than they appeared.

"Your mom?" I asked, masking my discomfort with curiosity. "You didn't want to see me?"

"No, that's not, I mean, yes," Clem stammered and blushed. "Of course I wanted to see you!"

There was a moment of uncomfortable silence as we wrestled with the implications of what we'd both said. Whatever there was between us was too big and complicated for me to get my mind around. We were friends, I had no doubts there. Clem had stood by me during the worst time of my life. She'd never stopped believing in me.

"I'm glad," I said finally. It seemed the easiest and least obnoxious thing to say. "That you came. If I'd known you were there, I would have made the guards let you in."

"You were busy." Clem shrugged. "You had twenty fights that day, I think. I'm surprised you could stand up when it was over."

"Some days I couldn't," I said, glad she'd steered the conversation toward safer ground. "They had trainers and medics keeping an eye on me every day and night. Massages, saunas, ice baths, jinsei treatments—you name it, they used it to keep me going. It was nice, but man it was tiring."

"That must have been something," Clem said, her voice distant and distracted.

Had I said something wrong?

"Oh, there's Abi!" Clem pointed down the hall, her voice suddenly bright with relief.

We'd entered the common area at the same time as our friend. His white uniform stood out in stark contrast to the other students, and when he waved all eyes turned toward us.

"My friends," he said as he met us in the center of the room. "You caught me on my way back to the portal station after my break. How are your rooms?"

"Great," Clem said. "At least mine is. We were on our way to check out Jace's digs."

"I'm sure mine won't be as nice as Clem's," I said. "The Thunder's Children are of much higher status than the Shadow Phoenixes."

"Don't be a dork," Clem said. "All the clans are treated equally."

"Sure," I said, but we all knew that wasn't true. Even if the Phoenixes had gained popularity since I'd become champion, they'd spent years getting the short end of the stick. If my rooms were even half as nice as Clem's, I'd be shocked. "Hey, Abi, I bet the portals are way more interesting than my stupid bedroom. Wanna give us a tour?"

My friend took a moment too long to respond. He stared intently at me through the silence, as if looking for a secret I was keeping from him. Finally, he let out a faint sigh and shook his head.

"It's not allowed, I'm afraid," he said. "Security is the tightest it has ever been. I'm scarcely allowed to view my assigned portal, much less show anyone else around. Maybe when the protests calm down."

His scrutiny prickled my nerves, and my core wanted me to strike him down for the raw suspicion I'd seen in his eyes. Abi had been pleasant enough earlier in the day, but he clearly didn't trust me.

"Sure," I said, struggling to hide my irritation. "Well, we won't keep you."

"Thank you." He sketched a hasty bow and took off toward a hallway on the other side of the room.

"Busy guy," Clem said.

I nodded and tried to push the anger aspects out of my aura. Abi had every right to be suspicious of me after what had happened in Singapore. He wasn't the only one who watched me with wary eyes since that day.

I just wished he'd be more open with me. His secretive stares and cryptic comments were already getting on my nerves, and the first day of school wasn't even over yet.

# THE COTTAGE

THE SHADOW PHOENIX DORMITORY TOWER surprised me in a lot of ways. I'd expected the same sort of gloomy, dark wood walls and floors that had dominated the new initiates' quarters. Instead, the main hallway was lit by bars of ivory light shining from the ceiling. The walls were a pale cream color, covered in a faint pattern that reminded me of both scales and feathers. As Clem and I walked down the hall, the pattern took on a rainbow sheen of blues, greens, purples, and reds.

"This is different," Clem said. "I don't see your name on any of these doors, though."

She was right. Each door had its occupant's name emblazoned across it in letters that glowed with the same hypnotic hues as the wall. We were three-quarters of the way down the hall, and I hadn't seen my name yet.

"Maybe they kicked me out," I teased.

"That's not very funny." Clem frowned.

"It is, now," I said with a grin. "It wouldn't look very good for the School to kick out its champion after a record-breaking winning streak, would it?"

"They could still try," Clem said, her voice low and urgent. "Winning a bunch of fights isn't the same as winning people over. You think Grayson Bishop's friends are willing to let bygones be bygones after what you did?"

That question had haunted me throughout the Five Dragons Challenge. Every city we stopped at was another opportunity for an enemy I didn't even know to take a shot at me. And yet, no one had.

Maybe security had been tight enough to scare off would-be assassins or anti-Flame thugs.

Or, maybe they were biding their time until my guard was down.

"I'm sorry," I said to Clem. "You're right. I should keep my mouth shut about stuff like that. There's probably a line of people waiting to knock me down a few pegs."

"Hey," Clem said, suddenly excited. "There's your name."

The only doors that remained were a pair of ornate ivory slabs at the very end of the hallway, their surfaces engraved with an elaborate scene of a fiery bird engaged in mortal combat with a serpent of some sort. There was a nameplate to the right of the doorway, and Clem was right.

I couldn't believe it, but this was my room.

I traced each letter of my name, one at a time, and the illusory fire changed color as my finger moved through it. A wellspring of emotions bubbled up in my chest, and I bit the inside of my lip to hold it back. This wasn't the time to go to pieces over seeing my name in lights. Clem wouldn't understand how much it meant to me to have proof that I was worthy to be at the School. I'd look like a blubbering fool.

"Let's see what's inside," I said.

The doors opened at my touch, sliding back into the walls on either side in utter silence. I'd expected a room like Clem's or Eric's.

Instead, I saw no room at all.

The double doors had opened to reveal a shaded walkway that wound its way between serpentine rows of tall, slender trees. Curious creatures somewhere between a squirrel and a fox perched on branches, their enormous amber eyes fixed on Clem and me. The air that gusted out of the unexpected forest was clean and clear, a faint, crisp chill on its breath.

"This day is just full of surprises," Clem said. "Ready for a walk?"

"I guess," I said. "I didn't expect a portal here."

I stepped onto the walkway first, unsure if there were any defenses that might bother Clem if she tried to go in ahead of me. There were no stone lions, but that didn't mean something else wasn't lurking beside the path. There was plenty of shrubbery and undergrowth to hide a snake, or even something larger.

When we reached the first bend in the walkway, I looked back and found the doors to my private sanctuary closed behind us. No one would be following us.

More of the squirrel-fox things peered out from the tree branches as we continued down the path. They were soon joined by birds with jewel-toned plumage, butterflies with wingspans wider than my chest, and swarms of tiny creatures I'd originally thought were hummingbirds, but which turned out to be tiny dragons.

"This can't be real," I said. "Thumb-sized dragons?"

"Niddhogg's not much bigger than your thumb," Clem said with a giggle. "I've never heard of itty-bitty dragons, though. Or those squirrel things."

"It must be an illusion," I said and reached out toward the nearest tiny dragon.

Most of the swarm buzzed away from my hand. One of the little creatures, though, zipped over closer to me. The wind from its wings was cool and gentle against the backs of my fingers. Its tiny tongue, ruby red and forked, flickered out to taste the air. Golden eyes with slit pupils focused on me, and then the creature landed on the tip of my right index finger. It weighed less than a feather, and its tiny claws put scarcely any pressure on my skin at all.

"That is a convincing illusion," Clem said.

The tiny dragon puffed out its chest as if in pride, tilted its head back, and unleashed a thin thread of violet fire. Despite the flame's small size, its heat warmed my face and ruffled my hair.

"I don't think it's an illusion," I whispered.

Satisfied with its display of dominance, the tiny dragon leaped out of my hand and zipped away from me. It circled once around Clem's vibrant pink hair, then buzzed away to join the rest of the swarm deeper in the forest.

"The school must really like its champions," Clem said with a laugh. "I wonder if Hank had a room like this last year."

Hank and I had spent a lot of time together during the tour. After I'd beaten him during the first fight of the challenge, he'd tagged along to keep me company and helped me navigate the etiquette that surrounded the tournament. There were a surprising number of political leaders and entertainers who wanted to meet the School's champion, and Hank had saved me from making a fool of myself a hundred times during the summer.

But in all of our talks, he'd never mentioned any of the perks of this position.

"If he did, he never said anything about it to me." I shrugged. "Maybe I got it because I went undefeated."

The pathway spilled out of the forest onto the banks of a small lake. A bridge extended from the shore where the walkway ended all the way out to an island in the center of its dark waters. There was a quaint and cozy cottage perched in the middle of the island, its front porch no more than three yards from the shore. Like the School itself, the little building was a mishmash of styles common and exotic. I'd never seen anything quite like it, from its solid porch to the walls ringed by Roman-style friezes to the pagoda-like roof.

Clem and I stopped for a moment, just to stare at the thing.

"They gave me a whole house," I said at last. "What is going on?"

"You know what they say about gift horses," she said. "Don't look in their mouths or they'll bite you."

Getting bitten was exactly what I was worried about. This could all have been some sort of elaborate trap designed to lure me away from the School of Swords and Serpents. Clem and I had no idea where we really were. If we disappeared, how long would it be before someone noticed?

My Eclipse nature surged to the front of my thoughts, and I had to take a deep cleansing breath to keep from snarling. Clem would certainly freak out if my eyes went black and serpents burst from my core. I had to control myself.

And the urges that came from the darkest part of me.

There was no point in worrying about hidden dangers. If something dangerous popped out of the lake or sprang an ambush on us inside the house, I'd deal with it. I was much stronger than anyone suspected.

Fortunately, no one tried to kill us as we crossed the lake. Enormous Koi fish glided through the water under the bridge, white bodies dappled with patches of red, gold, and black scales. The smallest one we saw was at least five feet long, and the largest had to be triple that size.

"I wonder what they eat," Clem said.

"Curious Thunder's Children," I said with a wink.

The island was covered with a thick blanket of lush green grass. Tiny flowers the color of the pale blue sky over our heads poked up from the emerald blades in scattered patches. Ladybugs bigger than my fist took to the air on either side of the path as we made our way up to the porch. Their wings stirred up faint breezes, carrying the scent of the lake to my nostrils. It was hard to believe a place like this existed, and even harder to believe it was my home.

At least temporarily.

"Let's see what we've got," I said and opened the front door with a flourish.

The room inside the door took up the entire width of the cottage and was about ten feet deep. The walls were covered in cream-colored plaster divided by heavy wooden beams that joined the supports of the arched ceiling. Globes of light floated in the air, unconnected to anything we could see, not even a script to power them.

They drifted around the room, adding a warm, comfortable light that left few shadows.

Six comfortable-looking easy chairs were arranged in a perfect circle around a low wooden coffee table in the center of the room. There was nothing on the table, but I imagined a coffee or tea set would fit perfectly there. It was a nice space to sit with friends and relax away from the bustle of the School.

An imposing stone fireplace dominated the wall to the right, and a wide picture window took up most of the front wall. A trophy cupboard filled with pictures and memorabilia from past Five Dragons Challenges occupied the left wall. A quick glance showed me that, yes, there was a picture of me in the cupboard. That was embarrassing.

I glimpsed the kitchen through a doorway on the far wall and motioned for Clem to join me. I'd rather have her with me than staring at the trophy wall. I'd feel like a moron if she thought I'd had anything to do with putting my picture up there.

"Maybe there's some food in here," I said.

"Do you ever think about anything else?" Clem asked.

I stopped at the question, and she bumped into my back. I turned around, just inside the kitchen, and leaned my hand against the doorway.

The pink top of Clem's head was just below my chin. She looked up at me with wide eyes, surprised that I'd suddenly stopped. Her lips were the color of bubble gum, slightly parted to reveal the even white lines of her teeth. Her fading grin lingered in the upturned curls at the corners of her mouth.

I didn't know why I'd stopped. I just stared down at her, frozen in place.

"Yes," I said.

She blinked, cleared her throat, and arched her eyebrows quizzically.

"Yes what?" she asked.

"Yeah, I think about other things," I said.

Before I could embarrass myself any further, I spun on one heel and headed deeper into the kitchen.

I wouldn't be cooking any award-winning meals in the small space, but it was more than enough for a student. A refrigerator stood in the far corner, next to a tall, narrow window that looked out over the lake. Granite countertops lined the wall next to the appliance, broken only by four burners on a stainless steel plate and a microwave that was so clean I wondered if it had ever been used. Cabinets covered the wall above the countertops, and a quick peek inside showed they were full of spices, boxes of food, and a coffee set.

"Oh, they stocked the fridge, too," Clem said from its open door. "They put steaks in here. Good ones."

"I'll have to figure out how to cook them," I said with a grin. "Let's check out the rest of the house."

A single door to the right of the refrigerator led into a narrow hallway. A carpet runner ran down the center of the hall, its surface stitched with a big black bird with fire around its eyes and wings locked in a battle with a black serpent.

A staircase off the kitchen led up to the cottage's second floor. Every one of the steps creaked under our feet, a chorus of squeals and groans that filled the house with unexpected noise. We both laughed at how surprised we were by the noise and shook our heads at how jumpy we were. There was no one here to hurt us, no traps waiting to spring on the unwary. The cottage was exactly what it looked like: a nice and cozy place for the School's champion to relax alone or with friends.

This year was suddenly looking up.

The upper floor of the cottage was an open bedroom. The king-sized bed was situated at the back of the house, under a wide picture window. The wall to its right held a closet with sliding doors. I took a peek inside and saw a selection of sleek black robes draped over wooden hangers suspended from a rail. A small shelf above my clothes held my personal effects, including the *Manual of the New Moon.* I slid the closet's doors closed before Clem spied the book; she'd go crazy trying to get a look at the thing. I didn't want to go down that road.

A heavy desk of dark-stained wood crouched at the front of the house under another window. A laptop, clearly one of the quantic models, sat in the center of the desk's uncluttered surface. A black-covered notebook sat to the left of the laptop, and a red-lacquered pen lay on the desk to its right.

What grabbed my attention, though, was the golden envelope on top of the computer.

"Oh, that looks intriguing," Clem said. "Open it!"

I didn't need any further encouragement. Maybe it was a reward for being the only undefeated champion in the past hundred years. Maybe it was a letter from my mother.

Excited, I snatched the envelope off the laptop and turned it over in my hands. It was surprisingly heavy and sealed by a thick disk of black wax. There was no monogram or sigil pressed into the seal. With a shrug, I cracked the stamp and collected the brittle black remnants in my left hand.

The envelope didn't so much open as unfurl. Its top flap curled away from the bottom flap, and the other seams unfolded so quickly I scarcely had time to realize what was happening. In less than a second, the envelope had opened into an origami phoenix, its beak slowly opening and closing, its wings gently flapping up and down.

"We humbly request the presence of the School's honored champion," the phoenix said in a deep, sonorous voice. "Would you do us the kindness of joining the elders of the Shadow Phoenix clan?"

My breath caught in my throat. The elders of my clan had sent Hagar to kill me less than a year ago. But my standing in Empyreal society had changed since those dark days, and the power that had gone into creating this elaborate invitation could just as easily have gone into a simple bomb that would have blown me to shreds the instant I opened the envelope.

"You should say yes," Clem advised. "Seriously, not everyone gets to meet their clan elders."

"Fine," I said. "Yes, I will join you."

The world unraveled around me, opening and unfolding just as the envelope had. The cottage vanished, its simple walls suddenly replaced by darkness. The smell of smoke and fire filled the air, and when I spun around, Clem was gone, too.

# THE ELDERS

THE WORLD WHIPPED AROUND ME IN A DIZZYING whirlwind of sights, sounds, and smells. The rich scents of seared meat, exotic spices, and woodsmoke replaced the clean, clear scent of my island cottage. The bright walls of my bedroom had transformed into dark wood paneling with heavy velvet curtains the deep red of wine. I no longer stood on a wooden floor, but on a carpet so thick and deep I sank half an inch into its pile.

Most alarmingly, I was no longer alone with Clem.

"Ah, here he is," said an older man with a wispy gray beard waxed to a sharp point.

He sat at the head of a long table, an empty plate in front of him, his fingers steepled against his chest. Though I'd never seen the man before, the raw power that radiated from his form made it clear he was one of the clan elders. He appraised me with sparkling gray eyes, and his attention bore down on my aura like a hydraulic press.

There were other powerful men and women at the table. The three chairs on the left side were occupied by a striking woman with tightly braided black hair who looked like she could have stepped off the pages of a fashion magazine. Her robes clung to her curves in ways that made my heart race and my thoughts stumble over one another. She smiled, a dazzling expression that sent a rush of warmth through the chamber. Her dancing amethyst eyes sized me up much more gently than the old man's had. I scarcely felt the touch of her against my aura before she shifted her attention away.

The man next to her did not wear the traditional black robes of our clan. His pinstripe suit barely contained his muscular bulk, and the heavy gold rings on his fingers clattered against the tabletop. His tailored clothes and fashionable haircut couldn't hide the danger in his black eyes or the tension that held his body ready to leap into action at a moment's notice. His stare was as rough and abrupt as a choke hold, and my core writhed in protest at its unrelenting pressure.

"That's enough, Claude," the next man on that side of the table said. "He's our guest, not a threat."

"You're too trusting, Brand," Claude said. "This boy nearly destroyed our entire clan with his antics last year. I'm not ready to disregard the damage he's done just yet."

Brand rolled his eyes and adjusted his robes. His clothes were stiff with embroidered scrivenings, and power radiated from him like a bonfire's heat. No matter how he turned his head, his face seemed wreathed in shadows that made it impossible to make out his features. His eyes might've been brown, or blue, or green; I couldn't tell.

"Welcome to our little club, Jace," Brand said. "Don't mind Claude, he's paid to be paranoid."

"He's paid to keep us safe," said the only person seated on the right side of the table.

The elderly woman towered over the rest of the elders. Her long, slender torso was perched on a collection of skeletal mechanical legs that splayed out around her, taking up more of the floor than the table. She did not even look at me, instead focusing intently on Brand across from her. She shook her head, and the long mane of her gray hair danced around her shoulders.

"Mr. Warin," the man at the head of the table said. "Please, have a seat while I make the introductions."

The only chair that remained was at the table's foot, and I eased myself into it. My legs were still a bit wobbly and my head spun from the unexpected jump through a portal, and I was glad to get off my feet before I fell off them.

"I am Elder Sanrin," the man said, his tone surprisingly informal. "This lovely woman on my right is Elder Hirani. Elders Claude and Brand have already introduced themselves to you, and the last member of our illustrious counsel is Elder Ariana. It is our pleasure to welcome you here, to our private meeting room. I do apologize for the abrupt method of transportation, but the Portal Defense Force has been finicky, and it was easier to use our private resources than attempt to negotiate the unnecessarily complex public alternative."

"And, this way," Claude said quietly, tugging at his bushy sideburns, "no one knows you're here."

"Quite right," Ariana said. "Discretion regarding our conversation here is quite important. In fact, before we continue, will you agree to a geas of silence regarding everything said at this meeting?"

I wasn't sure what a geas of silence was, but it was clear I wouldn't get any more answers without agreeing to one.

"Of course, honored Elder," I said with a slight bow in her direction.

A coil of jinsei wound itself around my core the instant I said the words. It was terribly uncomfortable for a moment, then faded away to a vague throb. It only took me a moment's examination to understand what it had done. I simply wasn't able to discuss anything said in this room with anyone. My core rebelled at the idea, but it was a little late for it to complain.

"Can we at least eat before we beleaguer the poor boy with our demands?" Brand asked. "I don't know what time it was when we snatched him, but I haven't eaten in what feels like days."

"It was getting on toward lunchtime," I said. "And I'm hungry, myself."

"Then let's eat." Sanrin snapped his fingers, and unseen hands suddenly pulled one of the velvet curtains aside to reveal an open archway.

Young men dressed in black pants, white shirts, and black vests immediately entered the room. They each held a sword-like skewer of steaming meat, the pointed ends resting on trays supported by their other hands. Without a word, each of the men took up a position next to one of us at the table, placed their tray on the table, and drew a long knife from their belt.

I was the only one that flinched, and I barely restrained my Eclipse nature from lashing out at the weapon nearest me. That would have been extremely embarrassing, at best, and deadly at worst. I couldn't imagine how the Elders would react if an Eclipse Warrior suddenly appeared at their dinner table.

"Easy, Jace," Brand said from my left. "They're just going to carve the meat."

I blushed and stared down at my plate, too embarrassed to say anything. I'd never seen this much meat in one place outside of the School's dining hall, and maybe not even there. The servers quietly announced the names of their dishes, sliced meat from the skewers, and then moved one position to the right to repeat the process.

In a matter of minutes, my formerly empty plate was stacked high with thick slabs of herb-crusted prime rib, slices of picanha so thin I could practically see through them, bundles of bloody rare filet mignon wrapped in crispy bacon, and hunks of pork loin crusted with a layer of seared Parmesan cheese. Another set of servers, women wearing black skirts and white tops, swept into the chamber behind the meat course and deposited small dishes containing mashed potatoes sprinkled with chives and swimming in butter, spears of asparagus lined up like soldiers next to them, carrots glazed with a sauce that smelled both spicy and sweet, and tiny loaves of bread smeared with garlic butter.

"May the Shadow Phoenix bless us all," Elder Sanrin said.

The elders dug into their food without another moment's hesitation. As nervous as I was, my stomach goaded me into doing the same. I devoured bite after bite of succulent meat and savory side dishes, stuffing my belly to help calm my suspicious Eclipse nature. It sort of worked until the elders began speaking.

"Who veiled your core?" Claude asked without preamble. "No one's been able to penetrate it."

"I don't know," I responded. "It's been like this my whole life."

Half that statement was true. After the tribunal at the end of last year, the dragon Zephyr had strongly suggested that Tycho Reyes had veiled my core, though I had no proof that was true. Even dragons could be wrong, and I wasn't sure why the elder of the Disciples of Jade Flame would have gone to such extravagant lengths to protect my secret from everyone.

Elder Ariana skewered a nugget of filet with her fork. She fixed me with a cold stare, pulled the meat off the silver tines with perfectly white, even teeth, then chewed slowly as if considering my answer.

"He is telling the truth," she said at last. "I think. The veil is insidious, and it is difficult to read the boy."

Elder Sanrin idly stroked the waxed length of his beard as he considered this.

"The veil is a work of considerable skill and immense power," he said. "It is hard to believe someone would do such a thing without a very good reason. And yet, no one will admit to being the mastermind behind it. Perhaps that will work in our favor."

The other elders watched me patiently, as if expecting some sort of reaction. When I kept right on eating, they turned their attention back to their own plates.

The silence stretched over the table for an uncomfortably long time. The only sound was the quiet clink and scrape of cutlery against plates and teeth, and by the time I'd cleared my plate I was afraid if someone didn't say something soon, I'd burst.

"That was amazing," Brand said. He dabbed at the corners of his mouth with his napkin, pushed his plate toward the center of the table, and sat back further in his chair. "As always, my most sincere compliments to the chef. I see our guest has finished, as well. Perhaps it's time to get down to business."

He said that last in a tone that was either ominous or joking, and I couldn't tell which. The other elders glanced at one another, then at me, and also pushed their plates away.

"You gave us quite a scare last year, Jace," Elder Hirani said in a voice as smooth and soft as silk. "We do hope you forgive us for sending Hagar to... deal with the issue. But we really had no choice. You seemed rather intent on disrupting our plans."

"Because he wouldn't bend the knee?" I was surprised that Claude jumped to my defense so quickly. The man hadn't seemed to like me at all. "You can't fault the boy for doing his best."

"It's water under the bridge," Ariana said sharply. "We did what we had to to protect ourselves and our long-term plans, Jace. Unfortunately, your discovery at the end of the last school year has done more to unravel those plans than winning challenges ever could have."

I carefully placed my knife and fork on my empty plate. I really wanted to ask for more picanha but decided that would have been rude. Instead, I settled for the thing I wanted next most in the world.

Answers.

"I'm very sorry, honored Elders," I said, choosing my words carefully. "I don't understand any of this. I know I attracted a lot of attention to the Shadow Phoenixes last year, and that was the reason why you sent Hagar and Deacon to kill me. Honestly, I was more than a little worried that you planned to finish the job today. What's changed?"

Sanrin chuckled at my question and leaned forward to eye me down the length of the table.

"Jace, I want to be very clear about two things. First, Deacon was not acting on our orders. He's been relocated to another educational facility this year to learn the error of his ways. Second, everything has changed since our botched assassination attempt. You discovered a member of the Locust Court hidden within the School of Swords and Serpents," he explained. "You revealed one of the most important members of Empyreal society was a traitor and a heretic."

"Which embarrassed the hell out of Claude," Brand said with a smirk. "He's been hunting heretics for decades without as much success as you had without even trying."

"I am not taking the bait, Brand," Claude said. His hand tightened around his knife, knuckles popping loudly. "Jace was lucky, and Bishop was lazy and careless."

"I still don't understand." The combination of so many powerful cores and a belly filled with delicious, rich food had me feeling dazed and slow. "I don't understand anything about heretics or the rest of what you're talking about."

"Ah, we don't have much time. I'll give you the short version," Elder Hirani said with a warm smile. "Our forebears committed a horrible crime, Jace. We've been trying to undo that wrong ever since. We have agents scattered throughout Empyreal society. They are tasked with finding and eliminating threats to the Empyrean Flame. Since the discovery of the Locust Court's emissary last year, those threats have become more active."

She had to mean the anti-Flame activists. Protestors had vandalized government buildings and temples. The news I'd seen about the attacks never offered much information on what the protestors hoped to gain or even meant. There'd been some rumors of protest marches in the undercities, but I'd never seen one.

"It's a difficult and demanding job," Elder Ariana continued. "Primarily because our agents risk discovery with every mission. If an operative is revealed, they become useless to us as a covert asset."

That made sense. Once a secret agent's identity was no longer secret, they weren't much good.

"Our adversary has also gotten much cleverer these past months." Sanrin scratched his beard and entwined his fingers in front of him. "Their surveillance has become more sophisticated and relies heavily on jinsei techniques we haven't been able to counter. A single glimpse of an agent's core is often enough for them to identify him or her."

A cold hand of dread closed around my heart. I knew where this conversation was going, and I didn't like it.

"You want me to be one of your agents," I said. "Because of my veil."

Anxiety welled up inside me at the thought of working so closely with the elders. The veil had hidden my core from others, which was the only reason no one knew I was an Eclipse Warrior.

But if I had to work side by side with elders, I wasn't sure I could keep the truth from them. They were decades, maybe centuries older than I was, armed with skills I could scarcely imagine. They might figure out how to crack my veil. Or I could lose control of my Eclipse nature and reveal myself in a moment of stress. This was an incredible opportunity that was incredibly dangerous for someone with my secrets.

"Yes," Hirani said. "You can be a great help to us all, Jace. The anti-Flame activists threaten the very fabric of Empyreal society. We've kept the worst of their actions out of the public eye, but if we don't find their leaders and stop them, soon, things will spiral out of control. We need your help to stop them, Jace. It will be dangerous, don't let anyone tell you otherwise. But your work will save lives, and there are other, more tangible rewards, as well."

Every eye in the room was fixed on me. My core stirred, restless as a nest of hungry serpents. Even the amount of food I'd shoveled down my gullet couldn't calm it when I was so anxious. My Eclipse nature worried this was a deadly trap that would expose it to others. Neither of us wanted that.

"I need some time to consider it," I said. "This is a big decision."

"Of course," Sanrin agreed. "We don't want to rush you into anything. Take your time, Jace. When you make your decision, tell Hagar and she will convey your answer to us."

"Thank you, honored Elders," I said. "I will."

"I must also remind you that you are bound by a geas not to speak of this meeting to anyone other than Hagar," Elder Sanrin said. "We look forward to working with you, Mr. Warin."

And that was the end of our little meeting. Sanrin waved his hand in my direction, and the world dissolved into darkness.

# THE ARTS

I T WAS LATE AFTERNOON WHEN I RETURNED TO the cottage on the lake. My bedroom was empty, and when I called out for Clem, there was no answer. Not that that was much of a surprise. She'd probably gone down to get some lunch for herself.

That left me with a few hours until dinner to occupy myself. I looked around the room for inspiration as to what to do next and spotted a scrap of paper on top of my laptop.

"Sorry! I borrowed some of your notebook," I read to myself. "I got too hungry to wait anymore. Come find me when you get back from your meeting. I want to hear all the gory details!"

I chuckled at Clem's enthusiasm and boundless curiosity. Then I grimaced when I realized I couldn't tell her anything about what had happened. My expression deepened into a sincere frown at the thought of how Clem would respond to more secrets. She would dig and dig at whatever I didn't tell her until I'd want to scream.

It would be awesome to not have to carry around a bunch of secrets.

The fact that I was an Eclipse Warrior.

The fact that what had happened in Singapore wasn't exactly self-defense.

The fact that the Shadow Phoenixes served the Empyrean Flame as covert operatives.

And, of course, the fact that my clan wanted to recruit me as one of their secret agents.

Those dark thoughts churned up dark worries from my Eclipse nature and set me to pacing the confines of my tiny bedroom. That wouldn't do. If I didn't calm down, soon, I'd spend the rest of the day fighting dark urges. It was time to center myself.

I crossed the room, opened the closet, and pulled the *Manual of the New Moon* off the shelf. I hadn't had access to the Internet the entire time I'd been on tour. The trainers and handlers hadn't thought it was a good idea to clutter my mind with current affairs or social media, so I'd spent my nights reading, hanging out with Hank, and working out. I'd been dying to do some research about Eclipse Warriors, and now I finally had a chance.

It took me all of ten minutes to reread what I'd been able to understand from the *Manual*. Most of the book was just indecipherable to me, and I wasn't sure what would let me understand more of it. Armed with what little information I had about the Eclipse Warriors, I turned my attention to the quantic laptop.

The computer was far more advanced than the crappy desktops I'd struggled to use in the labor camp schools. My worry that I wouldn't understand the operating system turned out to be baseless. The laptop instantly joined with my core when I laid hands on it, and my vision shifted to show me a dark background littered with icons. I mentally selected the browser symbol, and the whole World Wide Web was at my fingertips.

With the sparse information I had from the *Manual of the New Moon* as a guide, I was able to research some more information about the Eclipse Warriors and the Utter War. The information I could gather was scattered all over the place, and it was hard to verify how much of it was true, but one thing was obvious: the Empyreals had been terrified of the warriors they'd created.

I finally found a report of a battle involving a small squad of Eclipse Warriors that helped me understand why the other clans were terrified of their defenders. It was frustratingly vague, but included a line that filled me with a mixture of excitement and dread.

"Alone and faced with impossible odds, the Warrior made his last stand at the portal. While the Expeditionary Shock Force from the Resplendent Suns retreated from the Far Horizon, the lone Eclipse held the portal against a host of Locust Court warriors for seventy-three hours before reinforcements arrived. Though the name of the heroine of the Dire Portal battle has been lost, her deeds will never be forgotten."

I tried to imagine that battle and couldn't see it. Even with a fusion blade and serpents, one Eclipse Warrior would have been torn apart by so many enemies. There had to have been some technique known only to those with an Eclipse core. Something that would allow them to survive a horde. I made a note to look for that, later, and went on with my research.

After the Dire Portal conflict, the handful of Eclipse Warriors that had remained on Earth were kept on military bases or in research labs. And then they'd been betrayed by the people they'd saved.

Frustrated by what little I'd been able to unravel of my real clan's past, I headed to the bed. I sat cross-legged on the mattress, the *Manual* in my lap, my hands on its cover, and began focused breathing to initiate my meditation.

The process was difficult at first. My Eclipse nature was built for action and didn't like the quiet introspection of meditation. Even with the *Manual* nearby, it took me most of an hour to settle into the calm rhythms that pushed jinsei through my core in steady pulses that cleansed my aura and emptied my thoughts of worries and fears. In the darkness behind my closed eyelids, I filled my core a little more with each inhale-and-exhale cycle. The sacred energy pushed against the walls of my core, swelling it, pushing it to capacity.

My Eclipse nature roused itself and demanded I do something with all that power. It wanted to hunt and kill. There were enemies out there that needed to be destroyed.

Rafael.

Professor Ishigara.

Hagar.

The jinsei I'd gathered during meditation fueled the urge to lash out at those who'd wronged me. Before I could stop myself, I shoved the *Manual* off my lap and lurched to my feet next to the bed. I made it halfway to the stairs before I regained control of my body and froze in my tracks.

"No," I said, loud and clear. "I'm in charge here, not you."

My Eclipse nature raged at the words and nearly broke free again. The jinsei at its disposal made it so strong.

With a shout of frustration, I forced the jinsei out of my core and into my body's channels. I poured it through my aura and into powerful serpents. My fusion blade consumed more of the sacred energy, leaving my core only half full.

That was better. My Eclipse nature receded into the shadows at the back of my thoughts. Satisfied my darker self wasn't going to rip free of my control and go on a rampage, I banished my serpents and blade and flopped back down on the bed, frustrated and worried.

I'd struggled with this all summer. To advance my core, I had to fill it with jinsei beyond its limits. But when I tried to do that, my Eclipse nature forced its way to the surface. Every time I thought I was close to a breakthrough, I had to break off my meditation and fight back the urge to do something horrible. It was a frustrating cycle that I didn't know how to break free from.

The problem tumbled through my thoughts as the light of the afternoon sun faded from golden red to the velvet purple of dusk. I was still no closer to an answer and closed my eyes to rest them. Just for a moment...

A shrill bleating exploded next to my head. The sound jolted me upright, and I bounced off the mattress and onto the floor in a fighting stance. My Eclipse core churned inside me, eager to fight off whatever had surprised it. Serpents burst from my core, and my fusion blade appeared in my hand unbidden.

The alarm clock on the nightstand next to the bed unleashed another shrill tone, and I groaned. I'd fallen asleep.

It took me a few moments to figure out how to shut off the alarm clock, by which time I was ready to kill the thing. At least I'd never have to worry about oversleeping and missing class with that obnoxious noise blasting in my ear.

"Five in the morning?" I groaned. Who had set my alarm clock for such an ungodly hour?

A dull booming echoed through the cottage. I went to the front window of the second floor and peered out through the glass. The booming repeated, and a faint flash of yellow-green light washed across the terrain outside my cozy little home. I couldn't see through the trees, but I instinctively understood the origin of the noise came from someone banging on my door.

"Ugh," I growled. The rich meal from the day before had left me feeling sluggish. I wanted to crawl back into bed and sleep off the meat hangover.

The booming came again.

"I'm coming," I grumbled.

I shrugged out of the robe I'd fallen asleep in and crossed to the closet. There were a dozen robes inside, and I flicked through them to find something suitable.

Three of the robes were long and formal, my name scrivened down the left lapel in glowing thread and the words "School Champion" embroidered down the right lapel. A double string of glossy black buttons ran from the high-collared throat all the way down to the hemline. Fancy, but impractical.

The next three robes were still long, but the buttons only went down to the waist, and they had a pair of matching black pants, perfect for more casual occasions.

The next group of three robes also opened in the front, with a shorter skirt that would have hit me just above the knees. Rather than buttons, they had a concealed zipper that vanished when they were closed. The pants that went with these were loose-fitting and comfortable, perfect for everyday wear.

The final three sets hardly qualified as robes at all. They didn't even have sleeves, and the skirt was so abbreviated, it barely dropped below my waist. There weren't even buttons or zippers. The super casual outfits were made from a fabric so stretchy I could just pull them over my head. The pants were knee length and made of the same material. Those must have been meant for workouts.

A sudden rush of excitement ran through me at the realization of what those were for. I snatched the exercise gear off its hanger, pulled it on quickly, and slipped my feet into the short black shoes on the floor of the closet.

The booming came again, and I rolled my eyes and took off down the stairs. The cottage's door had no lock, and it didn't need one. No one could get into my private quarters without going through the dormitory tower's front door, and that wouldn't open for anyone but me.

The booming came twice more as I ran across the bridge and wound my way through the forest. The trip back to the dormitory tower was much shorter than the trip to the cottage had been. I wasn't sure if that was because I was more familiar with the area or if there was some sort of time and space bending weirdness going on. It wouldn't have surprised me either way.

"You're going to make us all late for our first martial arts class," Eric said when I threw open the tower's door. "Let's go!"

"Lead the way." The doors slid closed and locked with a click behind me as I stepped into the hallway. "Far be it from me to keep anyone waiting."

Eric took off, and Abi fell in beside him. Clem and I followed them, and she slowed down to let them get far enough ahead of us that we could speak without being overheard.

"Where did you go?" she asked. "I saw the portal suck you away, but not where you went."

I wanted to be honest with Clem, but the geas would only let that go so far. I mulled over what I could tell her for a moment, then rolled out an abbreviated version of yesterday's events.

"The portal took me to a fancy meal with the elders," I said quietly. "They want me to work for them."

Eric's single-minded determination to get to class on time pushed the School's shifting architecture harder than I'd ever seen it before. We didn't take a single corner or go down any steps. The hall rearranged itself just ahead of us as we made a beeline from my dormitory tower to the dojo. I filed that little tidbit away for later experimentation. If it was possible to get through the School faster, I wanted to learn that trick.

"What do they want you to do?" Clem asked, her eyes wide with curiosity.

"I learned a lot of stuff working for Tycho last year," I said honestly, then lied. "They want me to do the same sort of stuff for them."

"Are you going to do it?"

"I don't know," I said, which was also the truth. "It would take so much time, and I don't want to spend another year slaving away. I want to enjoy at least some of my time at school, you know?"

"This is a big opportunity for you," Clem said thoughtfully. "Working directly with the elders of your clan will be a prestigious feather in your cap."

"Maybe," I said with a shrug. Everything I did would be a secret. I wasn't sure how much of a reputation boost that would give me. Still, it would help people, and that was important, even if it was dangerous. I just wasn't sure what I should do.

"I'm sure you'll make the right choice," Clem said. She threw an arm around my shoulders and gave me a quick squeeze. "Oh, we're here."

The School's dojo had an elaborate arched gateway instead of a door. The wide opening in the stone wall revealed an open floor covered in a soft, somewhat springy material. Older students were already practicing with one another, while the younger upperclassmen had gathered in small groups where they chatted nervously.

While no initiates ever saw the dojo, we'd all heard stories about what went on there, and spotted upperclassmen with bruised faces and bandaged limbs at mealtimes. This room was where Empyreals truly learned how to harness their martial capabilities.

As soon as we passed through the gateway, a gong reverberated through the dojo. A tall man with his long gray hair pulled up into a topknot entered through a door across the room from us. His robes, like those worn by the rest of us, were clearly intended for comfort and ease of movement. His gaze swept across the fifty students gathered in his domain, then stopped to meet mine.

A faint smile quirked his lips, and he gave me a short nod.

"Welcome to the dojo," the man said. "I am Professor Song, and I'll be instructing you this semester. Please, form a semicircle around me. I'd rather not shout to be heard."

The professor waited until we'd gathered around, then launched into the first class's teachings.

"You should all be familiar with your aura, serpents, and swords." He crossed his arms as he spoke and paced back and forth inside the semicircle. "Your aura is your defense against jinsei attacks. Your swords are your most potent offense and will become more so as your cores advance. Finally, your serpents are the most flexible tool at your disposal, capable of attack or defense, and so much more. My goal for this semester is to help you understand how these three work together to become more than the sum of their parts. Today, we're going to start by having you integrate your serpents into your defensive maneuvers."

I'd already covered most of what the instructor had explained with Hank and my trainers during the Five Dragons Challenge. While Professor Song explained how to summon serpents quickly, an art I'd mastered weeks ago, my mind drifted back to the conversation with the elders.

Their offer was an opportunity for me to do real good for Empyreals. Stopping the anti-Flame protestors would make everyone safer and stabilize a society that had been dangerously upended by my actions last year. And, if I did a good job, maybe the Shadow Phoenix Elders would help me find my mother. The danger from defying Tycho had passed, and I wanted to bring her in from the cold. She deserved a better life.

There were so many dangers to the job, though. If anyone discovered who I was, they could go after my friends or the School. They might even hunt down my mom to use against me. And then there was the very real danger that someone would discover my Eclipse nature.

I had no idea what I was going to do.

"Now that I've explained the concept to you, let's see it in practice," Professor Song said. The sudden weight of his attention on my core dragged me out of my thoughts. "Mr. Warin, would you care to help demonstrate the use of serpents as a defensive measure with Mr. Vilrose?"

"I'd be honored to be part of your demonstration," the Disciple of the Jade Flame said as he stepped out of the semicircle and up to Professor Song. "I will be the aggressor."

"As you wish, honored Professor," I said. My friends clapped me on the shoulder as I stepped forward. "I suppose I'll be on defense."

Everyone chuckled at that, including the professor. He stepped back, letting the Disciple and me square off with one another. It had only been two days since my last fight, and I fell easily into a ready stance.

The Disciple's eyes burned with excitement as he raised his clenched fists to protect his head. Aspects of energy and anticipation flickered in his aura along with a few dark sparks of fear. He was looking forward to his chance to prove himself in front of the rest of the students. If he could land even one punch on the undefeated School champion, his clanmates would consider him something of a hero.

That wasn't going to happen.

"Jace." I offered my opponent my hand.

"Kyle." He gave my fingers a squeeze but decided not to try to crush my hand when I squeezed back.

"Good, good," the professor said as he stepped into the space between us. He raised a hand to each of us. "This isn't a fight, it's a demonstration. Mr. Vilrose, your goal is to strike Mr. Warin at no more than half strength. Mr. Warin, you will defend yourself using only your serpents. Ready?"

We both nodded.

"Begin!" the professor shouted, and leaped back.

The Disciple pushed jinsei into his legs to fuel a gliding step that covered the space between us more quickly than I'd expected. More of the sacred energy glowed around his right fist, which was cocked back to his shoulder. The power grew in intensity as he approached until the entire length of his arm shone like polished gold.

That was a lot more than half strength.

My Eclipse core responded to the threat instantly. The Borrowed Core technique lashed out to rats beneath the dojo's floor. The connections clicked into place easily, and I cycled beast aspects through my core and into my aura with a single breath. My training during the Five Dragons Challenge had made me much more efficient with my use of aspects, and I used the minimal amount I'd gathered to conjure a pair of thin serpents.

The Disciple planted his feet, and his fist rocketed toward my face. The golden glow around his arm shifted to a deep shade of red as he activated a potent striking technique. He grinned with wild glee, sure there was no way my meager defense could block his powerful assault.

My Eclipse nature raged at this unwarranted attack, and my serpents struck without conscious thought on my part. One of them looped around the Disciple's arm, and the other speared into his core.

My blood ran cold. It was Singapore all over again.

The Disciple tried to push through the coils of the serpent I'd tangled around his arm. He leaned into his punch, beads of sweat sprouting from his forehead as he poured every ounce of effort he could muster into the attack.

Against most opponents, that might've been an effective tactic.

Against an Eclipse Warrior?

It was pointless.

My serpent leeched the jinsei out of his arm's channels before he knew what had happened. My unique power stripped the aspects from his technique and used them to harden my aura. In the same moment, my other serpent hit his core and began to siphon away the jinsei it found there.

If I didn't stop it, my Eclipse nature would suck every ounce of sacred energy out of the Disciple. He'd be dead in a heartbeat.

Darkness erupted across my vision. I blinked hard to drive it away and willed my core back into submission. The urge raged against me, hungry for the sacred energy in my opponent. It was confused and hurt by my unwillingness to finish my foe. The Disciple had attacked me, and it was my duty to defend myself to the utmost of my ability.

The Disciple gasped and fell to his knees. His face was white, and his eyes rolled back beneath fluttering lids. His breath came in shuddering gasps, and he collapsed onto his face.

I banished my serpents and severed the connection between me and my opponent. Denying the urge sent a shock of visceral pain through my core, and

I stumbled away, hands over my face to cover the darkness I knew had flooded my eyes.

"Give me room," Professor Song shouted.

"It was an accident," I choked out. "He was going all out. I had to defend myself."

"Class dismissed!" Professor Song barked. "Jace, we'll talk about this later."

My heart raced as I pushed my way through the semicircle of students and headed toward the dojo's door. Clem called my name, and Eric and Abi echoed her.

I didn't stop. My control over my Eclipse nature felt weak and uncertain as the stress inside me mounted. Denying the urge had felt like tearing my core in half. I wasn't sure I could do it again so soon. I needed space.

I didn't want to kill anyone else.

# THE OFFER

MY CORE THRASHED AND CHURNED WITHIN ME as I stormed out of the dojo. It urged me to go back, to make sure my fallen foe wouldn't rise again. To the Eclipse Warrior, winning wasn't enough. Any foe who still lived could be a threat again in the future.

I was beginning to realize why the other clans had been so terrified of people like me. Every time I slipped up, someone got hurt.

"Jace!" Clem called as she raced up behind me.

"I need to be alone," I said. "Please."

Clem ran ahead of me, then turned around and planted her feet in my path.

"Jace, what happened?" she asked. "It was over so fast."

Eric and Abi caught up to us and flanked Clem. Eric looked confused and upset, while Abi just looked angry.

"He activated a technique," I said. "Two days ago, I was fighting in the Five Dragons Challenge against contenders who didn't follow rules like half-strength. When I saw that attack coming at me, I overreacted."

"You saw him activate a technique and reacted before it could hit you?" Eric asked. "No wonder you won all those fights. All I saw was a flash of light and then Kyle was on the ground."

"I think that's all any of us saw." Abi eyed me with open concern. "Will he be all right?"

"He'll be fine," I said defensively. "I used my serpent to deflect the jinsei from his technique. It stunned him, but he'll recover. Won't even have a bruise."

That explanation was mostly the truth. I'd done a lot of reading on the road and had learned there were several techniques that could temporarily disrupt jinsei. That had been a relief, because it made it easier to hide what I was really doing.

I hated lying to my friends, but no one could know the truth. I'd be dead before dawn if it came out that I was an Eclipse Warrior.

"You've grown very strong since I last saw you, my friend," Abi said with a rueful chuckle. He seemed to have accepted my explanation. "I'll be careful not to surprise you when we are sparring. I'd hate for you to take me down like that."

"It won't happen again," I said, too quickly. It couldn't happen again. "I guess I'm still not wound all the way down from the challenge. Would you guys mind if I took a little time alone? I need to meditate, clear my head. I'll catch up with you at breakfast if that's all right."

The three exchanged concerned glances, then gave me slow nods.

"Sure," Clem said. "Take however long you need. While we were all enjoying our summer, you were fighting contenders all over the world. Sorry, I should have been more considerate."

She blushed a pink that almost matched her hair and threw her arms around my neck. She squeezed me tight, and the hug caught me by surprise almost as much as Kyle's technique had.

At least my core didn't respond to the surprise as a threat. That was a big relief.

"We'll see you at breakfast, man," Eric said as Clem released me and stepped back. "Take it easy."

He offered his fist for me to bump, and I brushed my knuckles against his. Abi extended his hand, too, fingers open for a firm shake.

"I feel your turmoil," he said as our hands clasped. "If you need to talk, you know where to find me."

He held the shake a few seconds longer than was comfortable, then let go with a sharp nod of his head.

"Thanks for understanding, guys," I said. "I'll see you soon."

We all headed off in different directions, my friends dispersing along with the rest of the students, who were clearly glad to have some of their early morning free after I'd disrupted the class.

I caught more than a few curious glances tossed in my direction and ignored them. Let them wonder about what really happened. It might make all of them think twice before taking a shot at me to prove they were tougher than the champ.

I headed back to my room, where I could be sure I wouldn't be disturbed. I threw out connections from the Borrowed Core to the School's rats as I walked. Some of them recognized me and were eager to help. Others were from new litters, small and spry, curious, but cautious.

I passed the same message to all of them: find Hahen.

The rats scampered off to do my bidding and spread the word to their friends. Hopefully, the entire School's population of rodents would soon be searching for my old mentor.

On a whim, I changed course and headed for Tycho's laboratory. I focused my thoughts on my goal and fell into a light meditation in an attempt to mimic Eric's earlier speedy travel through the building's shifting structure.

I made good progress at first. The school returned me to the main hall in record time, and I slipped into the shadowed corner where Tycho's hidden doorway had been.

*Had* being the operative word.

The wall there was now completely solid, and a tall vase took up most of the corner. It was as if there'd never been a door there.

I scratched my head, shrugged, and checked in with the rats. They were searching, but it would take them a while. For all their speed and agility, their legs were still only a couple of inches long and the School was enormous. It might take them days to search the School, and that was if they didn't get distracted and forget what I'd sent them to do.

"Maybe he's down in the stacks," I muttered to myself. I'd spent weeks locked up there with dusty books and rats, with only Hahen to keep me company. I focused my thoughts on that destination and willed the shifting architecture to guide me there.

It took me less time than I'd expected to reach the older part of the School and the barred door that I'd once been trapped behind. My control over the path the School chose for me was growing stronger.

Unfortunately, my control over the dark urge within me was still tenuous at best.

It reacted to the sight of the prison door with a flurry of furious activity. It lashed connections to the rats beyond the door, then used their beast aspects to rip the bar from its brackets. It smashed the old wood to splinters against the stone before I regained control.

The outburst left me so shaken I had to lean against the heavy door to catch my breath. My hand shook, and beads of oily sweat oozed from my forehead and back. Old fears and dark memories clawed their way up from the dark spaces at the back of my thoughts, and it took me long minutes before I was able to steel myself enough to open that door.

The barrier opened easily despite its size to reveal—

Nothing.

The stacks of books that I'd dutifully organized into neat categories were gone, as if they'd never been there at all. The black spots I'd used to open the subterranean chamber where I'd found the *Manual of the New Moon* were gone, too. Even the strange hole in the floor was nowhere to be seen.

I summoned an orb of jinsei to serve as a lantern as I entered the chamber for a closer look. My feet stirred up clouds of dust from the thick layer that covered the floor, filling the air with shimmering particles that made me sneeze and cough. It was as if someone had replaced the stacks I'd spent so many weeks in with an identical, but very empty, chamber that had not been disturbed for decades.

Finally, after minutes of searching and wheezing on dust, I found something. Small footprints near the part of the room where my cot had once been. No, not footprints.

Pawprints. Two of them with a small round spot cleared next to them, as if a stick or a cane had rested there.

Hahen had been here.

"Hey!" I called out. "Anyone here?"

The only answer was the echo of my voice. There was no one here and no way to tell how long ago my former mentor had been around.

The last time I'd seen the rat spirit, he'd seemed distant and worried about the choices that lay ahead of me. Then he hadn't brought me my meals on the last day of school.

I'd spent the entire summer worrying that something happened to him, or that he'd gotten disgusted by the fact that I'd embraced the Eclipse core and abandoned our friendship. The idea that I might never see him again stung, and I quickly pushed it aside and headed for my room.

Other upperclassmen waved and nodded in my direction, and I did my best to be polite in return. I'd spent my whole first year at the School with my head down, trying to avoid fights and stay out of the way of the people who hated me. Now that everyone was friendly, I was having a rough time adjusting.

Rather than risk an awkward conversation, I nodded to everyone who waved at me, and hustled back to my room.

Where Hagar was waiting.

"I've never been in the champion's quarters before," she said. "Want to give me a tour?"

Hagar had literally tried to kill me last year. Now, she acted like we'd been lifelong friends. This would take some getting used to.

"Sure," I said cautiously. She was, after all, a warden and one of my clan's respected students. The least I could do was be polite, despite the growing urge from my Eclipse nature to make her pay for the pain she'd caused me last year. "Let me get the door, honored Warden."

The engraved barriers slid out of the way at a touch from my hand. Hagar gave out an appreciative little gasp.

"You first," she said. "I don't want to get zapped."

"Good point," I said with a chuckle. I still had no idea what kind of defenses protected this place, but I was willing to bet they were impressive.

The warden followed me into my private territory, and I led the way to the cottage. Our conversation was light and breezy, like we'd never fought before. It was jarring, and I had to keep checking myself because I really wanted to blurt out questions like, "You do remember trying to kill me?"

"This place is great," she said. "I knew the champion got something special, but I never imagined it was so awesome. I wonder if it's the same for all of you."

"No idea," I said. "Hank never said anything about this to me."

After a quick tour of the cottage, I busied myself with the coffee set in the kitchen while Hagar leaned against the doorway and watched.

"Where'd you learn to do that?" she asked.

"I made coffee for my mom, all the time," I said. "Back in the camp."

"That's right," she said. "It's easy to forget where you came from, champ. Things are sure a lot different for you now, aren't they?"

"In so many ways." I dumped beans into the grinder and pressed the power button. The clatter of the conical burrs drowned out any hopes of conversation for the next few seconds. Finally, the last of the coffee grounds emptied into the receptacle in the grinder's base, and I gave it a quick tap to make sure none of the vines would cling to its lip when I removed it. That would be a hell of a mess.

"About our fight." Hagar finally decided to poke the elephant in the room while I dumped the grounds into the French press and put the water on to boil. "It wasn't personal."

"It felt personal," I said, not quite ready to let her off the hook so easily. "You would have killed me."

"It was a job," Hagar insisted. "Like the one the elders offered to you."

"A job," I said. "Lots of people have done horrible things for a job. That doesn't make it all right."

"I know," Hagar said. She raked her fingers through her crimson Mohawk. "I want you to know I'm sorry about what happened. It turns out you were right, and we were all wrong. Even the elders admitted that."

While it was nice that Hagar and the rest of the clan no longer blamed me for everything that had ever gone wrong, it was hard to shake the anger at what had happened. My Eclipse nature wanted them to all pay for hurting me. It wanted to smash the coffeepot into Hagar's face and—I took a deep breath and shoved those dark thoughts aside. It hurt to deny the urge, but it was the right thing to do. Hagar and the elders had gone after me because they wanted to protect Empyreal society, not to hurt me in particular. Revenge would gain me nothing, while cooperating with them might help a lot of people.

Not to mention my mind.

"Okay," I said. "I accept your apology. Is that the only reason you came to see me?"

"I also wanted to be sure you were okay," Hagar said. "Word spread fast about what happened in Professor Song's dojo."

"I'm fine." I didn't want to talk about that. "Anything else?"

"I wanted to discuss the elders' offer," Hagar said. "Before you made your decision."

"I don't even really know what the job is." I checked the temperature on the gooseneck kettle and saw there were still a few minutes left before the coffee would be ready. "I'm not sure how much I'm allowed to tell you."

"You don't have to tell me anything," Hagar said. She opened and closed the cabinets until she found a couple of mugs, then came over to rest against the counter next to me. "I've been working with the elders since I was an initiate. They knew there was something going on at the School, they just didn't know what. I kept an eye on things for them, did a little snooping."

"And assassinations?" I said with a grin I hoped would take some of the sting out of my pointed question.

"Just you," she said, her cheeks glowing red.

I never thought I'd see Hagar blush.

"And this is what, your fourth year?" I asked.

"That's right," she said. "I spent almost four years looking for heretics, and you found them in one."

"They found me," I corrected her. "If Grayson hadn't come after me so hard, I probably would've never figured out what was going on."

"If you don't mind my asking, why did he hate you so much?"

"My mother and father knew him before I was born," I said. "Honestly, that's all I know about it."

I didn't feel the need to tell Hagar about my family's disgraced past, the fact that my father had been exiled before his death. That was personal, and I still didn't completely trust the warden.

"Family stuff," she said with a sigh. "I know how that goes. My parents were both Resplendent Suns. They weren't very happy when Mama Weaver made me a Shadow Phoenix."

I'd never considered the fact that Hagar might not have been born a Shadow Phoenix. The Resplendent Suns were the exact opposite of my clan—proud and noble, well-respected and treated like royalty pretty much everywhere they went. To have a kid ripped out of that sort of privilege and dumped into the lowliest group of misfits in Empyreal society had to have stung.

"It's not like you had a choice," I said.

"Well, sort of." Hagar frowned. "I could have—"

The kettle's shrill whistle interrupted her. She stepped back to give me space to pull it off the stove top and pour the water into the French press.

"You're right that I didn't get to pick my clan, no one does. But, if I'd been a little more like my parents and maybe less nosy and skeptical about everything, who knows where I might've ended up." She handed me a mug, and I filled it with coffee. I handed it back, and she gave me the empty one, which I also filled.

"There's cream in the refrigerator, and I saw some sugar with the rest of the coffee gear." I put the kettle on a cold burner. "If you want anything in your coffee, that is."

"Black is fine," Hagar said with a wink. "It matches our robes."

"True," I said and took a sip of some truly excellent coffee. I'd gotten used to having the finer things on the challenge tour, but I had to admit that this brew was something special. I'd have to find out where the beans came from and make some for my mom. Whenever I found her again.

"Anyway," Hagar said in a sudden rush, "I just wanted you to know that working with the elders is important. There's a lot of bad people out there who aren't what they seem on the surface. The Empyrean Flame has a lot more enemies than you might think."

"How is that even possible?" I asked, suddenly skeptical. "The Flame is the source of all our power. Why would anybody endanger that?"

"Because some fools believe the Empyrean Flame is blocking our true source of power," Hagar confided. "And, because the Flame didn't do a great job of protecting us during the Utter War. If it hadn't been for…"

She left the half-finished thought between us, and I didn't pick it up. Most Empyreals knew nothing about the Eclipse Warriors, or at least pretended they didn't. I guess when you blow up an entire clan, it's easier for everyone to pretend that it never happened than to own up to what felt like a dangerously dishonorable act.

I hid my thinking face behind another drink from my oversized mug. Working for the elders would be a giant pain, I knew that. I'd be running all over the place, constantly exhausted, struggling to keep up in my classes.

I'd also be protecting everyone from threats they didn't know existed. I'd be doing good work.

And, maybe, working so closely with the elders I might learn something that would help me control my core and keep everyone safe. Maybe they'd even be inclined to do me a favor if I joined the team.

"They need you, Jace," Hagar said. "They won't tell me why, but the elders think you're our best hope at finding the next big problem before it blows up in our faces like the thing with Grayson."

"I'll do it." I realized I wanted to be a good guy, use my powers to do the right thing. But that didn't mean I couldn't get something out of it for myself. "On one condition."

"I can't promise you anything, but I'll tell the elders what you want," Hagar said.

"I want to find my mother," I said. "I want her taken care of."

"That's all?" Hagar asked, her tone vaguely suspicious.

"Yes." There was nothing else that mattered as much to me.

"I think we can do that," Hagar said. "You don't have to tell me why you don't know where your own mother is, Jace, but you will have to tell someone, eventually, if you want her found. If you're good with that condition, then I'll do my best to fulfill your request."

"Then I'm in," I said.

Hagar put her mug down on the counter and pulled my mug out of my hand to set it down next to hers.

She wrapped her arms around my waist and pulled me into a tight hug. Her breath was warm against my neck, and the stiff ruff of her Mohawk tickled my nose.

"You won't regret this, Jace," she said. "You're going to be a hero."

# THE DISCIPLE

THE REST OF MY FIRST REAL DAY BACK AT THE School of Swords and Serpents rushed by in a flurry of new classes, new professors, and hurried meals. It seemed that upperclassmen had much busier schedules than we'd had as initiates.

We met Professor Shan, our Intermediate Scrivenings instructor, after breakfast. She was a short, severe woman from the Thunder's Children clan who vowed to whip all our crude scrivenings into shape. She clearly favored Clem, who had become well known for her skill in this art last year, and just as clearly thought I was going to be trouble.

"You'll have to work harder in my course than you did in Professor Ishigara's," she warned me with a stern wag of her finger. "Not even the School's champion gets a free ride here. Stick with it, though, and your work will far surpass the crude scribblings you were capable of last year."

Which admittedly wasn't a very high bar to get over. Scrivening was easily my weakest subject, and I hadn't had much time or inclination to practice it while I'd been out cracking skulls during the Five Dragons Challenge.

That lack of summer study made the first day of Intermediate Scrivening two hours of pure torture. We practiced the same basic forms over and over until my arm felt like it was going to fall off and my hand cramped into a useless claw.

After Professor Shan dismissed us it was time for Intermediate Alchemy. I'd been looking forward to this class because I was sure it would be a breeze. Professor Ardith introduced himself with a flourish and assured us that even though he came from the Resplendent Sun clan, there'd be no favoritism on his watch. That, of course, was immediately disproved when he grouped all the Suns together as lab partners and then split the rest of us up so no two members of the same clan worked together.

My friends and I all grimaced as we were split up. Eric headed over to the Suns, who greeted him with enthusiastic slaps on the shoulder as they paired up and took seats on the right side of the big classroom. Clem ended up with a tall, thin Disciple of Jade Flame who offered her a nervous smile as they sat in a pair of seats near the front of the room. Abi paired off with a girl from the Thunder's Children clan who beamed as she fingered the lapel of his Portal Defense Force uniform.

I was shocked when my partner turned out to be Rachel Lu. The short girl grinned and threw a weak punch into my shoulder when she plopped down in the chair next to me.

"Bet you didn't expect to see me here," she said.

"You're right," I said. "I thought you were an initiate."

"Really?" She frowned at that. "I know I'm short, but I didn't think I looked that young."

"You weren't here last year," I countered. "And you fought in the challenge. If you didn't need to win a spot at the School, why risk fighting me in the tournament?"

"Well, for starters, I thought I could beat you." She raised her fists into a mock fighting position. "I was known as a bit of a scrapper back home."

I found that hard to believe. She might've been ninety pounds dripping wet, and her showing in the arena had not impressed me.

"If you're a fighter, I'll eat my robes," I said with a shake of my head. "Seriously, what's your deal?"

"Okay, you got me." She laughed. "I was at the Golden Sun Academy. My mom got a promotion and used her raise to transfer me over to the School of Swords and Serpents during the summer. My dad thought it would be a good idea for me to at least try the Five Dragons Challenge so I'd come in with a higher standing. That did not work out."

"You lead with your chin," I said, and jutted mine toward Rachel to show her what I meant. "You also flinch when a punch is coming…"

Professor Ardith cleared his throat to get everyone's attention and wrote our first assignment on the board. It was a simple aspect identification project, hardly worth my effort. Rachel and I pulled the sealed flasks from under the workbench and arranged them in front of us according to the diagram the professor had drawn on the board.

"I'll start," I said, and scooped up a clay flask with a wide bottom and a narrow mouth. I tugged the cork from its mouth and took a quick breath of its contents. "Ice aspects."

Rachel filled in the first blank on the worksheet we'd found with the flasks.

"My turn." She lifted a heavy frosted glass beaker and unscrewed its top. "Yuck, smells like garbage."

"You said you came from the Golden Sun Academy," I said. "Where is that?"

"New York Undercity," Rachel said with a shrug. She took another sniff and wrinkled her nose. "I don't know what this is. Anyway, the Golden Sun was hardly glamorous, but it got me through the basics."

"They have schools for people who live in the undercities?" The idea boggled my mind. I'd had no idea such a thing existed.

"Seriously?" She shook her head. "You make a lot of assumptions about people, Jace."

"What?" I didn't know what she meant. "You said you went to a training school in the undercity."

"That's where the school was, not where I'm from," she said, her voice almost a growl. "Not that there's anything wrong with being from the undercity. You came from the camps and look how well you turned out. Also, I can't figure out what this stuff is."

"I'm sorry, I didn't know." Her anger had caught me off guard. I took a sniff from her beaker. "That's rot aspect."

"Thanks." Rachel blew out a frustrated sigh. "I shouldn't have snapped at you. It's not your fault you made the wrong assumption. It's the whole society. People who weren't raised as Empyreals think we're all rich and spend our time lounging around in the overcity while servants feed us ice cream. But some of us work for a living. The assumptions are frustrating."

That was news to me. Every student I'd met at the School was far wealthier than I'd ever imagined I'd be. I'd thought this was the only school for Empyreals because that's what I'd been told. Now, I realized how foolish that was. For the students at the School of Swords and Serpents, this was the only academy of sacred arts because none of the others would even be on their radar. My fellow students were the rich kids.

I'd spent my whole life believing there were only two classes of people: Empyreals and everyone else. Now, I was starting to see that the Empyreals were divided into different groups, too. It was an eye-opener.

Rachel and I finished our assignment, and she gave me a quick hug when class was over.

"Thanks for helping me with this stuff." She grinned. "If you want to see something cool, come to the eastern door of the upperclassmen common area between the last class and dinner."

"What is it?" I asked, genuinely curious.

"You'll see," Rachel said with a wink. She slipped through the crowd of students before I could ask her any more questions.

Abi, Eric, and Clem descended on me and dragged me off to lunch.

"Feeling better?" Clem asked after we'd filled our plates and staked our claim on a table.

"Yeah." That was the truth. Deciding to help the elders had taken a weight off my shoulders, even if I knew it wouldn't be easy. "I guess I hadn't realized how all that fighting had taken a toll on me. It's hard to get used to the idea that not everyone is a competitor out to beat me into the ground."

"Most of us are," Eric said and flicked a pea off his fork into my forehead.

At least, he tried to. I snatched it out of the air an inch from my face and flicked it back at him. The green orb bounced off his forehead, leaving a sticky smear of butter above and between his eyes.

"You have to be faster than that," I said with a grin.

Abi let out a long, low whistle and shook his head. "They'll make a prizefighter out of you if you're not careful."

The rest of lunch went by far too quickly. I'd forgotten how nice it was to just hang out with people who liked one another. There was no pressure while I was with my friends, not even from Abi. His suspicions seemed to have eased off a bit, even if I did catch him watching me from the corner of his eye while we ate.

"I'll see you guys at dinner," he said when he'd cleared his plate. "Guard duty."

He waved as he headed off to his assignment, and the rest of us trudged to our next classes. Clem and Eric split off to their Empyreal Philosophy course, while I made my way to Professor Engel's Military History course. I'd hoped to learn more about the Locust Warriors, even if only by the gaps the professor skipped over. Engel, on the other hand, seemed much more interested in regaling us with stories of her time serving in the Horizon Expeditionary Squadron after the Utter War.

After two hours of that nonsense, I bolted out of class and headed back to the upperclassman territory. Rachel had piqued my curiosity, and I couldn't wait to see what surprise she had in store for me. I willed the School to take me to the common area as quickly as possible and was a little surprised when it did exactly that. I was getting better at visualizing where I wanted to go, which seemed to help the School grant my wishes.

Rachel was nowhere in sight, so I decided to do a little exploring before I headed off to meet her.

I picked a hallway at random and found one with a floor of white ceramic tile, while the walls and ceiling were seamless acrylic. Through the transparent walls I saw students working on projects in small alchemical laboratories, fiddling with strange mechanical devices on workbenches, and arguing in front of whiteboards filled with theoretical scrivenings I couldn't even begin to read. It was nice to know there were so many workshops close at hand, though it seemed most of them were in use at the moment. When I reached the end of that hallway and found nothing new, I turned around and headed back to the common area.

I waved to the other students gathered there, and several of them nodded back. A small cluster of Disciples of the Jade Flame eyeballed me. They seemed more curious than hostile, though their eyes were wary. Clearly word of what happened to their clanmate in Professor Song's class this morning had spread through the ranks of the upperclassmen.

The next exit I chose was narrow and low-ceilinged. Lightstones along the baseboards provided the only illumination, and even that glow was dim. Locked doors pierced the hallway's walls at regular intervals. When I finally found one that opened, I peered inside to find a tall, rectangular room lined with bookshelves. A small desk occupied the center of the miniature library.

I made a mental note to come back here when I had more time. I was sure the School had purged all mentions of Eclipse Warriors from the books in this chamber, but that didn't mean I couldn't find something else of use. I closed the door quietly and returned to the common area.

It was an hour or so before dinner by that point, and I decided it was time to meet Rachel. I headed down the eastern hallway, which soon transformed into a twisting stone corridor with veins of lichen crawling along its walls. The air there was damp, and the stone floor gave way to dirt after a few yards. Not many steps after that, I stood on a wide pathway that wound its way through hills capped by flowering trees the likes of which I'd never seen.

The air was alive with buzzing aspect sprites, their prismatic wings throwing out fiery sparks, tiny forks of lightning, miniature blizzards, and even sprays of light and darkness. The creatures seemed to have no interest in me and fluttered away as I approached.

"Rachel?" I called out.

"Over here!" she shouted back. Her voice came from the path ahead of me. I followed the trail and wondered if there'd be another cottage, or something else interesting at its end. At the very least, a nature walk would calm my nerves and help ease my core. My Eclipse nature seemed to be soothed by the great outdoors. I'd have to remember that the next time I was feeling pent up.

By the time I reached the hills, the terrain had already begun to change. The air was cooler and crisper, and the number of aspect sprites had grown considerably. They gathered in thick clouds above my head, chittering in a language I didn't understand. The dark urge grumbled at their presence, and I felt the familiar ache of its hunger. It wanted to devour the tiny sprites.

"Not now," I whispered to it.

It retreated into the darkness at the bottom of my thoughts, and I let out a sigh of relief. No one would miss a few sprites out of the dozens I'd already seen, but I wouldn't know how to live with myself if I let my core eat them.

"This way!" Rachel's voice came from ahead of me.

Past the hills, the ground grew rocky, and the path angled sharply upward along the flank of a towering mountain. I glanced back, and the hills were right where I'd left them. That was odd, because I certainly hadn't seen this mountain from the other side of them. I didn't know how that was possible, considering the great stony face rose thousands of feet above me and should have been easily visible as soon as I'd stepped onto the path.

The School was a weird, weird place.

Rachel's laughter spurred me on, and I chased it up the mountain path. The world shifted around me as I made my way along the path, the mountain rising and then falling away to be replaced by a rocky beach strewn with pumice stones the size of my head, before that, too, was replaced by a rolling plain haunted by fireflies bigger than my clenched fist.

A forest came next, and I drifted through the trees like a ghost, Rachel's giggles luring me deeper into the woods. I lost myself in the pursuit, happy to have something, anything, to distract me from all the worries and stress that swirled around me. Rachel didn't have any expectations from me. She'd given me a great gift bringing me to this place and giving me something pleasant to think about.

The forest path was blissfully, completely peaceful.

Too peaceful. Where had all the aspect sprites gone?

Something hurtled through the trees behind me. I'd been so lost in the beauty of the place even my Eclipse nature was caught by surprise. My attacker collided with me and knocked me off balance. I took a staggering step back, braced myself with a jolt of jinsei through my legs and back, and then turned the tables on my attacker.

I grabbed my attacker by the neck and belt of their robe, yanked them away from my body, and twisted hard at the hips to throw them onto the ground. My Borrowed Core technique lashed out and tore aspects from the creatures of the forest, and my serpents seized them from my aura and burst from my core. The Eclipse nature's black rage bubbled up from the darkest part of my mind, ready to slaughter whoever had been stupid enough to attack me. There would be no mercy, no second chances for this fool.

My assailant hit the ground with a pained grunt and curled into a fetal position. They wrapped their arms around their head and kept their chin down to their knees to ward off my retaliation. They were slender, dressed in the robes of Thunder's Children, a skinny black braid curled in the dirt behind their head like a question mark.

"Jace!" My attacker shouted in a panicked voice that blasted a cold shock up my spine.

Rachel.

The urge boiled in my core, far too powerful for me to resist. There was no time, and I had no strength to prevent my Eclipse nature from lashing out. Something had to break.

The best I could hope was to decide what that something was.

My serpents swept through the forest behind me and ripped through swarms of aspect sprites. The tiny creatures popped out of existence as my Eclipse core sucked away the jinsei and aspects they'd held in their tiny bodies. One moment, they'd been happily flitting through the trees. The next, they simply ceased to be.

Experience had taught me that my Eclipse nature was sated in the moment immediately after it had fed. I took advantage of that to force it back into its cage and push the darkness from my eyes. The combination of fresh jinsei and terror that I'd hurt Rachel was more than enough to give me the upper hand over the darkness.

For the moment.

"Are you okay?" My voice shook with adrenaline and fear. I offered Rachel my hand and helped her to her feet. I brushed the dirt off the shoulders of her robes and stepped back to give her some space.

"I'm fine, I think," she said. "You're a lot faster than I expected."

"You should've known better." I tried to force some humor into my voice, to hide the fact that I'd almost killed her. I wasn't sure she bought it. "I did trounce you in the challenge."

"You did not trounce me," she said with mock indignation. She smoothed her sky-blue robes and shook the fallen leaves from her hair. "Thanks for not killing me just now."

Rachel's words stung more than a little. I tried to brush them off, but the look on her face told me I wasn't exactly successful.

"Are you okay?" she asked.

"Yeah," I said. "There was an incident this morning. Kind of the same thing that happened here. Still not out of that competitor mindset, I guess. I keep lashing out when I don't mean to."

Rachel's hands flew to her mouth, and she pressed her fingertips to her lips. After a few moments, she shook her head and continued.

"That was dumb of me," she said. "I was only playing, but I should've thought about what that would be like for you."

"It's okay," I said, trying to console her. I felt terrible about what I'd done, and I felt even worse that she was blaming herself. "It was totally my fault. People can't be walking on eggshells around me all the time. I've got to get it together."

"Let's walk a little before dinner." Rachel smiled, a warm and welcoming expression that made me feel worse still. I'd been seconds from killing her. I was a monster. "That helps me think, sometimes."

"Sure," I said. And it did sound like a good idea.

We walked in silence for a while after that, until my stomach started to grumble, and I steered us back toward the rest of the School.

"I didn't mean to hurt your feelings," I said. "Earlier today, I mean. In class."

"Hurt my..." Rachel laughed. She leaned up and kissed me on the cheek. "You didn't hurt my feelings, Jace. I shouldn't have gotten upset when you assumed I wasn't an Empyreal. You don't have the background to know all the weird stuff that goes on in our society, and I shouldn't have snapped at you. But…"

Rachel stopped and let her words trail off. She looked up into my eyes and took my right hand in both of hers. She chewed on the inside of her lower lip, wrestling with the words she wanted to say.

Water aspect sprites flitted past us, misting our faces with tiny droplets of dew from their wings. Rachel laughed and the tension of the moment vanished.

"Don't take everything the Empyreals tell you at face value, Jace." She paused, then stood up on her tiptoes to kiss my cheek again. Her lips were warm and damp from the aspect dew. "There are people with a vested interest in keeping things just the way they are. Just… be careful who you believe."

With that, Rachel released my hands and took off down the path.

"Dinnertime," she called over her shoulder, then disappeared around a bend in the forest.

I wrestled with what she'd told me for moments longer, unsure of what to make of the spunky girl, who was so much more than she'd first appeared.

# THE PATH

I SPENT THE REST OF THAT DAY AND ALL THE NEXT on pins and needles. After she'd promised to take my decision back to the elders of the Shadow Phoenix clan, Hagar seemed to have vanished from the School. I'd knocked on her door so often her neighbor finally promised to tell Hagar I was looking for her if I'd go away.

That was easier said than done. I had no idea if Hagar had taken my message back to our clan elders or been sidetracked by some other mission. I was going nuts waiting on their response.

The inevitable meeting with Professor Song also had my nerves tied in a knot. I had no doubt he'd want to grill me about what had happened in his class. But he hadn't brought it up in today's class. I kept waiting for a tap on my shoulder that would summon me to his office for a sure-to-be-awkward heart-to-heart, but it never happened.

Rachel Lu was almost as elusive as Hagar. I spotted her here and there in the School, and we waved as we passed, but there was no time to talk and we didn't share any courses outside of Alchemy. I wanted, no, I needed to talk to her again. Our two brief conversations had filled my head with confusing thoughts, and everything I thought I knew about Empyreal Society had been topsy-turvy ever since. I had huge gaps in my knowledge and was sure she could help me fill them.

Plus, she was nice. And she smelled good. Like mint and something sweet...

"Oboli for your thoughts?" Clem asked as she caught up to me on the way to our early morning martial arts class. "Must be something serious judging by the thunderheads on your forehead."

"You know me," I said with a chuckle. "Lots of stuff to think about."

"Don't strain anything," Eric said as he threw a fake punch into my shoulder. "You're not a bookworm like Clem."

"I'm not a bookworm," my pink-haired friend snapped back. Then she grinned. "Okay, I am."

We all laughed at that, and Clem winked at Eric to show him there were no hard feelings. We entered the dojo together, still laughing.

Kyle stopped chatting with the small group of classmates around him the instant he saw me enter the dojo. He raised one hand to wave me over, and watched me intently as I headed in his direction.

My stomach tightened into a knotted fist, and my core reared like a cobra about to strike. Kyle was the only one who could have possibly known what I'd really done to him. If he hadn't been too rattled by all the strength leaving his body, he might have noticed me drain the aspects out of his technique and the jinsei from his core. If he had, there'd be questions.

My core grumbled inside me, urging me to finish what I'd started and put the Disciple in the ground. Its logic was sound; if I'd killed Kyle, he wouldn't be around to tell people what I'd done.

But I wasn't a murderer. I held my temper in check, braced myself for a confrontation, and walked over to the group with a fake smile plastered across my face.

"What's up?" I asked.

"Me, finally," Kyle said with a laugh. "You're going to have to show me what you did to me. It really knocked me for a loop."

"It wasn't all that impressive," I said, doing my best to downplay what had happened. "I redirected your attack with my serpent. You had expected to discharge your technique into my face. When that didn't happen, you must've lost control of it and all the jinsei used to activate it. That kind of shock can take down even a trained fighter."

"Ha," Kyle said. He scratched the side of his chin, tilted his head, and considered what I'd said. "I guess that makes sense. I've never thought about it like that, but I really did put everything into that punch."

"And that is why I asked you to only fight at half strength," Professor Song said wryly as he sauntered over to us. "Had you been more restrained, Jace would not have had to respond so harshly, and you would not have been injured."

"I really am sorry," I said to both my professor and fellow student. "It wasn't my intent to hurt anyone."

"I'm fine," Kyle said. "It didn't even leave a bruise, just made me want to stay in bed all day yesterday."

"It took your core some time to replenish the jinsei you wasted on that technique," the professor said. "It could've been much worse. You were lucky. Next time, you may not be."

With that, Professor Song bowed to us and took his place at the head of the class.

"Good morning, students," he called. "Line up. Ten wide, five deep. Let's hustle. We have a lot to discuss today."

I ended up sandwiched between Clem and Abi, with Eric in the row ahead of us. I'd have preferred to be at the back of the group, where I wouldn't be surrounded by other students who could irritate my Eclipse nature, but my friends had other ideas, and we ended up in the middle of the pack. I took a deep, cleansing breath, purified my aura, and sternly reminded the dark urge to not eat anyone.

"While your serpents, core, and aura are all separate," Professor Song continued, "the true sacred artist uses all three of these tools in unison. Every path will of course have a focus on one area or another, but it is only the fusion of all that will allow you to realize your potential."

The professor demonstrated what he meant in a flurry of motion. With a single deep breath he inhaled jinsei loaded with wood aspects from the walls, resilience from the floor, and even light from the globes that illuminated the dojo. I was surprised by how much he'd been able to gather from the air he breathed. I could only glean that many aspects by using my Eclipse core to tear them out of my surroundings. That caused a lot of damage. If I could learn how to do it the way Professor Song had, it would be much, much easier to hide my nature.

Our professor filled his aura with the aspects he'd harvested. Wood strengthened it like natural armor. He pushed the resilience aspects into his serpents, which coiled around him like a living wall. A split second later, the light aspects combined with Professor Song's unique aspect, and his fusion blade burst to life. He twirled the slender, elegant weapon over his head before he brought it down with its tip an inch away from the front rank of students, who gasped in surprise.

"This is the heart of martial arts." Professor Song banished his fusion blade and serpents as quickly as he'd summoned them. "When you're truly in tune with yourself and understand your own abilities, the three fragments of your Empyreal essence will work together as one."

A skinny guy with thick glasses and a tangled mop of black hair raised his hand. His arms were so scrawny that his robe fell down all the way to the shoulder, and I wondered if he was getting his fair share of the food in the dining hall.

"Yes, Mr. Lynn," the professor said. "What is your question?"

"How do we know which martial arts path to pursue?" the skinny guy asked. "I know the basics, but I'm not sure what comes next."

Professor Song raised one finger in front of his face and closed his eyes to consider the question.

"Your path is your own," he said. "It is not like your clan, or even your natural affinities for reading, writing, or arithmetic. One of the purposes of this class is to explore your individual path, and in that way find the proper trail for your feet to follow. When you are on the correct course, you will know it. Your core and the world will be in tune, and you will be at peace."

While most of the students in the dojo seemed confused by Professor Song's words, I understood what he meant. I'd learned the Borrowed Core technique of the Pauper's Dagger path the year before, and that had given me the ability to forge links between my core and the core of smaller creatures. I'd mostly focused on rats, because there were so many of them in the School and it wouldn't attract much attention if they acted a bit strangely. At first, I'd only been able to bond my core to a handful of rats. As I pushed my abilities to their limits, I'd expanded the number of rats I could control again and again.

And then, during my battle with the harbinger of the Locust Court, I'd pushed the Borrowed Core beyond even that limit, to unlock the Thief of Souls technique of my path. The power had allowed me to rip the core out of the spirit we'd faced and forge the Eclipse core inside me.

That had granted me abilities I didn't fully understand yet. My serpents could steal the aspects and jinsei out of anything they touched. It was an incredibly powerful ability, and it was the secret to my success in the Five Dragons Challenge. No foe could stand against me if the slightest touch from my serpents was enough to sap their strength or rob their techniques of the jinsei they needed to function.

That power had also caused the disaster in Singapore...

Before I could fall down that rabbit hole of angst, Professor Song's lecture abruptly changed direction and demanded my attention.

"... like for you to do is pair up and practice your attacking and defending with a martial technique," the wiry professor said. "Go slow, half strength only. The goal here is for you and your partner to explore your techniques and gain a deeper understanding of them. If you're observant, and you push yourselves in the right ways, the next step along your path will reveal itself to you."

"This would be a lot easier if he would just tell us what to learn next," Clem grumped. "All this mushy-feely stuff isn't really teaching if you ask me. Wanna partner up?"

"Of course," I said gratefully. Clem was methodical and careful, which was why she was annoyed at Song's intuitive approach to combat mastery. She'd much rather be given instructions to follow or books to study. That was also why she was a perfect partner for me. Clem wouldn't push the limits; she'd do exactly as we'd been told.

No surprises meant no accidents.

"You may begin when you have a partner," Professor Song said.

Pairs of students fanned out across the slightly springy dojo floor, giving all of us plenty of space to try out our techniques. I noticed Clem and I were given a wide berth, and I wondered whether that was because her mother was an adjudicator or because I'd just about murdered Kyle in front of all of them.

Probably a little of both.

"Do you mind if I go first?" Clem asked with a mischievous grin. "I've been working on an idea, and so far it hasn't worked out. Maybe you can see where I'm messing up."

"I'll be happy to try," I said, and dropped back into a defensive stance. I'd ditched all the beginner forms I'd relied on last year. The Gliding Shadow and Darting Minnow stances were useless against trained fighters, and the Tantrum Flail and Stunning Slap strikes weren't powerful enough to do much more than sting. I'd adopted a variant of the street-fighting style somewhere between boxing and karate. Its basic defensive stance was the cross-armed guard. It provided excellent head defense against any lucky shots from Clem, and it was an awkward stance to launch a counterattack from, so I couldn't inadvertently punch a hole through her chest.

Perfect.

"Look at Mr. Prizefighter over here," Clem said. Her stance was loose and sloppy, one foot behind the other, hands dangling at her sides. I wasn't sure if it was a ruse, because the Thunder's Children were chaotic fighters who didn't adhere to many traditional fighting styles. "Okay, this is supposed to be a defensive sweep. Something to push my opponent back and give me space to set up for a counterstrike."

"Let's see it," I said, and braced myself for the attack.

Clem pivoted on her rear foot. She flung her lead leg up and out to its full extension. A flare of jinsei burst from her core and roiled down her leg like an avalanche. The sacred energy flowed into her heel well before the sole of her foot was pointed in my direction. The momentum of her sweeping horizontal kick fanned the jinsei away from her leg in a wide arc tinged with wind aspect.

My Eclipse nature instinctively understood the technique's intent. The wind aspects would form a swathe of turbulence to push her opponent back or even knock them down if their core was significantly weaker than hers.

Fortunately, Clem and I both had initiate cores. Her attack was no real threat to me, and my Eclipse nature saw it more as a curiosity than a threat to be dealt with.

As Clem moved through her kick at low-speed, the scything curve of wind aspects rushed away from her. It reached me with enough force to push me back half a step. If I'd been unprepared or in the midst of an attack of my own, that might have been enough to pitch me off balance and set me up for a strong counter.

"Nice!" I congratulated Clem. "I think you've almost got it."

"Maybe," she said, her brow furrowed. "It takes so much of my jinsei to harness the wind aspects that I could only do it once, maybe twice in a fight."

"If you do it at the right time, you'd only have to do it once," I said. "Catch your foe in the middle of a roundhouse kick or a leaping kick, and you'll knock them flat. Then it's ground and pound time."

She grinned. "Unless I'm too slow and they knock me down first."

"That's what practice is for," I responded. "Do it again."

We spent the entire class working through Clem's new technique. By the time Professor Song dismissed us, Clem was sweaty and almost wiped out.

"Nice workout, Professor Warin." Without warning, she threw a hug around my neck. "I'm going to grab a shower before breakfast. Thank you so much for helping me with that technique."

"You're welcome," I said through the shock. For a moment, I'd thought Clem had something else in mind when she'd moved in to hug me.

"Clem and Jace, sitting in a tree," Eric said in a singsong voice, "K-I-S—"

"Better watch out," Abi said with a belly laugh that warmed my heart even though it was at my expense. "You keep that up, Jace will knock you out."

"He'll try," Eric said, his grin spreading so wide across his face I thought the top of his head might flop off.

"You're just jealous," I said. "Because no one likes you."

We roughhoused out of the dojo, and for the first time since I'd returned to school I felt really good about myself and my core. I'd held the Eclipse Warrior in check through the whole class, even when it had urged me to eat Clem's wind aspects and send them back to her with a roundhouse punch that would have knocked her flat.

The rest of the day went just as well. At the end of our last class for the day, Abi took off for Portal Defense Force duty while Clem, Eric, and I all agreed to grab dinner after we dumped our books in our rooms.

It was a great dinner. We laughed and teased each other, ate too much, and then headed back to my cottage to drink coffee and watch the sun set.

By some amazing stroke of luck, I managed to string almost a whole month of those magical days and nights together without my Eclipse nature trying to kill anyone. The urge was still there when I meditated, but I was learning to mitigate surprises and anxiety during the school day.

The extra time I started spending with Rachel also went a long way toward pushing back the tension that could trigger the urge. She was amazing and had so much to teach me about what life was like for Empyreals who weren't rich or connected. It was an eye-opening experience, and I loved every second of it. I wanted to introduce her to my friends, but Rachel always had some excuse about why she couldn't eat with us or hang out after school. She was very, very busy.

I started to believe that the year would be perfect.

And then it all began to unravel.

# ᴛHE SPY

HAGAR AMBUSHED ME IN THE HALL OUTSIDE MY room on the first Friday in October.

"Get the door open," she said, her voice tight and urgent. "I don't want us to be seen together."

"Thanks," I said sarcastically and opened the door for her. "And here I thought I was the popular one. You worried about your reputation?"

Hagar rolled her eyes and slipped through the door. When I joined her on the forest path, she threw a half-hearted punch into my left shoulder.

"It's not about my reputation, it's about our clan's enemies," she said.

"That sounds melodramatic," I said. "Come with me, I need to drop my stuff off."

"It's best we leave from inside the cottage, anyway," Hagar agreed. "I don't want to leave the port stone outside where someone could stumble across it."

"No one's going to stumble across anything in here," I said. "These are my private quarters. The door's locked."

"Because the Locust Court or heretics care about locks," Hagar said, rolling her eyes.

I didn't have an answer for that, so I just shrugged and led her down the path, across the bridge, and into the cottage. I dropped my books on the coffee table, rolled my head on my neck, and crossed my arms over my chest.

"What's going on?"

Hagar held up her index finger, fished out a thin crystal rod from her belt, and raised it over her head. A thin trickle of jinsei leaked from her core, ran up her spine, then went through her arm and into the crystal. The rod lit up with the pale green radiance, shifting slightly to blue, before it faded to white.

"Good, we can talk without anyone hearing us," Hagar said. "Today is your first mission."

Well, if I'd wanted any further confirmation from the elders that they'd accepted me, I guess this was it. There'd been a month of silence and Hagar hiding from me, and I'd been sure the elders had decided they didn't need me.

Guess I was wrong.

"This is happening really fast," I said. "I was supposed to meet Clem and those guys for dinner—"

"Sorry to disrupt your plans, but this can't wait. You'll be back before morning, but I'm afraid dinner is off the books," Hagar said. "Control can have something sent over when you get back."

"Back from where?" I asked.

With a flick of her wrist, Hagar made the crystal rod disappear, and a thin piece of pale white stone appeared in her palm. She crouched down and placed the disk on top of my books, twisting it this way and that until she was satisfied with its position. Then she stood up, snapped her fingers, and pointed at the stone.

A beam of light speared from the stone into the air over the coffee table. It unfolded in beams of light until a three-dimensional wireframe model of an office building hovered in front of me.

"This is a storage facility," Hagar explained. "We have reason to believe it is being used by a cell of anti-Flame heretics."

"Okay," I said slowly. "And you want me to do what?"

"Break in, use an eye-snapper to take some pictures, and then get out," Hagar said as if all of that was the simplest thing in the world.

"By myself?" I asked. "I don't have any experience breaking and entering. And whatever an eye-snapper is, it sounds painful. Maybe you should find someone with more, I don't know, thievery skills to do this."

"Jace," Hagar said with a faint smile on her lips. She reached out, took my hands, and squeezed them. "You'll be fine. And let's not pretend that you don't have experience taking things that don't belong to you."

That jab stung a little harder than I would've liked after what I'd gone through last year. She was right, though. I'd stolen things, sneaked all over the campus, and even fought a messenger from the Locust Court. I probably could get into a storage facility without too much trouble.

"Anything in particular I'm looking for?" I asked.

"I'm your handler on this one," she said. "I'll be right there with you in the eye-snapper. Just look for papers, computers, anything with information. When you find it, look at as much as you can without making a mess."

"All right." I squared my shoulders and stiffened my spine. I'd volunteered to be a hero. It was time to get to work. "Let's get on with it."

"Perfect," Hagar purred. She pulled two more small items from her belt, and I wondered how she'd managed to hide so many things inside the thin strip of cloth around her waist.

The first item she retrieved was a small black half sphere. She handed it to me, and I found it smooth and cool to the touch, though the flat side was a bit sticky.

"That's the eye-snapper," she said. "Press it to your right temple, just below your hairline. I need to calibrate this before you can leave."

A faint rush of disorientation staggered me when I adhered the device to the side of my head. My vision blurred, doubled, then righted itself. The first faint throbbing pain of a headache sprouted behind my left eye. The pain was tolerable, though if it got any worse I'd be in trouble.

"One moment," Hagar said.

She closed her eyes, and when she opened them they were covered with a faint oily sheen. She held very still, as if she didn't trust herself not to fall over if she moved.

"Turn your head to the left," she instructed. "Now to the right. Now face away from me. Hold out one or more fingers in your line of sight. Oh, that finger?"

"You saw that?" I asked.

"The eye-snapper sees all," she said in an ominous tone. "Or at least everything that you see. And while it's operational, I see everything through your eyes. Now, time is running short, we need to get moving."

By the time I turned around, Hagar had banished the shine from her eyes and held what looked like a fancy laser pointer in her right hand. The slender silver tube was covered in tiny dials, screws, and buttons. Its tip glowed ruby red, growing brighter and dimmer in regular pulses.

"This is a key wand," she explained. "Very rare, very expensive. No touchy. Like the eye-snapper, this is Shadow Phoenix jintech. None of the other clans know about this, and we'd like to keep it that way. Our little toys give us the edge we need to keep an eye on the heretics. Consider all these gadgets to be part of your geas. Don't breathe a word about them. We don't want the traitors to the Grand Design to know our capabilities."

"You keep saying that," I said. "What does it mean?"

"There's no time for a full explanation. The short version is that the Empyrean Flame has a great design," she said. "It gives each of us a purpose and protects us from the dangers that lie outside our society."

I wasn't sure how I felt about all that. The idea of some mysterious entity laying out a long-term plan for my life without my input didn't really appeal to me. Mostly because it hadn't really worked out very well for me, so far.

Then again, being eaten by the Locust Court's hungry spirits wasn't very enticing, either.

"Okay," I said. "What's next?"

Hagar fiddled with her key wand for a moment. She pressed a button, and a beam of scarlet light lanced out from the wand's tip onto the wall between the sitting room and the kitchen. She sketched a narrow archway on the wall in crimson light.

My heart caught in my throat when she completed her drawing.

There was a hole in the wall.

As strange as that was, what lay beyond the hole was even stranger. The sounds of city traffic reached my ears, and the faint soothing scent of a recent rainfall teased my nostrils. The side of a building, its damp concrete surface glistening with the green glow of a reflected stoplight, blocked my view of anything else through the arch. A rat, as big as my foot, peered back at me, then scurried off into the darkness.

"That building's your target," Hagar said. "I have to close the portal behind you for security, but I'll be watching the whole way. As soon as you find what we need, I'll open another portal to bring you back."

"How am I supposed to get into the building?" I asked.

"The storage facility is technologically inert. The heretics use a lot of jinsei tricks that don't work well with modern gear," Hagar said. "There's no standard alarm system, no closed circuit television, nothing like that. Find a fire escape, break out a window, and slip right in."

"There are no defenses on this building at all?" I asked.

"I didn't say that," Hagar said. "But this is why we brought you in, Jace. The spirit guardians who watch over this place use supernatural senses to find intruders. You shouldn't have any trouble slipping by them with that veil around your core."

"If I get killed," I said to Hagar, "I'll haunt you forever."

"Yeah, yeah," she said with a dismissive wave of her hand. "Get moving. You only have a window of twenty minutes or so before the human security guard makes the rounds. You need to be gone before then. Your target's on the eleventh floor, unit one one one five. This will be a piece of cake for you, Jace."

"Wish me luck." I hoped Hagar was right.

I stepped through the portal and across a few thousand miles. An illuminated billboard written in Spanish glowed from the sky on the left end of the alley I'd landed in. Puddles in the street reflected the advertisement's brilliant light. The opposite street was darker, lit only by the sullen red glow of traffic lights I couldn't see from my position.

Wherever I'd landed, it was darker than it had been back at the School. That told me I'd traveled east, but that wasn't much use to me. I stood still for a few seconds, fully expecting someone to show up and ask me what I was doing in the alley.

The portal vanished with a faint pop.

It was time to move.

There was, indeed, a rickety fire escape near the end of the alley. Its rusted bars glowed purple and pink in the neon lights from businesses across the street, and I hoped no one would see me as I scrambled up its lowered ladder. My hands picked up dirt and grime from the rungs, and I wished I'd thought to bring some gloves. I'd have to be very careful not to leave fingerprints behind once I was inside. My core was veiled, but the rest of me wasn't.

The fire escape rattled and banged against the side of the building as I hurried around and around the flights of metal stairs leading from floor to floor. I hunched my shoulders and tried to quiet my steps, to no avail. I expected someone to stick their head out through one of the windows I'd passed and yell at me to knock it off or get lost, but it never happened. Maybe Hagar had planned this thing right after all.

I peered through the window on the eleventh floor. The dirty glass and reflection of neon lights from surrounding businesses made it hard to see much. I could just make out an empty hallway on the other side of the glass. It was now or never.

The window was locked, which was just my luck. I looked down at the sidewalk and didn't see any passersby. Hopefully it was late enough no one would hear what came next.

I grabbed my right fist in my left hand, turned my back to the window, and slammed my right elbow through the glass.

It shattered, and chunks of square safety glass bounced away in every direction. The glittering greenish cubes cascaded down the fire escape like balls in a pachinko machine. Their echoes rattled through the alleyway for what felt like half an hour. I froze, sure that someone had to have heard that and would come investigate. I took a deep breath, then another. No one came.

The window had broken cleanly from its frame, and I stepped over the wooden sill into the hallway. The carpet in the narrow passage was old and rubbed through to bare concrete in places. The dropped ceiling was splotched with brown water stains, and the paint on the walls had peeled like old scabs to reveal patches of rotting drywall. The stink of mildew filled my nostrils, and I fought it by taking slow, shallow breaths through my mouth.

It only took me a few minutes to find the right unit. The heavy door that barred my way was held in place by a thick padlock. The numbers on its dial had been almost worn away by years of twisting and turning. Despite its obvious age, the lock's U-shaped hasp still looked sturdy and unmarked by rust or wear.

I gave it an experimental jerk. The lock scarcely rattled, much less opened.

"Okay," I said, "I guess we do this the hard way."

Like every building in every city, the storage facility was teeming with rats in its hidden spaces. It took no effort at all for me to forge connections to dozens of the hardy little creatures. I cycled my breathing and pulled their beast aspects into my aura, where I could put them to use.

Individually, the rats weren't terribly strong. Combined, though, and properly focused, the strength I had taken from them was more than enough to do the job at hand. My serpents flowed out of my core and hovered above my shoulders like hooded cobras. My thoughts refined their shapes, narrowing their tips until they were flattened wedges less than half an inch across.

I pushed the heads of my serpents into the half-circle opening formed by the hasp. I closed my eyes, concentrated, and used them like a pair of crowbars. It wasn't subtle, and I hope Hagar wouldn't be angry with me for leaving a trace of my presence. On the other hand, she hadn't given me the lock's combination, and I didn't have time to figure it out by trial and error. The heretics would just have to know someone had rifled through their stuff.

The metal groaned, and the serpents pushed against one another and the metal in a frenzy of activity. Beads of sweat dotted my forehead, and the effort left my aura feeling bruised and battered. Finally, when I felt as if I couldn't push any harder, the latch on the door gave way with a terrific squeal and the broken lock fell to the floor.

"Okay, then." I slipped inside the door and pulled it closed behind me. "Let's see what we've got here."

The darkness inside the cube made it impossible to see anything. A sliver of light leaked in under the door from the hallway. When my eyes finally adjusted to the darkness, I stumbled toward what looked like a lightbulb hanging from the ceiling in the center of the unit.

And promptly barked my shins on something. I yelped in pained surprise, then clapped my hands over my mouth. I took a long, slow breath, then let it out, and the pain eased away. I reached up to the lightbulb and groped at its smooth surface. My fingers found the switch on its socket and turned it sharply to the right, careful to use my knuckles rather than my fingertips to avoid leaving prints.

The bulb turned on with a loud click and filled the cube with a warm glow. It was ten feet on a side, though most of that space was unused. The room's only furnishings were the desk that had attacked my poor shins. It crouched in the center of the bare concrete floor, the lightbulb directly above it. The walls were naked cinder blocks streaked with glistening rivulets of rust-colored water that leaked through the dropped ceiling's spongy tiles.

"What's in the desk?" Hagar's voice crackled in my thoughts.

I jumped at the unexpected question and got to work.

To keep my fingerprints off anything in the room, I pulled the sleeves of my robe down to cover my hands. Being a little clumsier was a fine tradeoff for not making it obvious who'd been in here.

The desk's shallow sliding drawer held a pair of fountain pens that had leaked black ink from their exposed nibs onto a sheet of pink blotter paper. There was nothing else in the drawer, and its back seemed solid when I rapped against it looking for secret compartments.

The file drawer to the right of the seat, though, was filled with hanging folders. I had no idea which of those held important information, so I took a seat in the chair and pulled half of them onto the desk in front of me. I made a neat stack at my left hand, took the top folder off it, and dropped it on the desk. It held a short stack of plain white paper covered in dense rows of handwritten block letters.

"Look at a page, then blink to take a picture," Hagar advised me. "I'll store the pictures on my end."

A golden frame appeared around the page the instant my eyes focused on the text. When I blinked my eyes, the light stayed superimposed on the darkness behind them and flickered to green before returning to gold. I had no idea how Hagar could store the pages I sent to her, or what she'd do with the information. That was above my pay grade. I flipped through page after handwritten page, blinking at each one, taking time to skim only a few of them out of sheer curiosity.

What I saw was confusing. I'd expected to see some mention of the Locust Court. After all, those were the biggest enemies of the Empyrean Flame and its Grand Design. If they were notes from a heretic cell, I'd assume they would have reams of spirit propaganda.

Instead, most of what I saw seemed to have something to do with a technical theory of something called the Machina. There were hand-drawn diagrams, too, of some sort of complex mechanism. None of it made any sense to me, and I wasn't sure it would even if I took more time to read it.

I'd gone through three-quarters of the stack from the file folder when I saw something that stopped me. A list of names in two columns. My eyes landed on three names in the left column: Grayson Bishop, Tycho Reyes, and Eve Warin. They were near the top of the page, surrounded by names I didn't recognize. My interest piqued, I scanned the right column for any other familiar names.

Hagar Inaloti.
Elder Sanrin.
Melody Hark.
Jace Warin.

My name was the last on the right-hand list, in black ink where the rest of the list was in blue. I'd been added to this page last. The implications of that whirled through my thoughts. The bad guys knew my name, and it was on the same side as Hagar and Sanrin. That could mean the right column was their enemies list. But Adjudicator Hark's name was on that side of the list, too, and I wasn't sure she was working with the Shadow Phoenix.

And if the right side was the enemy list, then the left side would be friends. But that list had both Tycho's and Grayson's name, and they absolutely hated each other. It also had my mom's name, and—

A faint warbling sound from the hallway raised goose bumps on my arms and sent chills racing up my spine.

"Guardian." Hagar's thoughts were a faint whisper in my head. "Get out of there."

I restacked the folders and replaced them in the file drawer, then stood carefully from my chair so as not to make any noise. The guardian might just be on the prowl. If it didn't know I was in the storage unit, maybe it would move on by.

The strange sound was closer, now. It had to be right outside the door.

I reached up and covered the lightbulb with my hand to shield the light. Turning it off would have been better, if the switch hadn't made so much noise when I turned it on.

I held my breath, unsure what to do next.

The door creaked open and an amorphous haze drifted into the storage unit. The cloud twitched and pulsed in strange rhythms, extending tendrils from its mass to grope around the edges of the room. The warbling sound it made set my teeth on edge and amplified the headache the eye-snapper had started. I was sure those appendages would close in until they'd touched every inch of the cramped room.

My veiled core kept me hidden from the guardian for the moment. If it touched me, though, all bets were off.

"Hold still," Hagar said. "It didn't sound the alarm when it found the door open. Maybe it's just doing a cursory check."

The tendrils had finished with the walls and moved on to the ceiling and floor. They'd picked up the pace and spread out. Hagar was wrong. This thing would find me if I didn't do something.

The guardian had moved into the room and blocked the door with its amorphous body. Its tentacles were closing in on me from every direction. I had to make a move before it found me and sounded the alarm.

I leaped over the desk and used the dregs of the beast aspects I'd taken from the rats to fuel a knife hand strike. The blow drove my fingers deep into the spirit's body, and I strained to reach its core. Another inch, and the spirit watchdog would be dead.

The creature's tendrils lashed at my back in a pained frenzy. The beast's attacks were ineffective, so it switched to evasion. Its body morphed, and it pulled its core further from my grasping fingers.

My Eclipse nature responded instantly. It hungered for the core almost within my grasp and wasn't about to let the tasty morsel slip away. The urge pushed jinsei into the channels in my arm, and I used that new strength to thrust my hand deeper into the guardian. My fingers found its core and seized it like the talons of an eagle around its prey. The urge swelled inside me, demanding that I tear the core out and devour it.

For a moment, my mind flashed to Singapore.

No, I didn't have time for that. The guardian wasn't a person, it was a mindless spirit construct that would get me killed if I didn't destroy it. I ripped the spirit's core out of its body and threw it on the ground.

My Eclipse nature wanted me to snatch it up and devour it. The dark urge demanded I consume the core, take it all into me, and leave not a scrap to be wasted.

"No," I growled. Giving in to my shadow nature was a slippery slope. If I let the darkness have its way, it would demand more and more from me. Better to keep it shut away where it couldn't hurt anyone else.

Without its core, the guardian spirit's body began to dissolve into the raw jinsei that had been used to craft it. Its tentacles thrashed at the desk, overturning it and spilling papers everywhere. Then it flopped to the ground and let out a long, warbling cry. The sound went on for a long breath, then faded away.

Other curious warbles answered the guardian's death cry. They were far too close to my location for comfort, and I knew I was out of time.

I bolted out into the hallway and rushed for the broken window, heedless of the damage I'd left behind. There was no hiding the fact that someone had broken into the heretics' storage unit. The best I could hope was that they didn't know it was me.

I scrambled through the window and raced down the fire escape. My feet banged off each rain-slicked stair, making a terrible racket. I ignored the ladder at the bottom of the escape and dropped to the concrete with a single step.

The portal was back, its red glow comforting in the alley's darkness. I raced to it, took a deep breath, and threw myself back to my comfortable cottage.

Hagar scrambled out of the chair she'd been slumped in when I arrived. She aimed the key wand at the portal, and a blue light from the device banished the door behind me.

"That wasn't the most subtle thing I've ever seen," she said with a groan. The warden returned the key wand to her belt, then held her hand out to me. "Eye-snapper, please."

"Here." My headache receded the instant I plucked the black bead off my temple. I was glad to be rid of the thing. "What was all that stuff about the Machina in those papers? And what's the deal with the list of names?"

"I don't know," she said. It was hard to tell whether she was telling the truth or not. "I'll take all this back to the elders tonight. The analysts will go through all of it."

"When will they tell us what they find?" I asked. "My mother's name was in those papers, Hagar. I need to know—"

"Jace, calm down." Hagar put her hand on my shoulder. "You did good work tonight, and that's all you need to be concerned with. You got the information. What happens to it after isn't your job."

"You said they'd help me find my mother," I started.

Hagar shut me down with a quick squeeze of my shoulder and a shake of her head.

"That isn't how this works," she said. "If they find anything about your mother, they'll tell you. If they find anything useful for our next job, they'll tell you. But that's it. We compartmentalize the data we retrieve from the heretics to keep it safe. You can't know everything. I don't even know everything. Get some rest. Control put some food in the kitchen for you. Try to relax. I'll get back to you when I have anything."

Hagar surprised me with a short hug, then left the cottage. I stood in the main room, alone, and wondered what I'd gotten myself into.

# THE CLASH

WE KEPT UP OUR TECHNIQUE WORK IN MARTIAL arts class the next day, and it was my turn to attack Clem. My focus was on using the power of my Eclipse core to steal aspects, without triggering the dark urge that made me want to rip the core out of anyone and anything who got too close to me. My idea was to use my serpents to pull the aspects directly into my aura without also stealing jinsei from my target. That should, in theory, bypass my core entirely and not alert my Eclipse nature. I could then push those aspects back into my serpents to make them even stronger.

It was a pretty smart idea, if you asked me.

Unfortunately, I couldn't quite get it to jell together. The first part of it worked well enough, and I scooped aspects out of Clem's aura without her even realizing what had happened. Unfortunately, I couldn't stop small amounts of jinsei from entering my core at the same time. That woke my Eclipse nature and forced me to spend a minute or two calming it back down before I could try again.

Clem was understanding through the whole process, though by the end of the class her patience had begun to fray.

"Whatever you're doing seems awfully difficult," she said. "If you tell me what it is you hope to accomplish, maybe we can figure it out together."

"Maybe," I said with a dejected sigh. I couldn't tell Clem, or anyone else, what I was trying to do without revealing my Eclipse core. "Let me think about it some more."

"Up to you." Clem shrugged.

I knew I'd irritated her by dismissing her offer to help, but there was no getting around it. Until I came up with a suitable cover story for why I could only try the technique every couple of minutes, she'd just have to think I was being a jerk.

That sucked, but there wasn't an alternative.

I puzzled over my technique problem for the rest of the day, barely paying attention through history and struggling to keep my focus on the Intermediate Scrivenings course.

"Due to some unforeseen circumstances, Professor Ishigara will no longer be instructing the other half of your class in the fine art of scrivening. All second years now fall under my purview," Professor Shan said. The way she twisted her mouth into a disgusted little grimace told me she wasn't thrilled by the added responsibility. "As a result, there will be more group projects, starting now."

As if on cue, the door to the scrivenings hall opened and the rest of our classmates from the second year spilled in. They all looked around, confused and unsure of where to sit.

Except for Rachel.

She spotted me immediately and waved enthusiastically as she headed in my direction.

"It's going to get crowded in here," Clem grumbled from the chair on my right. "There goes all our individual attention from the professor."

"Like you need it," Eric said with a grin from Clem's opposite side. "You're the best in the class. This won't affect you at all."

"It's already affected me." It was hard not to notice that Clem's eyes didn't waver from Rachel as she spoke, and it was equally clear she didn't like what she saw.

The new students found seats, and it got more crowded by the moment as they filled in all the gaps. A burly kid I didn't recognize pushed his way past the other students, his eyes on the seat to my left. Fantastic. I didn't want to spend the rest of the year with an oversized neighbor constantly jostling me with his elbows. I had enough trouble keeping my temper under control in this class without the added grief.

"Taken," Rachel said as she slipped past the big guy from the other direction and plopped into the chair next to me. She pointed to an empty seat down near the front of the classroom. "Try over there."

"That was my seat," he protested.

"I don't see your name on it," Rachel said with a smirk.

"Making friends," Clem muttered.

Rachel turned toward my pink-haired friend and thrust her open hand past me.

"I'm Rachel Lu. You must be Clem. I've heard so much about you. I'm so excited to get to see the best scrivenings student in school at work in such close quarters!"

"Yes." Clem took Rachel's hand and gave it a firm shake. "It's nice to meet you too."

For a moment, the girls were very, very close to me. Their hands were clasped in front of me, their shoulders pressing against mine from either side. A faint wisp of perfume, delicate and citrusy, tickled my nostrils, but I wasn't sure if it came from Clem or Rachel. Their eyes sparked, and I felt a sudden tightness around my heart.

"All right, students," Professor Shan called from the front of the room, "looks like you've all got seats. Excellent. This is today's group assignment."

The professor flicked her hand toward us, and tiny squares of metal fluttered through the air like confetti. They grew as they spun across the room until they were three inches on a side. One of the squares landed in front of me, and another in front of the girl to Eric's right. More squares dropped onto the shared tables until exactly one third of the students had one.

"If you have a square, then your partners are to your left and right," Professor Shan continued. "It is up to each team to repair the scrivening on their square. Please have one member of your group bring me the completed assignment before the end of class."

Rachel and Clem both looked at the square, then at me. There was something strange in their eyes, and I didn't like it even a little bit.

"This will be fun," I said. I groaned inwardly and hoped the hostility I felt building between my two friends wouldn't explode into an open argument.

"Yes," Clem said, her voice cheerful. "It will be."

"It looks simple enough," Rachel agreed.

We all bent our heads over the square, analyzing the scrivening for its flaws. There were some obvious gaps in the connecting swirls, and a strange set of vertical slashes on some lines needed to be smoothed out.

"We should start here," Rachel offered. "If we inscribe a new connector between these two lines—"

"We'll end up disrupting this pattern here," Clem responded. "It's subtle, but these secondary effects are connected to the primary script through the border. We have to be careful not to remove those connections accidentally."

The two girls gave each other wide smiles filled with straight white teeth.

"Have either of you ever heard of the Machina?" I blurted out to draw their attention to me instead of each other.

"Just rumors," Rachel said. "The labor unions say it's some new kind of core that can be programmed to run a machine. It'll take a lot of jobs out of the undercity if it's true."

"That'll never work," Clem shot back. "Merging jinsei into traditional technology has never been done on any significant scale. The two types of power don't work well together."

"Is that what they taught you in your precious overcity elementary schools?" Rachel said, venom dripping from her words.

"Yes, that is what they taught us in the overcity," Clem replied, her eyes sparking dangerously. "It's simply a fact of Empyreal science. Combining different types of energy work can have unpredictable results."

"And no one wants to be unpredictable," Rachel said. "After all, if we start questioning the status quo, what would become of the traditions that keep the overcity's boots on the necks of all the little people?"

The temperature between my friends had risen several uncomfortable degrees. Anger aspects danced in their auras, and my stomach clenched into a knot. The two girls came from very different backgrounds and clearly had incompatible points of view on many, many things. I needed to distract them before things really blew up.

"I'll just do this," I said and dragged a polishing tool across one of the jagged slashes that marred the scrivening on our square. "It should—"

"No!" Both girls exclaimed together. Rachel snatched the polisher out of my hand, and Clem used her inscriber to redraw what I'd erased.

"Ugh, we're never going to get this right," Clem grumbled.

"It is a mess," Rachel agreed.

They both eyeballed me with irritation, which was an improvement over the boiling anger they held for each other. I could handle my friends being mad at me over something I'd done a lot more easily than I could handle them arguing with each other. Especially when I didn't even know why they'd decided to fight.

My partners put aside their differences and dove into a frenzy of activity to undo the mess I'd made of our scrivened plate. While I felt a teensy bit bad about what I'd done, I mostly felt relief. I didn't see any way for us to complete the work before the end of the class, especially because I kept asking questions so I'd understand what my partners were up to. That would cost us some points off on the assignment. On the other hand, I'd avoided a fight between two of my friends, who seemed much more interested in talking to one another when they both had something to gain.

"What if we added an inner border to connect these two pieces?" Rachel said excitedly.

"It is unorthodox," Clem said with a frown. Her expression brightened, though, when she saw how Rachel's unusual tactic could help them overcome one of the gaps in the scrivening. "It'll work! I've never seen anything quite like it, but there's no reason not to do it."

"I had to teach myself scrivening," Rachel confided. "We don't get a lot of textbooks in the undercity. Most of what I learned came off the Internet. The rest I sort of made up as I went along."

"I can help you," Clem offered, much to my surprise. "It won't be easy, but if we put in some extra time, maybe…"

"Oh, I couldn't trouble you," Rachel said. "I know you're very busy."

The two of them chattered on like that, bouncing ideas off each other, working feverishly to finish the assignment. I was shocked to see we'd actually finished with minutes of class time to spare.

"Nice work," Clem said as Rachel closed the final loop on the scrivening with a smooth, spiral flourish. "I didn't think we were going to make it."

Rachel grinned at my pink-haired friend and slapped a high-five into her palm.

"No, thank you," Rachel insisted. "I found a couple of shortcuts, but we would've never finished if it weren't for your knowledge of the more traditional techniques. There were sigils that I just didn't know were missing."

"There are advantages to traditional training," Clem admitted. "That's what helped me fill in the gaps. But without your intuition and shortcuts, it would've taken much longer to fix the damage that someone caused."

I raised my hands defensively but couldn't hold back a chuckle.

"I'm terrible at scrivening," I said. "They shouldn't even let me have an inscriber."

"We'll remember that for next time," Rachel said with a wink for Clem.

"I'll turn this in," she said. "I wouldn't want it to get messed up on the way down to Professor Shan."

"I wouldn't mess it up," I complained.

"No sense taking chances!" Clem said brightly and snatched up the scripted square of metal. She took off for the front of the classroom to turn in the assignment.

Rachel watched her go, a faint smile on her lips.

"I guess I'm the one who rushed to judgment this time," she said.

"What do you mean?" I asked.

"Clem," she clarified. "She dresses like a rebel, you know? The hair and those robes, I mean. It's not very traditional. I thought she was more like me."

"Well, she is," I pointed out. "You're an Empyreal from the undercity who taught yourself, and you don't like rules. She's from the overcity, but helped a kid from the labor camps survive his first year at the School of Swords and Serpents."

"Maybe we do have some similarities on the surface." Rachel gave me a faint grin. "You need to learn to look past that, Jace. Dressing like a rebel doesn't make you a rebel. And acting out doesn't always mean you don't like the rules. The truth is deeper than that. For all of us."

Before I could ask her what she meant, Professor Shan dismissed us. Rachel gave my shoulder a quick squeeze, gathered her books, and slipped into the stream of students pouring out of the scriptorium.

I watched her dark braid sway through the crowd as Clem climbed the stairs to retrieve her books, and I wondered if I'd ever really understand my friends.

# THE RAID

HAGAR PULLED ANOTHER VANISHING ACT AFTER our first mission. I rapped on her door every night, hoping the analysts had given her some information about my mother, but my handler never answered. None of the other Shadow Phoenixes had seen her around, either. Half of my fellow clanmates claimed to have no idea who Hagar was, and the other half didn't seem concerned about her vanishing act. I asked some professors if they'd seen her in class, and they all reprimanded me for asking them to violate student privacy rules. Even Professor Song, who seemed particularly open and honest, claimed he hadn't noticed her missing from his upperclassman courses. I sent the rats to find her, and they came back just as empty-handed as those who'd gone looking for Hahen.

Either Hagar had special permission to come and go from the School whenever she pleased, or her teachers and friends knew better than to question her absences. It was frustrating, and I vowed to get the truth out of her.

If I ever found her again.

And then, a month after I'd last seen her, the warden showed up at my doorstep.

"Stop asking so many questions about me," she said sharply. "It takes a lot of work to hide a missing student, and you're not making it any easier."

"Where did you go?" I asked.

"Not important, and also not for you to know," she sighed. "The only thing you need to know right now is that we've got a new assignment."

"Hold on," I said. "We go on a mission, then you go missing for a month? I thought you were hurt. Maybe dead. You can't just drop off the face of the world."

"I don't want to have this conversation in the hall," Hagar said, glancing up and down the empty corridor. "Inside."

She didn't say another word until we'd reached the cottage. Then she took a seat on the edge of a chair in my sitting room and crossed her hands on one knee.

"First off, I didn't go on a mission, you did," she said. "I stayed right here, in this chair, and watched. It was very intriguing. The analysts who looked over the footage noted that you did something very unusual to the spirit—"

"You said something about a new mission?" I interrupted. The last thing I wanted was to go into what I'd done with my Eclipse core.

"Yes, in about fifteen minutes," she said. "This one is going to be a little more intense, okay? We have a line on some vital material we need to recover. If we can get our hands on this, we'll leapfrog past the heretics. It will accelerate the elders' timetable by months, Jace. Unfortunately, it's in a secured facility behind a wall of core sensors."

"And you want me to sneak in and steal the stuff?"

"Not exactly." Hagar leaned forward. "You'll clear a path for the recovery team. Neutralize the guards, disable the core sensors, and get out."

"What kind of guards?" I asked.

"You worry too much. They're not heretics, just hired goons." Hagar's eyes burned into mine. "I've seen you fight, Jace. You're the champ. This will be a piece of cake."

Maybe she was right. Three months of fighting day in and day out had left me wired for combat even now, almost three months after the challenge had ended. I'd beaten the best contenders each city could offer. None of them had been able to take me down, and few of them had even landed a single blow. I doubted any rented security team would fare any better.

"What else do I have to worry about?"

"Cameras in the halls," Hagar said. "But we have a jintech helmet to hide your face from them. We've got a source on the inside who has patched us in to the security net. I'll be able to control the cameras and watch the guard patrols, though. Shouldn't be a problem. We can talk about all this on the way. Let's get you on the transport ahead of schedule."

"Transport?" I asked. "What are you—"

An angry hum rumbled through the air over the cabin. It grew louder by the second until the walls began to shake, and the lake's surface jittered and jumped outside the window. It felt like my teeth were about to shake out of my head.

Hagar grinned at me and rushed outside. I followed her and was immediately pummeled by the downdraft from some sort of bizarre helicopter. The vehicle descended to the shore on the far side of the lake. A set of stairs flopped out of a hatch on its side and landed at the end of the bridge.

The vehicle was thirty feet from nose to tail. Its body was long and slender, pointed at the nose, and flared out into a wide tail that supported a pair of vertically mounted rotors. Four mobile struts that extended from the top of the craft held the horizontal rotors, which still spun with furious force. Clearly, they were in a hurry to get moving.

The strangest thing about the vehicle, though, was its color. The entire craft was coated in a dark material that was difficult to look at for more than a few seconds. It was as if my vision slid off it without absorbing any details.

Weird.

"There's your ride," Hagar shouted. She rushed across the bridge ahead of me, and I hurried to catch up.

By the time I'd boarded the vehicle, Hagar had already thrown herself into a seat and grabbed hold of the armrests. There was a thump from behind me as the stairs retracted and the hatch closed.

"Grab a chair," Hagar warned.

And not a moment too soon. The instant I dropped into a flight seat, the angry buzzing became a roar and the transport lifted into the air. It took off with a sudden burst of speed that made my stomach lurch sickeningly. There was a bone-rattling bout of turbulence, and the deafening roar of the engines vanished.

"Where's the rest of the team?" I asked with a glance at the empty seats.

"They're coming in on a different transport," Hagar responded. "Stop worrying about the details."

"What if—"

"Let's get you kitted up." Hagar unbuckled her safety harness. "It should be a smooth flight from here on out. Unless you keep asking me questions I can't answer. Then I'll toss you out the hatch."

She jumped up and rummaged through the storage compartments attached to the walls of the transport. She found a black plastic package and dropped it on the seat next to me.

"Get your robes off, and put that on," she said. "I promise not to look."

The inside of the transport had ten seats, and they were all empty except for the one I'd taken. Each of the comfortable chairs had a flight harness dangling from its shoulders, and a few of them had heavy steel rings mounted to the ends of their arms. Cargo containers lined the sides of the roof, and other compartments occupied the spaces between the seats. The interior was lit by a thin strip of light overhead, and there were no windows. A bulkhead toward the transport's nose had a heavy, secured door in its center.

"Turn around," I said.

Hagar rolled her eyes at me and moved toward the bulkhead. She twirled her finger over her head.

"Hurry it up," she said. "We're on a tight schedule."

The plastic bundle held a simple black jumpsuit that unfolded as soon as I tore the packaging. The material was stretchy, with plenty of pockets on the thighs and chest, along with carabiners sewn directly to the fabric above the waist.

"Seriously, don't look," I said.

Hagar snorted.

I stripped out of my robes and tossed them on the chair to my right. The new suit fit like a glove. It was tight where it needed to be and still loose enough to allow an easy range of motion.

"I'm dressed," I said.

"Good to know," Hagar said. "We're getting close."

That announcement sent my thoughts in a dozen different directions. Where were we going that was within a few minutes' travel of the School? And how had they flown the transport into my private quarters?

Before I could ask any of the questions, Hagar returned to me with a black helmet under her arm.

"This will hide your face." She rapped on the helmet's mirrored full-face visor. "It's also got a full communication suite, encrypted, of course, and it can take a pretty good knock without cracking. We're using this instead of the eye-snapper this time."

"Why?" I asked.

"Not your concern," she said. "Focus up. Here's a picture of your guy. I'll put his apartment number on the HUD in your helmet. Focus on this, okay?"

"I guess," I said. "This is all happening pretty fast."

"That's how it goes." Hagar grinned. "Don't get distracted. We'll be back at the School before you know it."

"I'm not distracted!"

"Get your shoes on," Hagar said, pointing to the low boots I'd discarded when I took my robes off. "We're five minutes out."

"From where?"

"Stop asking so many questions," she said.

I slipped my boots on and tightened the laces. Hagar was right. The less I knew, the less chance there was I'd let something slip and screw it all up for the elders. I took a deep breath, cycled jinsei into my core, and purged the tension and anxiety aspects from my core on the exhalation. I cleared my thoughts and let all the questions go.

"Ready," I said.

"Good." Hagar took a seat and fastened her harness. She pointed at a rail over the hatch. "Hang onto that. We're coming down."

With that, the transport's nose tilted alarmingly toward the ground, and it spun into a sharp circle. The sudden motion made my stomach jump into my throat, and I hung onto the rail for dear life.

"Helmet on," Hagar called.

I grabbed the black armor from the seat and pulled it down over my head. There was a disconcerting moment as the cheek and neck pads tightened to secure the helmet in place. In the time it took for the helmet to adjust itself to the shape of my skull, the visor shifted from an impenetrable black to transparent.

A red circle floated in the center of my vision, obvious but not distracting. Smaller red triangles dotted the edges of my field of view. When I focused my attention on any of those, small words appeared next to them: cargo compartment, electrical access panel, restraint system, fire retardation nozzle, emergency oxygen mask.

I turned toward Hagar, and the circle flickered green.

She was now wearing a helmet, too, and a small keyboard rested on her lap.

"All right, champ," she said, "when the door opens, move out. I'll be right in your ear."

Her words were tinny and distant through the helmet's speakers. I decided I liked trading slightly less clear audio from my handler for the eye-snapper's headache.

The transport descended slow and silent, and a moment later I felt a faint bump as we touched down. The hatch opened, and the stairs tumbled down with a ratcheting noise I could barely hear above my own breathing.

"I'm out," I said and raced down the steps.

My Eclipse core stirred the instant my feet hit the flat tarred roof the transport had landed on. The skyscrapers that surrounded our landing spot told me we were in a big city. Most of the windows I saw were dark, and the sky overhead glowed with ambient light that blotted out the stars. I instinctively looked up for the bright flares of an overcity's lift crystals, but the only lights in the sky came from the city itself.

I tried to think of any big cities without an Empyreal presence. Nothing came to mind.

"I've highlighted your door." Hagar's voice disrupted my thoughts. "Once you're inside, give me a moment to secure our tie into the security cameras."

My HUD pointed me toward a door set into the side of a small cube of aluminum that jutted from the roof's top. I darted around ventilation fans and jumped over ductwork to reach it. I cycled jinsei as I ran, purging any stray aspects of tension or worry from my aura to keep my mind as smooth and calm as the lake that surrounded my cottage.

"The door is unlocked," Hagar informed me. "You can tell by the green light just below the handle. If you run into any doors where that light is red, do not try to open them. You'll set off an alarm."

"Good to know." The door's knob twisted easily in my hand, and it pulled open on silent, well-oiled hinges. "I'm in."

The small maintenance room I'd entered held a collection of basic tools on a pegboard against one wall, a tattered binder filled with yellowed paper on the workbench beneath them, and a set of stairs that led deeper into the building.

"One second, let me get these cameras oriented." A few seconds later, Hagar broke the silence. "All right, you're clear down to the tenth floor. I'll let you know if that changes. Move quickly."

My heart raced as I sprinted down the squared spiral staircase. My Eclipse nature was restless inside me, a tiger pacing its cage. I'd felt like this before almost every fight in the Five Dragons Challenge, and I'd never gotten used to it. There was a hunger in me now, a taste for violence I didn't want to indulge.

It dogged me all the way down the stairway, a constant clamoring to punch and kick and break things that just wouldn't leave me be. The dark urge knew there was a fight coming, and it wanted blood.

"Hold." Hagar's voice dragged me out of my thoughts. "There's a guard outside the door to your left, ten paces. Take him down, now."

"Take him down?" I said. "Why can't I just wait for him to move—"

"Now!" Hagar's shout rang in my helmet.

The panic in her voice broke through my hesitation. I glanced at the door's handle, saw the green light, and eased it open into the passage beyond.

The Borrowed Core technique forged connections to a dozen rats as I raced up behind the guard. Their breaths became mine, and their bestial aspects filled my aura. The serpents twitched inside me, ready to burst forth and do my bidding. As much as I didn't want to admit it, the rush of adrenaline felt good.

It felt right.

The guard wore a boring khaki uniform, complete with a heavy utility belt on his waist that held a holstered pistol on his right hip. A tactical harness covered his torso in a web covered with items I didn't recognize. He held a walkie-talkie in his left hand. I'd need to deal with that before he had a chance to call for help.

The guard heard me when I was less than a step away. Time slowed as he spun on his right heel, one hand dropping toward his holster, the other hand lifting the walkie-talkie to his mouth. The color drained out of his face at the sight of an intruder so close to him, and panic aspects leaped into his aura in a sparkling flurry.

If the guard's hand reached his holster, he'd have a weapon trained on me in the next second. If he got that walkie-talkie up to his mouth, there'd be a bunch more weapons trained on me not long after that.

My serpents exploded out of my aura. The first to emerge darted toward the guard's left hand, a chittering swarm of shadows that closed around his wrist in the blink of an eye. He yelped in surprise, and my serpent yanked his arm toward me.

Hard.

Off balance, he couldn't recover in time to defend himself. A right backfist knocked the walkie-talkie out of his grip and into the wall, where its black plastic housing shattered. My left hand slammed into his shoulder, knocking his hand away from his pistol's grip.

Before he could recover, I drove my knee into the guard's gut hard enough to bend him double.

My opponent's breath shot out of his lungs, and he fell on his tailbone, hard. My Eclipse nature wanted me to end the man's life to ensure he wouldn't cause me trouble later. If he raised an alarm, the whole mission would be in jeopardy.

Instead, I drove my fist into the side of the man's head, just behind his ear. The jinsei-amplified attack put the guard's lights out, and he flopped onto his side, unconscious. His breath stuttered, then resumed. He'd have a terrible headache when he woke up, but at least he would wake up.

"Pick him up," Hagar ordered. "There's a storeroom down the hall to the right. Hide him in there."

The guard and all his gear were heavier than I'd expected, and I fed a bit of jinsei into my back to make hauling him around easier. The unconscious man groaned as I carried him and started snoring when I leaned him against a stack of toilet paper rolls in the storeroom. I ran back to collect the pieces of his broken walkie-talkie and deposited them in a nearby trashcan.

"One down, twelve to go," she said.

"Twelve," I hissed with surprise. "That's insane."

"Good thing for you, then, it's only three." Hagar snickered. "Lighten up. Your next target is straight ahead and then left. Stop at the intersection. Wait for my go."

I hustled down the hallway, relieved and irritated at the same time. It was easy for Hagar to joke about this mess, as she was safely back on the transport. I, on the other hand, was neck deep in enemy territory. If anything went wrong, I'd pay the price, not her.

I wondered how heretics would deal with someone like me, then pushed all those thoughts aside. I'd seen too many TV shows where sneaking around ended up in torture. I pressed my back flat to the wall and cycled the nervous aspects out of my aura. No one was going to torture me. I'd get out of here in one piece.

"Wait for it," Hagar said. "Wait for it."

The guard walked with his head down and didn't even see me hiding in the shadows as he strolled along his rounds.

I reached out when he passed by my hiding spot, hooked an arm around his neck, and jerked him into the hallway with me. He tried to elbow me, but his webbed harness got in the way.

I slapped his hand away before he could reach his weapon, then pulled the gun from its holster and tossed it down the hall behind us. The whole time I kept up the pressure on his throat, my bicep and forearm digging into the sides of his neck. His struggles grew weaker, his grunts and wheezes less frequent, and finally he went still. Pinching off the blood supply to the brain hadn't killed him, but he and his friend would be eating aspirin together to soothe their savage headaches.

"No time to hide this one," Hagar said, her words hurried. "Your next target changed direction. He's coming from the left. Twenty seconds out."

"Great," I growled.

"Something's wrong," Hagar said, panicked. "There's another coming from the right."

My Eclipse nature surged to life, its animal aggression screaming for me to slaughter these foes and finish the mission. It showed me a vision of the future, blood splattered across the hallway, dead men at my feet.

It took me long, painful seconds to push the dark urge down and out of my thoughts. I wasn't going to kill these men who were just doing their job. There had to be another way.

"They're almost on top of you," Hagar breathed into my ear. Her voice was tight and twisted with worry. "Do something."

I lunged out of the hallway and rushed to the left. My Borrowed Core technique gathered in more rats to the fold, filling my aura with bestial aspects. Unfortunately, the guard heard me when I was still too far away for me to reach him with my serpents. He found his weapon, raised it, and drew a bead on me.

In the next second, he'd pull the trigger.

I was fast, but not fast enough to dodge a bullet.

My fusion blade appeared in my right hand at the speed of thought. I hurled it down the hallway at the guard, knowing even as I threw it my attack wouldn't be fast enough. He'd squeeze off the shot, and it'd punch into my chest. That would be lights out for me.

The guard flinched at the unexpected attack. As my unbalanced sword flew toward him, he jerked to one side and his shot went wide.

The gunshot's echo in the hallway was deafening. It felt like someone had slapped me on both ears with their open palms, and yet I still heard the whiz of a bullet as it ripped past my head. The guard's second shot followed hot on the heels of the first one, a wild and undisciplined squeeze that sent a bullet into the ceiling above my head.

My fusion sword slammed into the guard's chest, hilt first. The heavy weapon fell away from the guard, and he took his eyes off me for a moment to watch it hit the floor.

I hadn't stopped my headlong charge at the man. My serpents struck the instant the guard's eyes were off me, driven as much by my Eclipse nature's survival instincts as my conscious thought. They slammed into the guard's core, rocking him back on his heels and stripping jinsei out of his core in the blink of an eye.

The sacred energy, laced with aspects of panic and anger from my target's aura, hit my core in a delicious flood of power. I pushed the aspects back into my serpents, strengthening them and solidifying their grip on the guard's core.

It would be so easy to finish the man. I could let my core go for another second, maybe two, and the last of the jinsei would drain out of the man's body and into me.

Just like Singapore.

I ripped my serpents away from the guard, and my Eclipse nature roared. It filled my head with all the reasons the man needed to die. He wasn't out of the fight yet, which meant he was still a threat. He could shoot me.

"Halt!" the other guard shouted. He'd stopped twenty feet away, his weapon raised in a two-handed grip, legs spread, and shoulders squared in a stable firing platform.

"Abort!" Hagar shouted. "Get out of there, Jace. We've lost the element of surprise. They're coming for you."

Hagar was right. Hurried footsteps rang through the building. If I stayed where I was, they'd outnumber me in the next few minutes. One gunman I could deal with. Two was pushing my luck.

More than that?

Even a sacred sage could be taken down by enough bullets, and I was nowhere near that powerful. The smart choice was to run.

But if I cut and ran, we'd miss this chance to grab the material. That would put the elders' plans back by months, maybe years. Which meant they wouldn't be able to devote any resources to the most important thing to me: finding my mother.

"No," I said, my voice calm and quiet. I'd made my choice. I wasn't running. "I can still do this."

One of my serpents snatched my fusion blade from where it had fallen. The other looped around the downed guard's neck and bounced his head off the floor hard enough to knock him senseless.

The remaining guard's aura sparked with anxiety, dread, and violence. He didn't know who I was or why I was there—all he saw was his fallen friend. He could have fired, but he hadn't.

My Eclipse nature told me why. He was prey, paralyzed by the sight of a true predator before him.

I pushed the stolen jinsei into my legs and ran faster than the guard could track with his gun. I zigged to the left, then zagged back to the right as he fired into the space I'd just left. The bullets missed me by feet, not inches, and then I was on top of my foe.

My sword lashed out at the guard's gun, shattering his fingers as the weapon twisted free of his grip. Before he could cry out in surprise, I reversed my hold on the sword and drove its butt into his forehead. The jinsei-strengthened blow knocked the man off his feet, and his eyes rolled up into his head as he collapsed onto the ground.

"There are more guards coming," Hagar said. "We have to pull out."

"No," I demanded. "You told me this was a once-in-a-lifetime chance to get our hands on this material. Where's the target?"

"It's dangerous, Jace," my handler insisted. "We don't know what it can do. The extraction team has containment gear—"

"No time," I said. "Which way?"

Hagar debated whether to give me the location for what felt like hours. The sound of boots on the tiles rang through the building all around me. I was just about out of time.

"Straight ahead to the end of the hall, then right, first door on your left." Hagar's voice sounded hoarse. "The material isn't stable, Jace. If you touch it, no one knows what will happen."

"I understand," I said as I raced down the hall. "I'll do this."

The guard stationed in front of the door leading to my target had wisely held his ground despite the disturbance. He was there to protect what I'd come to steal, I was sure of that. Nothing was as important to him as keeping it safe.

He hadn't, however, drawn his gun, and he wasn't anywhere near fast enough to do it after he saw me. His hand hadn't even reached his holster before I was up in his face.

I snatched the guard's harness, dragged him away from the wall, then slammed him back into the drywall as hard as I could. The impact drove the air from his lungs and rattled his brain in his skull like a nut in a cup. The guard was out like a light.

I kicked the door in, and it bounced back on its frame to close behind me as I charged into the room. Like the storage unit, there wasn't much in this room. A naked lightbulb over a desk that held a small, strange cube beneath it. A manila folder lay next to the cube, opened to a sheet of paper inside it.

I wished I still had the eye-snapper and hoped that my helmet could capture at least some of what I saw. I rushed to the desk, looked down at the paper, and saw a bizarre mess of technical diagrams and handwritten notations. I couldn't make heads or tails out of the diagrams, but a tangled scribble on the right side of the page snagged my eye.

It was my mother's signature.

"Device needs more power," she'd written, then signed it with the same scrawl she'd used on the notes she'd written to my school when I missed a day sick.

The device on the diagram was clearly a match for the cube in front of me. Why would my mother have been involved in this thing's creation? I couldn't understand how all the pieces I'd gathered fit together.

"You've got guards coming," Hagar practically shouted in my ear. "You have to get out of there."

"Is this it?" I stared at the floating cube to make sure Hagar understood what I was asking.

"Yes," Hagar said. "But—"

We were out of time for buts.

I hooked my serpent around the cube and yanked it off the table.

A blinding flash of light exploded from the device. A blast of searing pain rocketed into my core, and for a moment I thought Hagar was right. I'd screwed up. I was dead.

Except, I wasn't.

As fast as the pain began, it vanished. A strange vibration poured out of the device, rumbling through my serpent and into my core. It was familiar somehow. Like I knew this thing. Or at least I should have known it.

"How do I get out of here?" I asked.

"Back the way you came!" Hagar shouted. "Go go go!"

I banished my fusion blade and ran like I was being chased by the world's angriest pit bull.

Jinsei flooded into my legs from my core, increasing my speed even further. A pair of guards drew their weapons at the intersection, and I ducked around them and kept running. Left, then right, I juked back and forth across the hallway, hoping speed and evasiveness would keep me safe.

Five feet away from the guards, they realized I wasn't going to stop and raised their weapons. At that range, there was no way they could miss.

Which is why I didn't let them fire.

My remaining tentacle smashed across the chest of one guard, knocking him to the ground. Before he regained his feet, I slammed the serpent across the other guard's knees. He went down with a grunt, and I was past them and around the corner.

"We've got company on the roof," Hagar said. "Two minutes, Jace. Then we have to pull out."

Another guard seemed to materialize from thin air in front of me. He raised his gun, and I threw out an elbow that caught him across the chin. He flew backward from the blow, his eyes unfocused. His pistol roared, and something tugged at my sleeve.

That had been too close.

My serpent slammed into the side of the man's arm, knocking the gun out of his hand, then spun back to bounce his head off the wall. His legs gave out, and he went down.

I crashed through the stairwell door and raced up one flight after another. The jinsei in my core was almost gone. I didn't have any left to pump into my legs. I wasn't going to make it. My lungs burned, and my muscles were on fire. Doors behind me flew open as more and more guards joined the chase. I'd never be able to outrun them.

"One more floor," Hagar shouted into my helmet. "You're almost there!"

My core ached as I wrenched a final drop of jinsei out of it to fuel my run. Finally, I reached the maintenance room and burst through its door onto the roof.

There were guards hunkered down behind ventilation fans and raised conduits, all of them with weapons trained on the transport. None of them had heard me over the growing roar of the vehicle's rotors. A barrage of gunfire was followed a split second later by the almost musical sound of bullets punching into the side of the craft's metal hull.

"Over here!" I shouted to Hagar.

I dragged myself on top of the entrance to the building and crouched down on its roof to avoid catching a bullet from the angry guards who turned to track the transport's flight.

The transport lifted into the air and screamed low over the rooftop. Its rotors were far too close to the guards for comfort, and the hired guns threw themselves flat to avoid being torn to ribbons. At the last possible second, the transport pulled up short beside my perch with its hatch wide open.

I jumped in and slammed into the back of the transport's interior as the pilot gunned the engines and roared away from the building before I'd even touched the deck. The vehicle's nose pointed toward the sky at an angle so steep it flattened me against the rear bulkhead.

Bullets continued to ping off the transport's hull for long seconds after we'd left the building. Finally, the barrage died down, and the transport leveled off.

"Too close," Hagar said. "Way too close."

"Yeah, but I got it," I said, a manic grin stretched across my features. My serpent raised the Machina to show her.

Hagar recoiled from the object. She held her hands in front of her face and closed her eyes as if the radiance that spilled from it burned her.

"Put it in one of the compartments," she said. "Hurry."

I was puzzled, but I did as she asked. The light hadn't hurt me in the slightest. I dumped it into the nearest cargo compartment and slammed the lid.

"You okay?" I asked.

"No," Hagar said. "My face hurts. My hands, too."

The parts of the warden's hands and face that had been exposed to the light were bright pink. She looked like she'd gone for a stroll through the Sahara without sunscreen.

"I'm sorry," I said. "I didn't know."

"It's okay," she said, her voice thin and tired. "I'm glad you made it out of there in one piece."

"Me, too," I said. The adrenaline was wearing off, leaving in its place the nagging worry about what I'd seen. I couldn't figure out why my mother's name would be on a technical diagram in a heretic storage cell. It made no sense whatsoever.

"What did you see in there?" Hagar asked as if she'd plucked the thought out of my mind. "Just before you grabbed the material, you were fixated on a diagram."

"I thought I recognized something." I shook my head. "I was wrong."

"Jace..." Hagar popped out of her flight harness and moved over next to me. She put her hand on my knee and squeezed. "What you did in there was incredibly brave. That material you gathered could make all the difference in our fight."

"Thanks," I said. "That's why I stuck around to finish the job."

"It was also really, really stupid," she said. "You're important, Jace. More important than any single mission. If we lost you..."

Hagar's eyes were strangely misty and distant. She was looking at me, but also at something else. Something, or someone, from her past.

Her Singapore.

I wrapped my hand over my handler's fingers and gave my friend a comforting squeeze.

# THE BROTHER

I T WAS HARD TO CONCENTRATE ON MY
schoolwork after the raid. Thanks to Clem's
help, my scrivening grades didn't slip, too much,
but I certainly didn't make any great improvements in
my skills there, either. I struggled to focus even in
martial arts class, and the technique I'd been chasing
seemed to slip further from my grasp with every passing
day. The breakthrough I'd been on the verge of just a few
days ago eluded me.

Things didn't get any easier when Hagar started
dodging me after she'd returned to classes following our
last mission. Every time I tried to catch up to her, she
ducked down the hallway or buried herself in
conversation with her friends. Every day, I hoped I'd
find her waiting in front of the champion's door. And
every day, I was disappointed.

We were most of the way through the first half of
the school year when I finally couldn't stand it anymore.
I cornered Hagar on her way into the dining hall for
dinner, and wouldn't let her past even when she waved
at one of her friends and tried to squeeze around me.

"We have to talk," I whispered.

"No, we don't," Hagar shot back, her face twisted
into a deep scowl. "You can't keep doing this, Jace. I'll
contact you when it's time. Until then, back off."

"Did you find anything out about my mother?" I demanded. "Did you ask the elders—"

Hagar recoiled as if I'd struck her. Her eyes darted back and forth to see if anyone had reacted to what I'd said. With a hiss, she dragged me out of the main hall into a shadowy side corridor.

"I know you're worried about your mom." Hagar's voice was low and stern, her eyes cold and flashing. "You'll be the first to know if I have anything."

"Why did the heretics have her name?" I couldn't let this go. My mom was out there in the cold because of me. Anything could have happened to her already. I had to know she was safe.

"Stop," Hagar hissed. "We're not in charge of this, Jace. The elders will tell me when it's time to tell you. In the meantime, stay away from me. People will start talking about us if they keep seeing us together."

With that, Hagar pushed past me and made her way into the dining hall. Frustrated, I watched her go with a frown stamped into my face. My expression stayed like that as I stepped into the main hall and headed for dinner.

"Oboli for your thoughts," Clem said, surprising me.

"Oh," I said, relieved it was my friend. "Just, you know…"

"Arguing with Hagar?" Clem said. "You seemed to be having a pretty heated conversation."

"No," I said, then corrected myself. "Sort of."

Clem nodded and waited for me to elaborate. When I didn't, she shrugged and pointed to the table where Eric was already waiting for us.

"I'm starving, let's get some food in our bellies," she said, and hooked her arm through mine. She dragged us into the hall, navigated around the initiates to the line reserved for second years and above, and threw a jaunty wave at Rachel as we passed her table. "She's nice."

"Rachel?" I asked. "Yeah, she is."

Clem handed me a tray, then grabbed one for herself.

"You think so?" she asked, in a voice that tried to be nonchalant and failed.

"I mean, yeah," I said. "I thought you two were getting along?"

Clem and Rachel had partnered with me during every Intermediate Scrivening class, though they never spent any time together outside of class. Rachel didn't eat meals with us, and Clem didn't try to insert herself into my almost nightly nature walks. The two of them seemed to have reached an uneasy truce. That's why Clem's question caught me off guard.

"We are," Clem said. She pursed her lips tightly after that and didn't say another word until we were back at the table with full plates.

"She's just sort of difficult," Clem said at last. "Rubs me the wrong way sometimes."

"Rachel again?" Eric rolled his eyes to let me know this wasn't his first time in this conversation. "I'm sure you're not all peaches and cream around her, either."

"I'm perfectly nice to her," Clem said, irritation clear in her voice.

Eric glanced at me warily, then gave me a short shake of his head. I wisely avoided feeding into Clem's simmering anger and turned the topic to something safer.

"How's Abi doing? Haven't seen him around for a while."

"He's on the late shift," Eric said. "I think he rotates back to his normal classes next week."

"They have tutors for the students on PDF," Clem said distractedly. "Good ones, from what I hear. I think Abi was promoted to operator, so he's been learning how to pilot the portals."

"Really?" That was surprising. "That's a big investment to make in a student."

We chitchatted about that for a while longer until the conversation ran dry. I was too distracted by my encounter with Hagar to be much fun, and Clem couldn't take her eyes off Rachel for more than a few minutes at a time.

"I'm sorry, guys," Clem said at last. "I'm beat. I think I'll head back to my room to study for a bit and then turn in."

"I hear you," I said. "I should probably do the same."

"My two best friends," Eric said, "Sleepy and Grumpy. You guys are the best."

Clem flicked a glob of mashed potatoes off her plate into Eric's hair, then giggled and ran off with her tray.

"You need to watch yourself with those two," Eric said quietly.

"What are you talking about?" I asked.

"Oh, man," Eric said. "Don't be so dense. They like you. They both like you. Clem's got dibs, so she's extra annoyed."

"Dibs?" I said, a little too loudly. Rachel caught my eye and gave me a quick wink. "You're crazy. Even if they were chasing me, I don't have time for this."

"I don't have time for the two prettiest girls in school," Eric said. "You're killing me, man."

"I gotta get outta here, clear my head," I said. "Maybe I'll bring a doggy bag to Abi."

"Yeah, he'll dig that," Eric said. "Tell him I said hi. And remember what I said. Those two will carve you up if you don't."

"Will do," I said, leaving my friend behind with a slightly sad, slightly disappointed look on his face. It wasn't what I wanted, but there was a lot of that going around. I needed to focus on my work with the elders. Nothing else was as important as fighting off the heretics and finding my mother.

I gathered up some easily portable foods in a takeout bag and felt a sudden pang of whatever the opposite of nostalgia was for the year that had passed. I'd entered the School a social outcast and had nearly been in exile by this point last year. This year, I had too many friends that I disappointed because I was distracted by my Eclipse nature and missions for the Shadow Phoenix elders. I wanted a happy medium, and it just kept slipping away from me.

Abi sensed the turmoil within me, of course. Even as I handed him the bag of still warm food, he furrowed his brow and wagged a finger at me.

"Thank you for the meal, my friend," he said. "But I would thank you more if you delivered it with a smile on your face. You are still so troubled. What is it that bothers you?"

I didn't know where to start. I had a soul-eating monster trying to bust out of my core. I was going on deadly secret missions with Hagar for the elders of the Shadow Phoenix clan. Clem and Rachel were competing for me, and I hadn't even known it.

"Girls," I finally admitted. That seemed the least dangerous of the real problems on my plate.

"Ah, yes," Abi said, his face split into a wide grin. "The girl problem. Eric and I talk about it whenever we can."

"I'm sure that makes both of you very happy," I said and jabbed Abi in the arm. "I put a couple of biscuits in there, a few chicken tenders, and some of those steak fingers you like so much. There's also an apple and a little cup of broccoli. Not exactly a balanced meal, but it's the best I could do."

"Thank you," Abi said sincerely. He put the bag on the little desk in front of him. "Did you hear the good news?"

"That you're becoming a fancy portal pilot?" I grinned. "Clem told me. Maybe you could take me for a spin over to Kyoto sometime. They have this awesome ramen place—"

"Do not even joke about that, my friend," Abi said, his eyes suddenly cold. He crooked a finger in my direction and leaned toward me. "They are only training us because there have been attacks on the portal network. Protestors put two of the pilots in the hospital last week. The network has been on a quiet lockdown since last night."

"Oh, man," I said. "I'm sorry, I had no idea."

"Few do," Abi said. "I apologize for being so abrupt with you. But even joking about using the portals without explicit permission is grounds for dismissal from my post. They could jail me for sedition."

"That's insane," I whispered. "Have things gotten that bad?"

"I hear bits and pieces only," Abi said with a shrug. "But the protests are becoming more brazen. And there have been attacks."

Suddenly, the work I was doing for the Shadow Phoenixes seemed even more important. Abi and I were finally on the same team, even if he didn't know it.

"That's terrible." I shook my head. "I'm going to leave you to it. Need to think about some things."

"You should meditate on your problems. It will help to clear your mind," Abi said. "Especially of girl problems."

Abi didn't know the dangers that came for me when I meditated, but he was right about one thing. I needed to clear my mind and really look at the problems I had. It was the only way to conquer them.

"You know what," I said, "that's a good idea."

We shook hands and gave each other half a hug, and I headed off to see if I could get my mind right. The cottage would've given me the most privacy, but it was too tangled up in everything for me to relax there. How could I concentrate on a peaceful mind in the same place where I'd been whisked away by a transport or stepped through a portal into a different city?

The library cells offered some privacy, but they weren't exactly comfortable. I needed some place natural, where I could feel a breeze on my face and smell the wind.

That was it. I knew exactly where to go.

I found the strange path that led to the shifting terrain off the upperclassman floor. It was the perfect place for meditation. I felt better and calmer as soon as I headed toward the first hill. The path took me in a slightly different direction this time, though it still ended up crawling up the face of the mountain. When the wind grew chilly, on the verge of becoming unpleasant, I backtracked a little and took a seat.

"Hey!" someone shouted in surprise.

I jumped back and fell into a defensive posture, hands raised in a cross guard to ward off a blow to my head.

"Oh, by the Flame," Rachel said. "I'm so sorry, I keep sneaking up on you like that."

"How long were you behind me?" I asked, suddenly concerned. If Rachel, who was really quite terrible when it came to the sacred arts, was able to sneak up on me so easily, I'd be easy prey for a more experienced practitioner.

"Not as long as you think." She chuckled. "I came out here to get some fresh air and saw you coming up the mountain toward me. I hid back here to surprise you."

She pointed to a small crevice hidden by shadow. I'd never have fit back there, but Rachel was so small she'd had no trouble squeezing into the tight confines of her hiding place.

"What a coincidence," I said. "I was coming out here to meditate."

"It's a good place for it," Rachel said. "You mind if I stay with you?"

I didn't mind, and that was the problem. If Clem and Rachel were both competing for me, I didn't know what to do. I liked them both, though not in the same exact way. Clem had done so much for me, and there was a deep bond that had been forged between us during the time when everyone else had turned their backs on me.

My relationship with Rachel, on the other hand, was new and mysterious. It was exciting in a way that intrigued me, but I wasn't sure if it would last. Then again, if I ran away from her, I'd never know what might have been. I knew that taking Rachel with me to meditate carried a risk. I could lose control of my darker self, and the Eclipse nature could rear its ugly head. But there was also a risk in avoiding this moment with Rachel. If I kept turning her away, she might not keep trying to spend time with me.

"Sure." I'd decided the possible reward outweighed the risk..

"Awesome." Rachel took my hand and gave it a squeeze. "Come this way."

She led me a bit further up the mountain onto an almost-hidden path that curved back deeper into the stone flank. We passed under a natural granite arch, and I was momentarily blinded by the transition from daylight to the much dimmer illumination provided by dozens of scattered electric blue specks.

"Have you ever seen anything like it?" Rachel had stood up on her tiptoes to whisper in my ear, and her breath sent a shiver down my spine.

My eyes adjusted to the strange light in stages. First, I could only see the specks of light in the gloom. Then the walls that supported the lights emerged from the shadows, curving around us in a cool embrace. Finally, the flowers that were the source of the glow took on more details. Their broad fronds were open wide to reveal the pistils and stamens that seemed to glowed brighter by the second.

"No," I whispered back. "I haven't."

Rachel guided me to the center of the chamber, then motioned for me to sit on the floor next to her.

Wordlessly, we assumed the classic meditation pose: legs crossed, spines straight, the backs of our hands resting on our knees with our palms facing the ceiling.

I'd expected the stone floor to be uncomfortable and cold. Instead, it supported us comfortably and reflected our body heat to keep us from getting chilled. It was as if this spot had been created specifically for us.

Soon, I fell into the smooth, even rhythm of meditation. My breaths pulled jinsei into my core, and every exhale purged impurities from the sacred energy and flushed them into my aura, where they could be used for serpents or disposed of as I saw fit. I ignored the aspects and concentrated on maximizing every breath to cycle as much of the jinsei as possible. That was the surest way to advance, and I wouldn't pass up an opportunity to do that.

Even when my core was filled with jinsei, I kept pulling in more and more of the sacred energy. I had to push myself past the limits that held me back. If I kept going, I'd reach a new, higher level of mastery and my core would become more powerful. The spiritual power was a thunderhead inside my core, flashes of lightning lancing from within it. Just a little further…

"Jace." Rachel's voice was a soft, early spring breeze. "We should go. It's getting late."

It was hard to release the power inside me, and harder still to claw my way up from the depths of my meditation. My eyelids felt like they weighed a hundred pounds each, and my heartbeats were slow and heavy. My breath was thick and wet in my lungs, as if I had to draw each gulp of air through a soaking wet cloth.

The outside world pushed itself into my thoughts and scattered the storm of energy that I'd gathered. My

Eclipse nature thrashed and raged in a confused tantrum at what it had been denied. It had felt how close we were to advancing and hated that I'd been distracted from my goal. Its hunger drove me to my feet, fists clenched, eyes narrowed into angry slits.

"Jace." Rachel backed away from me, one slow step at a time.

I realized my core had used the cold aspects in my aura to summon my serpents. The twin tendrils of frosty white light arched away from my shoulders, their heads weaving in Rachel's direction.

"I'm sorry," I said, stumbling over the words and banishing the serpents into clouds of ice crystals. "Please, I'm sorry."

Rachel stopped backing away, cocked her head to the left, then stepped forward until we were almost touching. She looked up at me, amber eyes glowing with a curious warmth.

"You're a dangerous man, Jace Warin," she said, her voice low and husky. I'd never heard that tone from Rachel. It was dark and surprising.

And exciting.

We stared at one another for a long moment, before she shivered and took my hand.

"It's late, we need to get back to the dorms." Rachel threaded her fingers through mine, and we started down the mountain path.

The trip seemed shorter going down than it had going up. I wasn't sure if it was the terrain or the warmth of Rachel's fingers laced with mine. It all seemed like a strange and pleasant dream, which would end as soon as we stepped off the path and back into the stone halls of the School of Swords and Serpents. Maybe that was the real reason the trip back felt like it only lasted a few minutes.

"What time is it?" I asked. The sky had shifted from a pale blue to a deep purple velvet, though the terrain was lit up as clearly as if it were still noon. The strange combination and the jarring return from my meditations had my sense of time completely out of whack.

"After ten," Rachel said, a faint blush on her cheeks.

"Oh," I said. "I had no idea. I've been so focused on strengthening my core that time just slips away from me."

While there was no curfew for upperclassmen, a pair of students, alone, out well past dinner might raise a few eyebrows.

"It's all right," Rachel assured me. She squeezed my hand in hers and smiled up at me. "I like hanging out with you. Even if you are a little scary."

I'd never considered myself scary. Intense, maybe. Driven, sure. But scary?

I wasn't sure how to feel about that.

We'd reached the end of the path. One more step would take us back into the stone halls of study and practice. We paused there, neither willing to be the one who broke the spell we'd woven around ourselves.

"I had a nice time." The words sounded lame even to my own ears.

"Me, too." Rachel turned toward me and took my other hand.

We were so close the fabric of our robes rustled against one another. Rachel's fingers were warm between mine, a tingling pressure that made my heart race. I'd always thought she was pretty, but standing there in the strange light, I realized how stunning she was.

She rose onto her tiptoes, bringing her face within inches of mine. Her lips parted and the warmth of her breath brushed against my face. I knew what she wanted. I wanted it, too.

All I had to do was lean forward and—

"Get away from my sister."

I recognized that voice.

Rafael.

The Disciple stood motionless in the hallway. His aura was filled with so many rage aspects it was nearly black. A flicker of jinsei danced from his hand, and I knew he was moments away from summoning his fusion sword.

My Eclipse nature swarmed out of the darkness, suddenly territorial. It didn't want to protect just me. It now regarded Rachel as part of the deal, and it was fiercely protective. If Rafael attacked, I wasn't sure I'd be able to wrestle my darker urges under control.

"Raph," Rachel said, her voice sharp. Anger and embarrassment aspects danced in her aura like sparks from a bonfire. "This is none of your business. Leave us alone."

I was stunned speechless. The fact that Rachel and Rafael were brother and sister had never occurred to me. They didn't look anything alike, and Rafael had been at the School while Rachel was studying at the Golden Sun Academy. None of it made any sense.

"You dishonored my family once," Rafael snarled at me. Other students had gathered at the end of the hall, drawn by his shouts. "You will not do it again.

I demand satisfaction. A duel. Tomorrow, at noon. In the exercise yard."

# THE FLIGHT

HE DAY AFTER RAFAEL'S CHALLENGE WAS Saturday, and the dining hall's breakfast crowd buzzed with excitement as rumors about it spread through the School's student body. Most of the upperclassmen were well aware of the last time Rafael and I had fought. It had not ended well for the Disciple of Jade Flame, and it had taken several weeks before he could summon his fusion blade again. While it was strictly against school rules, bets on the new duel's outcome were fast and furious. From what I heard while loading my plate with bacon and sausage, Rafael was the favorite by three to two.

Either someone knew something about Rafael's skills that I didn't, or people were giving way too much credit to his being a year older than me. The Disciple was a strong fighter, but he hadn't even been able to take me down when he got the jump on me last year. People were nuts to think he was that much of a favorite to beat me in a fair fight.

"I can't believe you accepted the duel," Clem said when we'd taken a seat at our usual table. She had a disapproving frown stamped on her face, and Eric and Abi wouldn't meet her eyes. "It's stupid and dangerous. You know Rafael will cheat. He'd do anything to defeat you."

"It's a sanctioned duel to three touches," Abi said. "Professor Song will officiate. No one will get hurt."

"You really believe that?" Clem savagely bit the end off a sausage link. "This is the same guy that tried to kill our friend last year."

She had a point there. Rafael had ambushed me in the hall one day, an attack that had seemed completely unprovoked at the time. I'd later learn that our now ex-headmaster, Grayson Bishop, had encouraged other students to come after me. If I hadn't destroyed Rafael's fusion blade and knocked him silly, he would definitely have murdered me in cold blood.

"I'm stronger now," I said. "He can do his worst, and I'll beat him again."

"That's the spirit!" Eric said, clapping me on the shoulder. "I mean, he's had as much time as you to get better, but you've had more practice, right?"

That wasn't terribly comforting. Rafael was older than me, which meant he had a full year of training in the martial arts that I hadn't enjoyed. On the other hand, I had fought hundreds of contenders in the Five Dragons Challenge. That had to count for something.

"All because of that girl," Clem said with a shake of her head. "I can't believe Rafael thought you'd do anything improper with his sister. I mean, she's nice enough, but really. You have much higher standards."

No one had an answer for that. Clem eyeballed each of us in turn, then returned her attention to her plate. Our conversation dwindled down to nothing, and by the time breakfast was over, the tension among my friends had reached truly uncomfortable heights.

"I need to meditate a bit," I said. "Cycle my jinsei, get my core ready. I'll see you guys after the fight, right?"

Clem's eyes met mine for a moment. There was something troubled in her gaze. Her lips parted slightly, as if she were about to speak. The moment stretched out into a taut line between us. I knew I should say something.

I just didn't know what.

"Yeah." Clem pulled a chipper grin tight across her face. "We'll be there to congratulate you when you beat him."

"Thanks," I said.

Clem looked away from me then, her eyes misty, suddenly very intent on the food in front of her.

Abi and Eric wished me well, and I left the dining hall almost as confused as I had been the night before. I'd rather face a whole squad of heretics than go through that weirdness again.

I found a quiet place to gather my thoughts, far from the hubbub of the dining hall. I reached out to rats all through the School, binding them to my core and sending them off on another search for Hahen. I really needed the little rat spirit's advice. I missed him and wondered if he missed me, too.

A solid two hours of searching turned up nothing. My rat minions didn't pick up even a trace of Hahen's scent anywhere in the School. It was as if he never existed.

Sort of like Tycho's lab.

Disappointed, I released the rats and meditated to center my Eclipse nature. It was restless, churning inside me like a tiger pacing its cage. It sensed what was coming and wanted me to unleash it on Rafael.

There was no way that was happening. I tried to impress upon the dark urge the importance of behaving when there would be so many students and professors watching the duel. If I lost control and something like Singapore happened again, everyone would know I was dangerous. It wouldn't be hard for the professors to put two and two together and discover I was an Eclipse Warrior.

And that would be a death sentence.

My core didn't seem to care very much about the danger and was still agitated when it came time for me to head down to the exercise yard. I kept cycling my breath, purging the anxiety and anger aspects from my aura as I walked. I needed to be cool and calm during the duel. Score the points, beat Rafael, and no one had to get hurt.

I reached the exercise courtyard just in time. The area was packed wall to wall with students, the air buzzing with their excited chatter. Rafael and Professor Song were already in the center of the open space, waiting for me to arrive. I hadn't intended to arrive at the last moment but was glad I did. My late entrance irritated Rafael and put him on edge.

That gave me an advantage.

Every eye in the place turned to me as I strode toward my opponent. An excited cheer crashed through the student body on either side of me, spreading around the courtyard in a rippling ring. The thunderous applause was peppered with boos from the Disciples in the crowd. That was good, too. I'd learned to feed on the haters while fighting in the Five Dragons Challenge. Whether the crowd was for or against me didn't really matter. It was their passion that fueled me.

Professor Song raised his hands and waited for the gathered crowd to settle down. It took longer than I expected, and I used the time to psych Rafael out. Where he was angry, I was calm. I'd nothing to prove in this fight. I'd beaten so many challengers in the past few months, one loss wouldn't do much to tarnish my reputation. I held the Disciple's gaze, showing him I was ready and more than willing this time.

Rafael's rage boiled around him. His aura was a confused cloak of anger and shame, the aspects churning around one another like sizzling oil and cold water. He wanted to defeat me not just because he thought I'd dishonored his sister, but because he hated my guts.

"All right, gentlemen," Professor Song said, his voice boosted by jinsei so everyone watching could hear, "this is a formal duel. The winner will be decided by three touches anywhere on the torso or head. I have inscribed a circle, and there will be no doubt about when a touch is legal and confirmed. I expect no injuries from this duel. Am I clear?"

"Yes, honored Professor," I said and bowed toward Song.

"Of course," Rafael said through gritted teeth. He bowed to the professor, too, then we faced one another and bowed again.

"Very well." Professor Song positioned himself between us and waited for Rafael and me to fall into our combat stances. "Fight!"

The professor dropped his hand in a vertical chopping motion, then leaped back out of the ring.

Rafael surged across the ring toward me, hands raised to guard his head and ready to strike. His steps were smooth and even, his feet scarcely touching the ground as he charged. He unleashed a jinsei-boosted bellow designed to rattled me when he came within striking range and frowned when I didn't so much as flinch.

I held my ground and my cross guard defensive position. My eyes remained focused on the center of Rafael's chest, which I'd learned was the first part of an opponent's body to move when it came time for an attack. My breath cycled smoothly and evenly through me, my core filled with jinsei. I was as ready as I'd ever be and had decided to let Rafael make the first move.

He didn't disappoint me.

The Disciple unloaded a flurry of punches that I deflected with my forearms. He transitioned smoothly into a spinning kick accelerated by a burst of jinsei. The air crackled around his heel as it sped toward my left side, so fast it was little more than a sparkling blur.

As fast as the attack was, my defense was faster. My left arm swept down and out in a powerful circle, catching Rafael by surprise. I pushed the jinsei from my core into my arm at the exact moment of impact, and the burst of sacred energy flung my opponent's leg away from me.

Rafael shouted in surprise as his body twisted out of his control. His foot slipped off the ground, and for a moment he was airborne. His shoulder slammed onto the grass, and he curled into a ball to protect himself from the follow-up attack he knew was coming.

I took a single step and rapped his forehead with my knuckles.

The ring around us flashed a brilliant blue, and a wall of sparks shot into the air.

"Point, Jace," Professor Song shouted.

Rafael sneered at my offered hand and kicked back up to his feet without my assistance. His aura was clotted with far more anger than shame now, and the dark aspects seemed to fuel him much as the crowd energized me. The Disciple turned his back on me and walked away.

Professor Song reentered the circle, glanced at each of us, then raised his hand again.

I didn't like the look in Rafael's eyes. Given the chance, he might just try to kill me again in front of everyone.

That wasn't going to happen.

"Ready," Professor Song said. "Fight!"

Rafael took a different approach this time. He walked toward me, hands loose at his sides, bobbing his head left and right like an undisciplined street fighter. He thrust his chin forward as if begging me to knock him out. He was on the warpath, and he wanted blood.

I needed to end this, quickly.

Without hesitation, I triggered the Borrowed Core technique and connected myself to the maximum number of rats I could control. A single breath filled my aura with beast aspects, and I held them at the ready.

"Come on, coward," Rafael snarled. "You think you can take me. Make a move and prove it."

"It doesn't have to be like this," I told the Disciple. "Whatever you think happened with your sister, you're wrong."

At the mention of his sibling, Rafael's eyes narrowed to hateful slits. His rage blossomed from his core, clouding his aura with pure hate.

I chose that moment to make my attack. I stepped up to Rafael and drove a punch straight at the middle of his chest. I boosted it with little jinsei to give it more speed, though I didn't put anywhere near my full strength into the attack. My goal was to score another point, not hurt Rafael.

My opponent deflected the blow with his forearm and snapped a kick toward my midsection in return.

The strike was too fast to block, forcing me to pivot to the side so it could slide past me without scoring a point. Rafael's extended leg right in front of me was far too tempting a target to pass up. I grabbed his ankle with one hand and his knee with the other. Jinsei poured from my core into my arms and hands as I prepared to snatch Rafael into the air and slam him back to the ground.

But as soon as my fingers closed around his leg, Rafael unleashed a technique I hadn't seen before.

All the anger he'd built up in his aura burst away from him in a powerful shock wave. It ripped my hands away from his body and threw me back toward the edge of the dueling ring. Worse, the furious wave smashed into my core and scattered half the jinsei I'd gathered.

The maneuver had also severed my connections through the Borrowed Core and sapped my strength. I was stunned and unsteady on my feet, hands wobbling uselessly when I tried to raise them to defend myself. Three shimmering Rafaels approached me, all blurry and indistinct, and I couldn't tell which one was the real threat.

And then, suddenly, one of the trio of enemies solidified. Rafael gave me a wide, hungry smile and drove an open-palm strike into the center of my chest.

Red sparks exploded around the dueling circle.

"Point, Rafael," Professor Song shouted. He motioned Rafael back, then grabbed my hands and looked into my eyes. "You okay to continue?"

My vision was still blurry, and my core ached from the lingering effects of Rafael's technique. I felt like I was standing on the deck of a ship in rough seas, my legs unsteady beneath me. I shook my head and cycled my breath, pulling on the beast aspects and hoping that would steady me. One breath, two, and I nodded.

"I'm fine," I said to the professor. "I'm good."

"Ready," Professor Song said, eyeing me warily as I assumed a defensive position. "Fight!"

It turns out I wasn't fine. My core was a jumbled mess and my aura was shot through with confusion and exhaustion aspects. Rafael hardly had to try to score a second point with a simple punch to my gut.

My Eclipse nature was strangely subdued when I needed its aggressive strength the most. The dark urge lay quiet beneath my thoughts like a slumbering alligator. I shook my head and purged as much of the weakness and confusion as I could from my aura. Adding more jinsei to my core helped, but not enough.

This was bad. If I didn't recover, soon, I'd lose this duel.

As we reset our positions and assumed our stances, my thoughts raced to find a solution to this problem. My darker nature was playing possum, for whatever reason, so I'd need something tricky. A thought occurred to me, and I clung to the sneaky tactic that had sprung into my thoughts.

"Ready," Professor Song called out once we'd assumed our fighting stances. "Fight!"

Rafael wanted to finish the duel and claim his victory. He was cocky, and that made him careless.

He walked toward me, no mind for defense, no techniques ready, the victory already secure in his mind.

"You're done," he said. "The big man, brought low by my hand."

Rafael's overconfidence gave me a tiny window of opportunity, and I took it. I pretended to stumble toward him, as if my legs could barely hold me up. The crowd gasped, sure I'd just lost the match.

My opponent raised his hands above his head, laced his fingers together, and swung a hammer blow down at my back.

Blue sparks exploded around the ring, and Rafael gasped and stumbled away from me. The front of his robes had a long, clean slice through them. A single drop of his blood ran down the fusion blade I'd summoned at the last possible second.

"Point, Jace," Professor Song said, clearly surprised by my maneuver. "Take a knee, Mr. Warin. I want to make sure Rafael is all right."

"No!" Rafael shouted. "I'm fine. He barely scratched me. Let's finish this."

The maneuver had worked, but it had cost me dearly. I'd use the last of the pure jinsei still in my core to summon my blade, and there wasn't time to refill. I was completely defenseless, now, and my body would only grudgingly and clumsily take orders from my mind. I wasn't sure there was anything else I could do.

Unless…

I settled into a low, defensive crouch. I held my arms tight in front of my chest, hands raised on either side of my face to protect me from a finishing blow. The next point would decide everything, and I wouldn't go down easily.

Rafael adopted a neutral stance. He kept his right hand across his torso, protecting himself from a body blow. His left elbow was just above his right fist, that forearm vertical so his hand could protect his face on that side. It was a balanced posture, good for either attack or defense.

Especially against an opponent he knew was weakened.

"Ready," Professor Song said. "Fight!"

I didn't move. My legs were still wobbly, and without jinsei to strengthen them, I didn't trust myself to take so much as another step. Instead, I cycled my breath through my core to calm myself and center my awareness. I'd struggled with this technique all year, and if it didn't work now, I'd lose the fight.

Rafael took his time approaching me. He was wary I'd cut him again and didn't want to give me the advantage like he had the last time. He balanced on the balls of his feet, head weaving back and forth like a snake sizing up its prey. Jinsei gathered around his hands in dark, shadowy clouds. If his next punch landed, it was really going to hurt.

My Eclipse nature roused itself at last. It wanted me to devour the jinsei and his core. It wanted blood and death. It hungered, and denying it in my weakened state was so very hard. It promised me an easy win if I let it off the leash. One moment was all it would take. Rafael would pay the ultimate price for his arrogance.

It would be Singapore all over again.

No. I'd rather lose than go through that again.

There was another way. I felt the technique at the edge of my mind, ready to unlock. It was now or never.

My serpents uncoiled from my shoulders, a roiling mass of beast, confusion, and exhaustion aspects. The tumbling mixture made a poor weapon or shield, and it was difficult to control. A precise strike was out of the question, and there was no way I'd be able to use the serpents to block Rafael's jinsei-infused attack.

That was all right. This technique wasn't about precision.

I took a deep breath, focused all my attention on what had to happen next, and waited for Rafael to strike.

"This is over," my opponent declared. "You're done."

His fist shrieked toward me, a shadowy trail of dark jinsei behind it. It was a brutal, ferocious attack. If it touched me, I'd end up with broken bones at the very least. With no jinsei to defend myself, it might even land me in the emergency room.

Professor Song seemed to realize that, too. He shouted wordlessly and rushed back into the ring. There was no way he'd reach us in time, but it was nice that he'd at least tried to save me from the crippling blow.

My Eclipse nature strained to burst free of my control. It wanted to stop Rafael, no matter the cost. It didn't care if it revealed itself, or how badly it would hurt my opponent. It wanted to survive.

But I couldn't do that. Killing Rafael over a duel of honor wasn't just monstrous, it was dangerous. Someone would find out what I'd done, what I was, and they'd kill me for it.

I pulled the serpents tight around me, like a cloak of churning jinsei.

Rafael saw the shield form and his grin widened. He saw the wispy protection and knew it couldn't stop his brutal assault. His fist hammered into the thin veil of the serpents.

Just as I'd hoped.

When Rafael's aura passed into the thin layer of serpents that protected my chest, I sprang my trap. I let the tiniest piece of my Eclipse core's hunger rip through the tenuous connection between us. A dull roar filled my head, and a seismic shift revealed a new level of martial mastery to me. The serpents were no longer separate from my core or aura; all three parts of my sacred arts were joined. The fusion strengthened every part of me, and I saw the end of this fight as clearly as I saw Rafael's sneering face.

Something in my core snapped, and a new technique burst into my thoughts: Thief's Shield.

For the briefest moment, my aura overlapped with Rafael's. In that split second, my Eclipse core stripped the aspects from his aura and drained the jinsei from his core. My dark urge wanted to absorb all of the sacred energy from my foe, and it took a shameful effort for me to stop the flow of power. A spike of black pain speared my core when I killed the technique, and I groaned and nearly fell.

Rafael went to one knee, eyes fluttering, chest hitching as he tried to catch his breath. The shock of losing nearly all of his jinsei and having his aura stripped of the aspects he'd leaned on to fuel his technique had stunned him senseless.

Professor Song reached us just as I ended the duel with a tap of my boot's toe against Rafael's chest.

"Final point, Jace!" the professor called as blue sparks shot into the air around the ring. Rafael toppled onto his side. "The duel is complete. Jace Warin is the winner."

The crowd roared, cheers and boos mingling together in a wave of emotion that tumbled over me. I raised my hands over my head, bolstered by the energy that poured out of the crowd. I reached down to offer Rafael a hand up.

The woozy Disciple stared at me for a moment, shook his head, and tried to stand on his own.

"I don't need help," he said.

"Everyone needs help," I said. "Take my hand."

Rafael glanced at my hand, then up to my eyes. Finally, he accepted my offer. I hauled him to his feet and raised his hand into the air with mine.

I'd won the duel without killing my opponent. I wondered if Rafael knew his prize had been the greater one that day.

# THE HIT

TIME SEEMED TO RUSH BY AFTER MY DUEL WITH Rafael. If I wasn't in class or eating, I tried to sneak away to channel and focus on advancing my core. That almost never happened, though, because Rachel and Clem had both gotten very good at ambushing me and hauling me off for some one-on-one time.

Clem insisted I practice my scrivening with her or help her with her martial arts. Rachel wanted to hike in the wilderness connected to the School or cook fancy desserts in the cottage's kitchen.

I definitely enjoyed my time with both of them, but it was all getting exhausting. While it was nice to be the center of attention, it was also nerve-racking. Anything I said to one of the girls would eventually get back to the other, making all our conversations fraught with potential peril for me.

That's why I was almost glad when the holiday break arrived. I could use the time alone to recharge my social batteries and prepare for the last half of the year.

For the next month, I read the *Manual of the New Moon*, searched for Hahen, ate with the staff who'd stayed behind for the holiday, and generally enjoyed the peace and quiet. It was a good month that came to an abrupt halt when an unexpected booming echoed through the cottage on the last day of the break. Someone had come to see me.

"Hey, stranger," Hagar said when I opened the door. "Guess what time it is."

"Let me guess," I said, closing the door behind her. "Another job?"

"Could be," Hagar agreed as we headed down the path to the cottage. "What I do know, though, is that the elders want to see you."

"Really?" I asked, suddenly excited. I'd finally get to ask them about my mom directly. "When?"

"Now," a familiar voice said from behind me.

Elders Sanrin, Hirani, and Claude were all standing in my kitchen. They wore identical dark cloaks with deep hoods and seemed amused by my surprise.

"How did you get in here?" First the transport, now the elders. It looked like my secret hideout wasn't very secret or secure anymore.

"This place is proof against most," Sanrin said, "but not against the likes of us. How are you doing, Jace?"

Sanrin and Hirani came into the sitting room to greet me, while Claude busied himself going through my cabinets and cupboards.

"I'm all right," I said. "Pretty good, actually. Though I wanted to talk to you about—"

"I'm making coffee," Claude called from the kitchen. "How do you all take it?"

"Black," Hagar called.

"A spot of cream," Sanrin said.

"None for me," Hirani called, "stuff makes me jittery."

"Black, too," I called. "Anyway, what I was saying was—"

"We have a very important job for you, Jace." Hirani took my hands. The cloak hid her hair, but it couldn't conceal the stunning beauty of her face. Her eyes flashed even in shadow, and the touch of her fingers against mine made my breath catch in my throat. "It is not, however, a very pleasant one."

"Okay, but—"

"We've discovered how the attacks are coordinated," Sanrin said with a frown. "The heretics have an informant inside the Empyreal security apparatus. We need you to silence him."

I felt sick to my stomach. They wanted me to assassinate another Empyreal?

"Don't misunderstand us," Hirani said quickly. "We don't want him liquidated. He is still useful to us, and will be even more useful if you can convince him that working as our agent will be much safer and healthier than working for the heretics. We'd like you to deliver that message to him. Forcefully."

And that was how I found myself sitting in a very expensive apartment, shrouded in a creepy-looking black cloak that masked my face in a veil of shadows. The elders had assured me that this would prevent anyone from physically identifying me, and my veiled core would protect me spiritually. I had no connection to Hagar this time because my handler was concerned that surveillance gear near the target's location would intercept it.

For the first time, I was all alone on a mission.

My target was a middle-aged desk jockey named Albert Hughes. The elders had teleported me across the world to his apartment in the Paris overcity, and I'd been waiting there for him to return ever since. Albert must've been a workaholic, because it was almost eight o'clock in the evening when I heard his key in the door's lock. The three hours I'd spent waiting for him hadn't improved my mood.

I waited for the portly man to close and lock his door behind him, then strode out of the shadows to greet him.

"Mr. Hughes?" I asked.

The poor guy almost bolted out of his skin. He spun to face me and slammed his back against the door. The chain rattled next to his head, and his eyes shot left and right like a mouse trying to escape from a hawk.

"Who are you?" he gasped, his heavy French accent making the English words almost unintelligible. "How did you get in here?"

"Albert, I need you to relax," I said. "I've been sent here because you've been a very naughty boy. My bosses say you've been telling stories you shouldn't have to people you definitely should not be seen with."

Recognition blossomed in Albert's eyes. His jowly face and paunch told me he wasn't much of a fighter, so I wasn't surprised when he whirled around to fumble with the chain in a futile effort to escape.

Before he could open the door, I grabbed him by the back of his coat and used a bit of jinsei to boost my strength. I flung him across the room to the couch, which broke when his not inconsiderable weight hit it at speed.

Albert's short legs churned the air as he tried to right himself. Flustered, he attempted to roll over and regain his feet that way. When that succeeded in tangling him in his cloak, he gave up and lay still.

My Eclipse nature recognized prey when it saw it. The temptation to strike the fool down and savage his core was almost too great to resist. I watched Albert pant and gasp, tangled in his coat like a fish in a net, and I struggled to force the darkness down into its cage.

I was glad Albert couldn't see me. By the time the urge finally passed, I was shaking and soaked with sweat. It took me several cleansing breaths before I trusted myself to speak again.

"I want you to understand that my employers don't want you dead," I told him as I sat on the edge of the coffee table in front of his battered couch. "But we need a promise from you, Albert."

"I don't know what you're talking about." He finally wormed free of his coat and managed to take a semi-dignified seat on the broken couch. "I'm only an auditor. I haven't done anything wrong."

"Ah, but you have," I said. "I'm going to cut to the chase so you'll know that lying to me is a waste of your time and mine. You have been selling important information to the heretics. They've been using that data to coordinate their attacks against the Grand Design."

Albert deflated and sank back into himself with every word out of my mouth. Now that his secret was in the open, he was broken.

"It's not like that," he said. "We're trying to save the Grand Design from itself. There's something much worse coming."

"Are you trying to tell me you're the hero here, Albert?" I said. "That seems unlikely, don't you think?"

"I'm no one," Albert said again. "I give my handler the information he asks for. They use it to stop the real threats."

It was time to get serious with Albert. He didn't seem to be getting the message.

I punched him, hard, in the stomach.

The auditor was no fighter and wasn't prepared for the sudden blow. He doubled over, retching, his face red, back heaving up and down as he tried to keep his dinner where it belonged. His breath panted in and out of his lungs in asthmatic wheezes, and the bald spot on top of his head turned the color of a maraschino cherry.

Hitting Albert made me feel dirty. I'd hurt my share of people, but most of them had been trying to hurt me at the same time. Albert, on the other hand, wasn't a threat. Hitting him felt a lot like slapping a child. There was no honor in that attack. I held very still for a moment and reminded myself that even dishonorable actions can lead to an honorable outcome. My mission wasn't about hurting Albert, it was about stopping a far more dangerous threat to Empyreal society.

"Listen," he gasped, flopping back onto the couch. "I don't know who sent you, but you have to believe me. There's something out there. Something coming. My handler tells me the Grand Design didn't account for this. We're the only ones who can stop it."

I felt an uncomfortable twinge of sympathy for Albert. He and I were both little fish in a very big pond, and only the carp in the waters below us had plumbed its depths. Maybe Albert believed he was on the side of angels. His handler could have told him anything at all to make him believe that.

"You're hurting people, Albert," I said. "Do you understand that?

Albert's eyes flickered to something behind me. His jowls quivered, and he raised both hands defensively. It was a rookie move, and I'd seen it dozens of times before in the arena. The poor guy really thought I would look behind me so he could make a break for it. Albert was a terrible bluffer.

Unfortunately for me, he wasn't bluffing.

I heard the whistle of something heavy tearing through the air just before it slammed across my shoulders. The force of the blow drove me forward, off the coffee table, and I caught myself with a hand against Albert's squishy stomach.

He coughed and gasped as I forced the air out of his lungs for the second time that night and shoved both his hands into my chest. It wasn't a strong blow, but it was enough to knock me off balance after I'd already been stunned by what felt like a lead pipe to the back.

Knowing there was an opponent behind me, I rolled on my shoulder and popped back up to my feet near the end of the couch in front of the entertainment center and its little TV.

Albert's rescuer was about my height, slender, and also dressed all in black. He wielded a pair of black tonfa, and his core glowed brightly with sacred energy.

"Don't make this hard," I said. "I just need to have a little chat with Albert, then I'll be on my way."

"Just leave," Albert pleaded. "No one has to get hurt."

Albert was wrong. I couldn't leave without making sure he understood how important it was that he stop providing the heretics with intelligence. The fact that he had a mysterious bodyguard willing to fight for him made that a much, much harder sell. The only way to make my point now was to put a serious hurt on the bodyguard.

Or kill him. That's what the dark urge really wanted, and its siren song was getting harder and harder to resist.

The tonfa-wielding fighter circled around the couch, weapons at the ready. He rotated the twin clubs around their offset handles so the end of one of the weapons jutted out from his fist while the other one ran along the outside of his forearm. That configuration gave him an easy way to attack and block while still protecting his hands and arms.

Albert's living room wasn't very big. I took one step back from the approaching fighter, and the backs of my knees were up against the auditor's entertainment center.

The bodyguard saw I had no room to maneuver and rushed me.

I grabbed the small flat screen television off its stand and ripped it loose from the power and cable lines attached to its back. In the same motion, I hurled the rectangular missile overhand at the tonfa fighter's face.

My attacker's left hand flashed out, and the tonfa along his forearm bashed the small television aside. The screen shattered, chunks of plastic broke free of the frame, and the whole mess slammed into the wall on the far side of the living room.

While my opponent battered the television into submission, I summoned my fusion blade and went to work.

My first stroke sheared the man's offensive tonfa off just above his knuckles. The severed end of the wooden club spun away and clattered across the kitchen's linoleum floor. At the end of that strike, I reversed the angle of my attack and swept the butt end of my weapon across my opponent's masked jaw.

The maneuver staggered my enemy and sent him backpedaling across the room. His shoulder slammed into the sliding door that let out onto Albert's balcony and sent a lightning storm of cracks racing through the glass. My opponent's core flared with a burst of jinsei that flashed out through his body's channels, restoring his strength and dulling the pain I'd inflicted. He swung his tonfa out to extend the club past the end of his fist, and lunged toward me with a series of short, sharp strikes.

There was no room for me to retreat. I deflected the rain of blows with quick parries from my fusion blade. Without more room to maneuver, though, I couldn't mount an offense. My blade's long handle and blade eventually proved my undoing. The weapon was too unwieldy to deal with the close-in fighting favored by my foe, and a series of jabs from his right fist slipped past my defenses and struck me in the gut. The blows were hard enough to hurt and distract me from a tonfa strike that caught me in the shoulder with enough force to push my defenses aside.

My foe saw his chance and pushed jinsei from his core into his tonfa. Scrivenings along the weapon's length blazed with blinding golden light. A similar glow surrounded my opponent's hand as he swung another punch toward my gut. His tonfa swooped for my head at the same instant.

Both of those attacks held enough sacred energy to cause serious damage if they landed, and I had no way to block both of them from my current position. One of the blows would land, and I was sure it would take me out of the fight.

My Eclipse nature raged at this horrible turn of events and demanded to be let off the leash. It didn't care if I was injured. The dark urge would push my wounded body past its limits just to take its revenge. If I let it go, my attacker would definitely be dead.

And I'd be in the hospital, or worse. Neither of those were good options.

But my opponent had made a terrible mistake. His aura was flooded with aspects and jinsei he'd used to power his attacks.

Just like Rafael had used against me in the duel.

My Thief's Shield technique snapped into place at the last possible instant. My unified aura, serpents, and core embraced the attacks. A terrible hunger washed out of me, stripping the aspects from my foe and draining the jinsei from their core.

My attacker went down to one knee, and his weapon fell from his nerveless fingers. His head sagged and his breath came in labored, hitching gasps. He was seconds from death. All I had to do was let it happen.

"Don't kill her," Albert begged. "Please."

Her?

"Shut up, Albert," the woman said, her words more than a little slurred. "Don't tell him anything."

The dark urge wanted me to end this, once and for all. It would be so easy to take the last bit of sacred energy from her core and channels. Maybe I should be an assassin. That would be the surest way to stop the heretics. Dead terrorists aren't nearly as much trouble as living ones.

My reflection glared at me from a shard of the broken television screen. My eyes were black, tarry pits surrounded by flickers of eldritch fire. A black, shadowy smudge surrounded me, and my hair stirred in an unseen breeze. The bones of my skull seemed too sharp against my pale face. A cruel smile twisted my lips.

"No." I tore my connection to the woman apart. I wouldn't become the monster I'd just seen in the glass. The separation stabbed through my core like a dagger. It felt like I was cutting myself in half, but it was better than how I'd feel if I turned into a murderer. "Get up."

The woman stood, slowly and shakily, her hands above her head. Her core was nearly empty, and she had almost no sacred energy left in her channels. It was amazing she hadn't passed out, let alone that she could stand up. There was no way she could hope to attack me.

Still, I kept my blade's tip aimed directly at the center of her chest. If she made a move, she'd regret it.

"Listen up, both of you," I said. "Whatever you think you're doing with the heretics, it stops today. You aren't to talk to any of them. Don't look at them, don't give them any information, and don't tell them I was here tonight. Because if you do, I'm coming back, Albert. Clearly, whatever security they've given you can't stop me. Keep that in mind."

"You've got it all wrong," the portly man pleaded. He stood up, hands behind his head, his voice wavering and afraid. "We're not heretics. We're trying to stop a threat no one else understands. Tell me who you are, tell me who sent you. I can give you proof. I can show your bosses that this threat is real. We could use your help."

For a moment, my conviction wavered. What if this threat Albert kept babbling about was the Locust Court? If he had proof of another invasion, I needed it. I could use it to convince the elders that we needed to make sure nothing came through the horizon.

No. The elders knew more than this pathetic fool. Whatever he believed, he wasn't right. If I revealed myself to them, the heretics would use that information to come after me and my friends. I'd be lucky to survive the week.

"That's enough talk, Albert," I said with a weary sigh.

His rescuer decided to take her chances. She lunged at me with her hands clenched into fists.

My Eclipse nature demanded vengeance for her stupidity. My head filled with flashes of blood and torn bodies, broken bones and shattered skulls. It wanted to empty her core in a single gulp, then hurl her body through the window.

And I almost gave in to it. The Eclipse way would have been easier, more final, than what I thought was right. Kill your foes, and they won't ever have the chance to raise a fist against you again. It made sense, especially in a war against terrorists.

But I wasn't a murderer. I choked back on the rage and anger, shoved the dark urge as far down as I could, and ignored the pain that caused my core. Every time I pushed back against the Eclipse nature, it hurt worse, like I was tearing myself apart.

My internal struggle had cost me a precious second, and my opponent had almost reached me. She threw a wild punch that glanced off my shoulder, then fell back into a sloppy defensive crouch.

I caught her square in the center of the face with a punch and felt something crunch under my fist. She staggered back, then fell hard on her tailbone. She grunted and collapsed onto her back.

Albert ran for the door, huffing and puffing, his arms and legs pumping for all they were worth.

Which, as it turned out, wasn't very much.

I intercepted him in the middle of the living room floor and swept his legs out from underneath him. He landed on his right shoulder, hard enough to knock the air out of his lungs again. Before he could right himself, I unleashed a quick flurry of punches to his back and midsection. He grunted with each blow and curled in on himself like a dead spider.

"Nod if you understand me," I said to Albert. "You're done dealing with the heretics. You won't give them any more information. If you do, I'll come back."

Albert nodded vigorously, his face smeared with spit and snot. I felt a little sick to my stomach at the sight of him and pushed that way down deep. These people were terrorists. The woman would've killed me if she'd had a chance. Albert had already killed plenty of people with what he'd told the heretics. He deserved what he got.

I repeated that again and again as I left his apartment and stepped through the portal waiting for me outside his door.

# THE KISS

HAGAR AND THE ELDERS WERE BEYOND HAPPY when I spilled the details, minus my new technique, of how I'd dealt with Albert and his unexpected bodyguard. If I'd felt uneasy about beating up an old man and his bodyguard, those feelings were banished by the praise heaped on me by my clan.

"Shame your handler didn't know about the bodyguard," Claude said to me just before they left, drawing a blush to Hagar's cheeks. "I had my doubts about you, kid, but you're all right. Stick with us, and we'll save the damned world even if it doesn't want to be saved."

"Language," Hirani called from the other side of the portal she'd opened in my kitchen.

"Right," Claude said, a faint blush visible through his bushy sideburns. "Be seeing you, Jace."

"Wait," I almost shouted. "My mother—"

Hirani gave me a small, sad smile and crossed the room to stroke the back of my cheek with her left hand. A wave of warmth and calm spread through me at her touch. It was obviously a jinsei trick, and I didn't care even a little. That simple gesture had made me feel good, down to my bones.

"We're looking for her," the elder said with a sincerity that touched me. Her eyes were misty with unshed tears, and her lips trembled as she spoke. "I, too, have lost ones I loved in this cold, dark world. I promise you we are doing everything we can with the resources we have available. When we find your mother, I will personally deliver the good news."

"Time," Elder Sanrin said drily. "Hirani is right, Jace. Finding your mother is a priority for us. For now, though, we must leave. I'm afraid we're on a very tight schedule these days."

"Hang in there, kid," Claude said as he stepped through Hirani's portal. "If anyone can find your mother, it's Brand. I'll kick his ass if he doesn't."

"Soon," Hirani promised, and followed Claude and Sanrin through the portal.

The glowing gateway vanished.

Hagar surprised me by throwing her arms around my neck and squeezing me tight. She clung to me for a long moment, her shoulders shaking slightly. With a start, I realized she was crying.

"What's wrong?" I asked, my voice muffled in the ruff of her Mohawk.

"I should have known," she said shakily. "I was overconfident and didn't think the guard routes would change. I should have anticipated it, I should have—"

"Hey, hey," I said, rubbing my handler's shoulders. "It's okay. I'm fine."

"But—"

"Stop." I held Hagar at arm's length, my hands still on her shoulders. "You did everything you could. Focus on what we're going to do, not what's already happened."

"Thank you." Hagar blotted her tears on the dark sleeve of her robe. "I'm still new at this job. It's been hard, but you're the best field agent I could have hoped for."

"You're new?" I chuckled and felt my cheeks blush at her praise. "You can't be as new as me. We'll learn together, though, right?"

"I'll do better," she promised. "I want you to know you can trust me."

"If anyone had told me last year that we'd be having this conversation…" I said with a grin. "The world is a weird place."

Hagar laughed and shook her head.

"You really are doing the right thing here," she said. "I know it can be confusing, and you feel like you're in the dark most of the time. But you've got a gift, Jace. Let us help you use it."

"Us?" I asked, raising an eyebrow. "I thought you were just my handler."

"Well, yes," Hagar said with a smile. "And, no. That's something else we'll figure out as we go. Take it easy, Jace. I'll see you sooner than you think."

Just like that, Hagar walked out my front door and headed across the bridge. I crossed my fingers and offered up a short prayer to the Empyrean Flame that this would all make more sense someday. For the moment, I had to satisfy myself knowing that I was fighting for the good guys. Every mission I completed against the heretics was one less problem we'd have to deal with down the road, and one step closer to finding my mother.

That had to be good enough.

Despite that it had been dark in my target's apartment, it wasn't quite noon on Sunday afternoon at the School. I busied myself in the kitchen making a cup of coffee, hoping the simple ritual would take my mind off the last mission. Albert and his bodyguard had both gotten what they deserved. They'd known the risks when they threw in their lot with the heretics.

It was the image of my face I'd seen in the broken television glass that had stuck with me. That was what I'd become if I gave in to the urge, and every mission it got harder to hold back. I was on a very narrow path, just as Hahen had warned me. If I ever fell off, all the good work I'd done for the clan might be undone by my darker powers.

I was half depressed and halfway through my cup of coffee when a knock echoed through the cottage. Someone was at my door. I had no idea who it could be. All my friends were supposed to be out for the holidays.

Frowning, I dumped the rest of my coffee down the sink and left my quarters to see what was going on.

"Hey," Rachel said when I opened the door. She held up a small wicker basket covered with a checked cloth. "How about a picnic?"

"That sounds great." I realized I was starving, and whatever Rachel had in that basket smelled delicious. "Where to?"

"Back to the path?" she asked. "Maybe we can go another way, see something other than mountains."

"Perfect," I agreed. "Why're you back so early?"

"Oh, that," Rachel said. "Portal tickets were way less expensive today than tomorrow. I figured I'd save my parents some money."

"Is your brother back, too?" I asked.

Rachel laughed as we headed down the hallway and shook her head.

"Oh, no," she said. "Rafael is snowboarding with his friends at Telluride. He won't be back until he absolutely has to be."

"I still don't understand your family," I said. "If Rafael came to the School of Swords and Serpents as an initiate, why were you enrolled at the Golden Sun Academy? And why does he get a trip to snow country while you're looking for portal bargains?"

Rachel didn't say anything for a few moments. She stared down at her hands and the basket she held. I didn't push her, afraid that I'd embarrassed her or made her mad. That hadn't been my intent. I just wanted to understand how two people from the same family could be so different.

"My parents aren't rich." Rachel broke the silence between us as we reached the hallway that led to the path. "Rafael is here on scholarship. He also does work for the Disciples of Jade Flame. He's like… I don't know how to explain it. Anyway, he's actually much better off than the rest of us. I see more of him here at School than I ever did back home."

I hadn't considered that I wasn't the only student who had someone else footing the bill for their education. It felt strange to imagine Rafael and I being so much alike. We hadn't paid for school, we were both doing things for our respective clans, and we were both on a secret payroll.

I had a dark thought about last year. Had Rafael's clan hired him to take me out?

That didn't seem like a very good question to ask his sister, so I pushed it away.

"Oh," I said. "That makes sense. Maybe he can get you in with the clan, too."

"That's not a great idea," Rachel said with a grimace. "I mean, yeah, I'm technically a Disciple. I don't fit in very well with the other ones, though. My attitude doesn't sit well with most of them."

She trailed off, then shrugged as we stepped on the path.

"I know what you mean," I said. "I'm part of the Shadow Phoenix clan, but they hated me last year."

"Rafael said everyone hated you." Rachel giggled. "It's amazing how becoming the School champion and kicking the snot out of a hundred contenders made you so very popular."

"Oh." I took a fork in the path and headed toward a forested area we hadn't visited together yet. "That's why you're with me."

"With you?" Rachel said with a faint grin. "I'm with you so we can have a nice early dinner. I'm just being nice to a poor Shadow Phoenix who stayed at school over the whole winter break."

We both laughed at that, and I felt more at ease than I had this whole year. There was something just right about hanging out with Rachel. She was nice, and sarcastic, and we had similar backgrounds. It didn't hurt that she seemed to get more attractive by the day.

"Well, thank you for taking pity on me," I said. "It gets lonely in my room by myself."

"It looks like a pretty impressive room you've got there." Rachel raised an eyebrow. "I don't think anyone else gets their own lakeside cabin."

"There are definitely perks that I'm going to miss when I'm not the champion anymore," I said. "Then again, last summer just about did me in."

"Here's good," Rachel said. We'd passed through a thin band of trees to a bluff that overlooked a rushing river. The ground was covered in a thick layer of springy moss that made a perfect place for us to sit.

Rachel placed the basket on the ground, and I sat across from her.

"Let's see," she said. "I stole most of this from the dining hall. There're some chicken tenders, biscuits, a little pot of honey, apples, cherries, a couple of kinds of cheeses. Oh, and this."

She lifted a bottle of wine from the basket and offered it to me across her forearm like we were in a fancy restaurant.

"A fine vintage," I said. "I think. I'm not much of a wine drinker."

"Me, either," Rachel said with a grin. "I figured this was as good a time to try it as any. Picked it up from a party during the break."

Fortunately, the bottle had a screwtop instead of a cork, because neither of us had a corkscrew. We ate and drank, filling our bellies with food and sipping the stolen wine. It wasn't long before my head felt fuzzy and warm, and my words slipped and slithered across my tongue when I spoke.

"Did you miss me locked up here in this big old place by yourself?" Rachel wiped wine from her lips with the back of her hand and handed the wine bottle to me.

"I wasn't alone," I said. "The staff were here. They're pretty nice during the breaks. Even fixed me a Christmas ham. Or, at least, slices of a ham."

"That's not what I meant," she said.

She glowered at me, then we both dissolved into a fit of giggles. It was hard to take anything seriously when my thoughts were tumbling around the inside of my head like a litter of kittens on catnip.

"I missed you," she admitted. "A lot."

Her cheeks were bright pink, though I couldn't tell if it was the alcohol or if she was blushing. If she was embarrassed, she didn't act like it. Her eyes sparkled, and she stared intently at me.

"I missed you, too," I said.

We gave each other goofy grins, our shared happiness both surprising and overwhelming. Something was changing in our relationship, and I felt a pang of guilt and regret mingled with excitement and mystery. Clem and I would always be friends, I was sure of that. What I had with Rachel, though, was very different.

"What happened to your hand?" Rachel asked. "I just noticed the blood."

I glanced down at my right hand and was surprised to see fresh scabs across my knuckles. I must've gotten them when I punched Albert's protector.

"Oh," I said. "It's nothing. I was doing some stuff with the clan. Moving boxes and junk while everyone was gone. Scraped the back of my hand against a doorframe."

"I see," Rachel said. "You work for the Shadow Phoenixes?"

"Yeah," I said. "Just boring stuff. I'm sure it's not nearly as exciting as what Rafael does for the Disciples."

"That's why you have those nice robes?" Rachel reached across to finger the black cloth of my clothes. I'd never really appreciated just how nice they actually were. She had a way of showing me everything through different eyes. "These must've cost a fortune."

"No, those are from being the champion," I said. "At least I think they are. They were in my closet when I got to my room."

She took a long swig of wine. The little that was left after she finished swirled around in the bottom of the bottle as she handed it back to me. Her lips were stained a deep red, dark and mysterious.

"I wish I could've met you before you were the School champion," Rachel said.

"Why?" I asked, honestly confused. I took another sip of the wine and handed the last of it back to her. "I doubt you would've thought very much of me last year."

"I bet you're wrong." Rachel gave me an honest, warm smile. "Rafael told me about you. How hard you struggled. How you had to fight for everything."

"All that is true," I said. "I was also a thief, and I nearly got my friends killed in the final challenge. Plus, I was a filthy camper. It wasn't much to see."

"Don't say that," Rachel said softly. She reached across the basket and brushed my cheek with the tips of her fingers. "We're all born with cores. We can all master jinsei and serve the Flame's Grand Design. The only difference between campers and Empyreals is money."

"That's a very big difference," I said. "Money changes everything."

"And that's why I wish I'd met you last year," Rachel said. She leaned forward until her hands were on either side of the picnic basket and her face was less than a foot from mine. "Which one do you think is the real Jace? The scrappy initiate or the confident School champion?"

I leaned forward, too, drawn to Rachel as if by magnetism. Our noses bumped against each other, and she giggled.

"I'm not that different now," I insisted.

"You just said money changes everything," she teased. "Maybe it changed you in ways you can't recognize. Maybe you're a different person than the one who came to school here last year."

"I don't think so," I said, mesmerized by Rachel's vivid eyes. "I'm still a kid from the undercity at heart."

"Let's see if you still know how to kiss like a camper," she whispered.

And then we did.

# THE BLUR

ERIC AND ABI CAUGHT UP TO ME AT BREAKFAST on the first day of classes after the break. Clem wasn't with them, and they both looked like they had terrible news to tell me.

"Oh, man," Eric said. "You've done it now."

"What are you talking about?" I asked. "I haven't done anything."

"Well," Abi said, "before break you fought Rafael for Rachel's honor."

"That is not what happened," I said. "He challenged me to a duel because he thought—"

"And now Rachel is talking to Clem," Eric finished. He tilted his head toward the far side of the dining room where the two girls sat across from one another at a small table. I couldn't see Rachel's face, but Clem looked very serious.

"Oh," I said quietly. "This isn't how I thought this would go."

"You really don't know anything about girls," Abi said with a grin. "How are you feeling otherwise?"

"Fine, I guess," I said. "Why? Do I not look okay?"

"You look fine," Eric said. "Apparently, extra fine, given the fact that you landed Rachel."

My two friends chuckled at that, then Abi's eyes grew more serious.

"I've been thinking a lot about you," he said. "About what happened at the duel. And with the Locust Court's emissary last year."

My blood ran cold. Had Abi figured out my secret?

"I talked to my father when I went home for break," he continued. "He is a very wise man, a spiritual leader for our community. He remembered seeing you in the challenge."

"Over the summer?"

"No," Abi said. "The first challenge. When you fought Hank at the Five Dragons Challenge."

That was surprising. I didn't even know that fight had been televised. Even after I became famous as the School's champion, no one had ever brought it up. That Abi's father had seen it, and remembered what had mostly been a pretty boring fight, surprised me.

"Anyway," Abi said as he topped off his plate with an over easy fried egg, "he thinks there is something very special about you. About the way you handle jinsei. And aspects."

"What's that supposed to mean?" I asked as I followed my friends toward our usual table. Clem and Rachel were still in deep conversation, and I pretended not to notice. There was no way that was going to be good for me.

"It means most people can't do what you do," Abi said as we sat down. "I didn't catch all of your technique, it happened too fast. But I did see you fill your aura with aspects faster than I thought was possible. That's a unique gift you have."

Abi's voice was low and grave. I couldn't tell if he was looking at me with suspicion, concern, or admiration. He was hard to read, and my paranoia didn't make it any easier to decipher his thoughts. He could have easily been congratulating a friend on learning something new.

Or, as a member of the Portal Defense Force, he could have been telling me that he knew I was an Eclipse Warrior and should watch my step.

"It's probably because I had to teach myself so many things," I said. "Being a camper and all, you know how it is."

I felt a twinge of shame at using my background to deflect the conversation. Campers made Empyreals very uncomfortable. Most of those who lived in the overcities would just as soon pretend the poor people in the slums beneath them didn't exist. Rachel said it was because they couldn't reconcile the fact that they lived in luxury only because most people couldn't.

"Oh, no," Eric said. "Don't look now."

I glanced up instinctively and saw Clem and Rachel headed in our direction. They walked side by side, their trays of half-eaten breakfast balanced on their hands, their faces carefully neutral.

"We should go," Abi said.

"Please don't," I pleaded.

"Hey guys," Clem said, her voice so pleasant I was sure she was being sarcastic. "Room for two more?"

"Yeah," Eric said uncertainly. "Sure."

Clem sat across from me, between Eric and Abi.

Rachel took the seat next to me.

That division felt a little too much like taking sides for my comfort. I traced aimless lines in the syrup on my plate and waited for the hammer to fall.

"We were talking," Rachel said with a nod toward Clem, who shot me a smile so wide and bright I thought she might bite me. "About us."

"Us," I said noncommittally.

"You know," Clem said, her grin growing wider by the second. "About your picnic."

"Yes," Rachel confirmed. "Clem's fine with everything. She says you were just good friends. And I want you to stay good friends."

There was a glimmer of pain in Clem's eyes at the words. Her smile tightened, just a little, almost impossible to notice.

But I saw it.

And it hurt.

"Yes," Clem confirmed, her smile painfully wide. "We're all going to be great friends, from now on."

Eric and Abi glanced at me with sympathy in their eyes.

Oh, man. What had I done?

As it turned out, things weren't nearly as bad as I'd worried they'd be. Clem and Rachel really did seem to get along. I didn't catch even a whiff of argument between the two of them after that. Clem never mentioned Rachel during our scrivenings tutorial sessions, which was both a relief and annoying. I was glad Clem hadn't been hurt by my choice but couldn't help but wonder why she wasn't at least a little upset.

But, as the days of January passed, the last of the tension between Clem and me faded and our group of four grew to five. We ate our meals together, helped each other with our classes, and spent more time goofing off at my cottage than we probably should have.

The only dark spot on those weeks was that Abi was gone more often than not. The Portal Defense Force kept him and the other students hopping, and more than once he and his fellow cadets all missed class on the same day. When that happened, I was surprised by how many students were working for the PDF.

It also made me wonder which of my classmates were secretly working for their clans or other, darker, forces. If Rafael, Hagar, and I were all working for our clans, it was very possible that there were other students who'd decided they wanted to be heretics when they grew up. I'd have to bring that up to Hagar.

Not that I saw much of my handler. She was out of classes far more than she attended, and I wondered how many of the professors and staff the Shadow Phoenix clan had paid off to keep her absences quiet. As days without Hagar turned into weeks, I threw myself into my studies and martial arts practice.

That, at least, turned out to be a good use of my time.

Professor Song started us on a new kind of meditation that involved the repetition of modified martial arts forms in a fluid cycle. It was supposed to bring our bodies and minds into closer unity, and I was surprised when it actually worked.

My Thief's Shield technique had shown me the key to integrating my serpents, aura, and core. What it hadn't done, though, was push my core to the next level. I'd been stuck at initiate all year, and the meditation techniques I'd tried seemed to make my dark urges more dangerous and forced me to back off before I lost control.

Professor Song's new meditation style changed that.

The regimented motions opened a new understanding within me. I suddenly understood how my core worked with my body to harness and direct the sacred energy that was the key to all life. The sweep of my arm wasn't just muscles and bones moving according to the demands of my mind. It was an extension of the natural flow of jinsei through the universe. When I was in tune with what the jinsei wanted to do, everything was easier, simpler.

That revelation allowed me to harness more spiritual power without enticing the dark urge to surface. On one crisp Wednesday morning in the middle of February, I found myself so deep in Professor Song's guided meditation that my core ached with the power it contained. The rest of my class disappeared from my thoughts as I filled my core to its limits.

And beyond.

My thoughts exploded out of the meditation. My back arched, and every muscle in my body tensed at once. Jinsei crackled in my aura like a living flame, spearing toward the roof of the dojo in a golden rush. The power carried me with it. I hung, suspended in the air by the forces that had rushed through me during my explosive advancement.

My core had transcended to adept level.

As the rush of power subsided and my feet settled to the floor, I took a deep breath and felt a surge of jinsei pass into my core. It was as if I'd spent my whole life up to that point breathing with only one lung.

A gasp rustled through the students in the dojo. The weight of their attention fell on my aura like tiny hailstones, a pinging rattle that I banished with a thought.

I only had to glance around the room to see that, except for Professor Song's, my core was the most powerful one in the dojo. The rest of my class were still initiates, much more powerful than the average person, but nowhere near as powerful as I now was.

Finally, all the grinding and frustration had paid off. I'd done it.

"Congratulations are in order, Mr. Warin," the professor called from his position at the head of the dojo. He strode through the other students, a smile beaming on his face, his eyes lit up with pride as he approached me. "That was an impressively quick advancement for a student."

He stopped a few feet away, and I bowed respectfully, my eyes never leaving his.

"Thank you, revered Professor," I said. "I've been working hard, and your teachings helped me find the right path."

"You honor me," the professor said, returning my bow, his eyes cast to the floor. "It has been my pleasure to instruct a student with such ferocious determination. Perhaps when you have some time, you can show me that technique you used in your duel against Rafael."

"It's not all that impressive," I said, trying to deflect the conversation. "My time in Mr. Reyes's lab taught me to gather aspects from the environment quickly. The technique is merely an extension of that."

"I see," the professor said. He thrust his hand forward, and I took it. "Again, congratulations on your advancement to adept. You may find the change disorienting at first. I'll dismiss you from class early and will let your other professors know not to expect you today. You should return to your quarters, meditate, and rest. Feel free to explore your new abilities, though it's important you don't push yourself too hard just yet. Your core is very sensitive after an advancement of this magnitude. A new world has opened to you—be careful not to trip when you cross its threshold."

Professor Song shook my hand vigorously and clapped me on the shoulder as the rest of the class burst into applause.

I let myself bask in their admiration and thanked the Grand Design that everything was finally going my way. Even my duel with Rafael had worked out for the best, because I'd learned a new technique. Clem and Rachel were, if not friends, at least friendly toward one another, and I had a girlfriend for the first time in my life. And the dangerous work I'd done for the elders was getting me closer to finding my mother while I made the world a safer place.

The advancement was the icing on the cake.

"Thank you, Professor Song," I said. "It has been my honor to be your student and learn from your teachings."

With that, I left the dojo. I'd grown stronger during my time in the Five Dragons Challenge, my body hardened by the combat training. But that paled in comparison to the strength I'd gained from my advancement. It was as if I'd been a child, and now I was a full-grown man. My strides were smooth and long, my legs carrying me with no effort at all. My robes felt tight against my biceps and across my shoulders, like I'd gained muscle mass.

Maybe I had. I'd never known anyone who'd advanced from initiate to adept. There was no telling what sorts of physical changes might accompany such a dramatic shift in mystic ability.

And that had increased dramatically. I noticed faint swirls of golden light at the corners of my vision as I walked through the halls, and when I focused on them, they snapped into sharper relief. The luminous threads crawled along the walls and floated in the air. The longer I stared at them, the more of them I saw.

With a start, I understood these were currents of jinsei. The School's walls were riddled with them, which made sense. The architecture could shift and move because it was built on a base of sacred energy. I'd just never realized how much jinsei was around me at all times. It was overwhelming.

I was still marveling over this new ability when I reached my quarters. My eyes followed the glowing threads as the door opened, and the inner workings of the mechanism were obvious to my new senses. Sacred energy not only parted the doors, it lubricated the tracks and dampened the sound of their travel. There was so much more to jinsei than I'd ever noticed before.

If the halls had been brimming with jinsei, my quarters overflowed with the spiritual power. The boundary between the School and the forest path that led to my cottage was surrounded by a rectangle of golden light so bright it was difficult to even look at. It had to be a portal of some kind, stable and fixed in place and filled with energy so it didn't have to be activated. The amount of time and effort that had gone into creating such a thing boggled my mind.

There was so much sacred energy in the air, I had to readjust my vision to ignore it. It was difficult at first, and I stumbled more than once when I misjudged where the ground was behind the swirls of power that emanated from it. The trip across the lake's bridge was nerve-racking, and I was relieved to make it to the cottage's front door without tumbling over the rail.

"I need coffee." I shambled through the sitting room and into the kitchen.

The advancement had filled me with jinsei, amplified my senses, and left me suddenly wiped out. It wasn't yet nine in the morning, and already I needed a nap. That wouldn't do. There were so many new things about my core I wanted to explore. Its capacity to store jinsei. The effect it had on my techniques. What it had done to my body.

I was pulling the coffee supplies out of a cupboard when a floorboard behind me creaked a warning.

A rough hand slammed my face into the cupboard. The coffee set fell from my suddenly nerveless fingers and shattered on the floor. A burst of stars exploded across my vision, and a terrifying weakness spread down my spine.

Fingers closed in my hair and drew my head back, then slammed my skull into the granite counter. With a snarl, my unknown attacker hurled me across the kitchen and into the side of the stainless steel refrigerator.

A few days ago, even an hour ago, that series of attacks would have killed me. With my new core, though, my body was more resilient and able to withstand the damage. The attack hurt, but my skull was intact, and my nose wasn't even broken. My rattled senses snapped back into focus, and I pushed jinsei out of my core and into my body's channels. If the intruder wanted a fight, he was going to get one.

I bounced away from the refrigerator on the balls of my feet just in time to avoid a brutal punch that smashed a dent into the side of the appliance. I almost hadn't seen the attack at all, because my foe was wrapped head to toe in a strange field of jinsei that obscured every detail of his form. The humanoid swirl of power jumped away after his missed attack and he threw his arms up to defend himself.

"Who are you?" I demanded, settling into a ready stance. It was hard to concentrate on the figure in front of me, as if the jinsei surrounding him didn't want me to see him at all. If I'd still been an initiate, the field might have made him completely invisible.

My advancement had just saved my life.

The assailant didn't waste any words. He lunged forward, throwing punches and kicks in a blistering flurry of raw aggression. Unfortunately for him, the kitchen was cramped, and that limited his range of attacks to easily blocked straight-line strikes.

I defended myself and cycled my breathing to bring my body, core, and aura into alignment. My opponent had pulled back to evaluate me more closely, and I wondered if he was surprised at the strength of his target. I found myself excited by the fight, ready to test my abilities against a serious opponent. There'd be no pulling punches in this sparring match.

My attacker switched tactics and summoned a fusion blade in the blink of an eye. It was a strange, spear-like weapon, and the attacker threw a blistering series of thrusts toward me. The jinsei-fueled attacks came fast and furious, forcing me into a defensive stance.

I kept the fusion blade's business end from punching holes in my chest and gut with counterstrikes and parries, though my defense cost me numerous cuts across my forearms and the backs of my hands. My

Thief's Shield wasn't enough to save me here. Even if I stripped the aspects and jinsei out of my opponent, the speed and savagery of his spear thrusts would leave me full of holes.

Summoning my own fusion blade wouldn't do me any good in the cramped quarters, either. The long hilt and blade would be useless for defense or offense, just as they had been in Albert's dinky apartment. Meanwhile, my opponent's short stabbing weapon was the perfect tool for poking a bunch of holes in an opponent at very short range, very quickly.

As if he'd read my mind, my blurry attacker executed a series of short, sharp thrusts that backed me against the kitchen wall. With nowhere to go, I slapped the first few attacks aside, took a cut across my forearm, and narrowly avoided losing an eye by jerking my head to the side at the last minute.

Through it all, I cycled my breathing, drawing in beast aspects from the catfish that swam in the lake around the cottage, the birds that nested in the building's eaves, and, yes, the rats that cavorted in the fields that surrounded the lake. While my opponent had focused on murdering me, I'd been preparing a riposte.

In the instant he extended himself to drive his spear's point through my face, I formed serpents from the beast aspects and struck.

Each of the glowing tendrils was as thick as my wrist and narrowed to a sharp tip. My first serpent looped around my foe's fusion blade and spiraled down his arm to stab his bicep. In the same moment, the other serpent speared into his core.

Or, they would have.

The jinsei that surrounded my assassin wasn't just camouflage, it was also powerful defensive armor.

My serpents bounced off it with a pair of loud cracks and recoiled as the sacred energy they'd struck lashed out at them with jolts of lightning-aspected jinsei.

The unexpected retaliation drew a grunt from me, and if I'd been any weaker, it would've stunned me into immobility.

Instead it just made me mad.

My opponent tried to free his weapon from my serpent, with no luck. Rather than continue the fruitless struggle, he let the blade dissipate and came at me again with his hands and feet. This time, the golden energy around him shifted to red and black, powerful destructive aspects from his aura flooding into the sacred power.

A counterpunch from my left hand drove his right fist into the side of the refrigerator, leaving another dent in the appliance. I trapped his right hand with a sweeping block that pulled it under my left arm and tight against my body. The buzz of his armor's defenses was annoying, though hardly enough to stop me.

"Who sent you?" I demanded in the brief space between attacks.

The assassin wasn't talking. He tried to headbutt me, and when that missed, he threw a knee at my midsection, grazing my ribs with little effect.

With one arm trapped, the enemy couldn't defend himself against my blows. I hooked a series of rapid uppercuts into his abdomen, lifting him off his feet with every strike. He grunted with the impacts, but didn't fall.

The damned armor was blunting my offense.

I unleashed the Thief's Shield technique and my aura siphoned aspects of fortitude and resilience out of my attacker. It wasn't the usual rush of power I'd experienced when using the technique against other opponents, though. It was a slow drip of aspects and jinsei. Enough to weaken my opponent. Not enough to drop him.

My attacker realized the new danger and tried to free himself with a sudden frenzy of activity. His knees bounced off the outsides of my thighs as I raised one leg then the other to fend off his strikes. His free hand clawed toward my face, and I slapped it to the side with a backfist. He gambled on another headbutt, and I stopped it cold with a short, sharp elbow strike across his chin.

My technique had drained enough power from my attacker's armor to let that attack through, and the blurred aura that had surrounded him faded. For a moment, I caught a glimpse of gray eyes between layers of black cloth. I reached for the man's mask, hoping to tear it free and get a good look at him. The elders would want to know who'd tried to kill me.

My Eclipse nature wanted to see its victim's face. The dark urge had been amplified by my advancement and rose up within me so quickly I didn't notice until it was almost too late. If the man hadn't been protected by his armor, he'd have been drained dry in that moment.

Instead, my Eclipse nature gorged itself on half the jinsei in his core and stole away the last of the protection aspects in his armor. He was vulnerable. I could disable him and haul him off to face the elders.

Unfortunately, my assassin had an escape plan. He knew when he was outclassed and decided to run away to fight another day. The masked man made a complex gesture with his free hand and vanished in a burst of red light. A cloud of thick, stinking smoke filled the kitchen.

I staggered back into the living room and took a deep, shuddering breath. I raced upstairs to make sure there wasn't another attacker hiding in my bedroom. The windows on either end of the upper floor gave me a good vantage point to confirm there were no other enemies hiding outside the cottage.

The assassin had come alone.

How the hell had he gotten into my quarters in the first place?

I stormed back to the School. Hagar and I needed to talk.

# THE LURE

I HAD NO IDEA WHERE TO FIND MY HANDLER, SO I started with her room. I banged on the door, and when that didn't work, I pounded at her neighbors' doors until someone answered.

"I'm looking for Hagar," I told a final-year student who looked more than a little annoyed to have been woken up before his first class. "Have you seen her?"

"You know what time it is?" he asked. "Have you checked the exercise yard? I know she likes to do her calisthenics before breakfast."

"Thanks," I said.

I hustled down the hall and willed the School to show me the fastest way to the courtyard. I was surprised to find how much more quickly I could move through the building, now. It was as if my advanced core exerted more control over the shifting architecture.

Hagar wasn't in the courtyard. Of course not, nothing could ever be easy.

I concentrated on my handler, fixing her image in my mind. When I had it as clear as I could manage, I demanded the school take me to her.

I wound my way up and down staircases, through twisting halls I'd never seen before, and up a spiral ramp lined with burning candles glued to the walls by ridiculous stalagmites of once-molten wax. I raised my fist to hammer on the door at the top of the ramp and almost punched Hagar in the face.

"What are you doing here?" she asked. For a moment, she looked as angry and displeased with me as the old Hagar.

"Someone just tried to kill me." I showed her my bloodied arms through the shredded sleeves of my robes. "In the cottage."

"That's not possible," she started, then shook her head. "Of course it's possible. It happened. You can't come in here. Let's go back to your cottage."

"What if they send another killer?" I asked.

"You defeated one, you can defeat another. Plus, I'll be there to back you up," she said.

"What if they send something else? Like a bomb."

"That's a fair point," she said. "Give me a second."

There was a loud clatter inside the room, and a series of grinding noises like Hagar was dragging furniture across the wooden floor. Light flashed under the doorway, red, green, and a shade of blue so bright it was nearly white. Finally, the noise stopped, and the door flew open.

"Come in," she said.

I followed my handler into a room that was as plain and boring as any I'd ever seen. The circular chamber had stone walls topped by a plaster-domed roof crossed by a heavy pair of dark support beams. There were no windows or furniture, and no decorations on the walls. The only door was the one we'd entered through, and the only light came from a single dim orb floating near the ceiling.

"What is this place?" I asked.

"A meeting area," Sanrin replied as he walked through the wall. "Tell me what happened, every detail."

I spilled my story for the elder and answered a barrage of very specific questions. Where, exactly, had the man been standing when he vanished? What did he smell like? Was he wearing gloves?

Finally, after a solid ten minutes of interrogation, Sanrin crossed his arms over his chest and closed his eyes. His lips moved slightly, like he was having a conversation in his dreams. After a few moments of that, he opened his eyes and nodded.

"Brand and Claude have secured your cottage. They didn't find any weapons or traps," he said. "We'll return there now to search for additional clues as to who attacked you, and why."

The transition between Hagar's secret meeting room and my cottage happened between breaths. It was so smooth it took my brain several seconds to catch up with my body. On top of the sensory changes I was dealing with from my core advancement, that was almost enough to make my empty stomach do a dangerous flip-flop.

Hagar put a hand on my shoulder to steady me and looked at me curiously.

"Are you all right?" she asked. "You don't look so good."

"Just a little disoriented," I said. "I'm not used to popping in and out of places without warning."

"Ah, yes," Sanrin said. "I often forget most don't often use that method of travel."

Truth be told, I wasn't sure how Sanrin had moved us. Portals were energy intensive and usually required static gates on either end to work. The fact that he could blink us across the School with seemingly no effort made me wonder who else knew that trick.

"We need to search this place," Hagar told me. "Go through everything, let us know if you find anything out of the ordinary. We'll help you."

Sanrin had already started rifling through my desk. He opened and closed the file drawers with calm efficiency, then started in on my closet. Hagar threw my bedclothes back, flipped my mattress, then shook my pillows out of their cases. From the rattles and banging coming from downstairs, Claude and Brand were doing the same search on the first floor.

I ducked into the restroom off my bedroom and flipped open the top of the dirty clothes hamper. It was Thursday and laundry wouldn't pick up until Saturday, so the hamper was filled with sweat-stiff exercise clothes, my informal robes for daily classes, and an assortment of underwear and socks. I shook out each article of clothing. I used my new jinsei sight to examine each item, hoping that would help me locate something of interest.

Nothing.

I opened the medicine cabinet over the sink and looked over its contents. It held my toothbrush, a tube of toothpaste, a stick of deodorant, and some ibuprofen for the muscle aches and pains that came from working out too hard. I checked the bottles, popped the top off the deodorant, and even squeezed a little paste out of the tube. Nothing there, either.

I went through the small cupboard under the sink next. There were some towels, a few cleaning supplies, and something dark shoved all the way in the back of the cupboard, mostly concealed by the plumbing.

I reached back into the shadows and pulled out a matte black jumpsuit.

The same one I'd worn when I'd attacked Albert and fought his bodyguard. I hadn't wanted the school laundry to find that, so I'd hidden it in the last place I thought they'd look. It had been under there ever since. My eyes roamed over the black material for a second, and a burst of excitement rushed through me when I caught a spark of jinsei where it didn't belong.

"Found it!" I rushed back into the bedroom, the jumpsuit in my arms. "Right here!"

A thin crystal square, no bigger than my pinky nail, was attached to the back of the suit's right shoulder. It was surrounded by fitful sparks of sacred energy, and its surface was cracked in two places. An intricate script had been carved into the square's surface, but was now almost obliterated by scorch marks.

"Well," Sanrin said. "Someone certainly doesn't like you very much."

"Is that an anchor?" Hagar said. "I've heard of them, but I've never seen one in person."

"That it is," Sanrin confirmed. "This is definitely how they breached your defenses, Jace. Where did you get this jumpsuit?"

"It's what I wore when I went after Albert," I said. "His bodyguard must've stuck it to me while we were fighting. I had no idea."

I felt both stupid and vulnerable. I should've checked the suit as soon as I returned to the cottage. Of course, at that time I was still an initiate without the advantages of an adept core's enhanced senses, so it would have been much harder to spot the crystal anchor. I also had no idea what an anchor was, or how they could have used it to track me, so it would have been easy to assume the square was just part of the suit. My frustration turned slowly to anger.

I'd been kept in the dark about so many things, and now one of those things had bitten me. Enough was enough.

"Maybe if people told me what was going on, I would have caught this," I said. "If that's what the assassin used to reach me here, then they could use it to send more of their people."

"No," Sanrin said. "The anchor is a onetime-use device. Though your assailant may not need an anchor to return. If he has a strong enough emotional connection to a location, a skilled portal pilot could get him here. From the sound of your fight, his emotional connection will be quite strong."

"That's great," I said. "I mean, really awesome. I'll have to move out of here. If assassins can pop in and out anytime they want, I need somewhere safer to live."

Hagar and Sanrin exchanged glances. I didn't like that look at all.

"You should stay here," Sanrin said. "I'll have Claude and Brand arrange for a security detail to be stationed outside the cottage. If there's another attack, they'll respond within seconds."

"I'll stay here, too," Hagar said. "We'll be safer together."

"We'll be safer where the assassins don't know how to..." I stopped, frowned, then glared at Sanrin. "You want me to stay here as bait."

227

"That is such a crude term," Sanrin said. "I prefer to think of you as a lure. I have no intention of letting the assassins get their jaws on you. When they make another attempt, we'll catch them. Our interrogation of their assassin will get us that much closer to cracking open the heretic network. And then we can put an end to this whole sordid chapter of Empyreal history."

That sounded incredibly dangerous to me. It also sounded like a way to speed things along and get the elders to focus on finding my mother.

"If I do this," I said, "then you'll start looking for my mother, right away. If she's out there and someone knows who she is, then she's in danger."

"You have my word," Sanrin said.

Something about the way he said those words made me hesitate. There was a strange evasiveness in his tone, as if he knew something he didn't want to tell me just yet.

We eyed one another warily. Then I nodded.

"I'll do it," I said.

# THE GARBAGE

THE ELDERS WANTED ME TO KEEP MY USUAL schedule. If I suddenly went into lockdown mode, whoever had sent the assassins would be much less likely to send another killer after me. Since the elders wanted the bad guys to take the bait, I continued to attend classes, spent time meditating with Rachel, had meals with my friends, and pretended I wasn't worried about another attempt on my life.

And that's how I found myself underneath the School of Swords and Serpents alongside the rest of the students in my Intermediate Alchemy class. Professor Ardith and Headmistress Cruzal had taken us down there on what they referred to as a "field trip," but the rest of us were quickly realizing it was an unpaid maintenance detail.

This," the headmistress said, "is the containment area for the School's waste disposal system."

"The garbage dump," Clem said, much to the delight of the rest of the class. "Honored Headmistress, I'm not sure what this has to do with our Intermediate Alchemy course."

Professor Ardith clapped his hands and tutted at the chuckling students gathered around him in the narrow, damp, and somewhat sticky stone corridor deep beneath the School's main campus.

"Quiet," he said. "That includes you, Ms. Lu."

Rachel giggled at Clem's statement, and was much slower to get her laughter under control than the rest of us. She fidgeted next to me, hiding her face behind her hands, her shoulders heaving as she struggled to stifle her amusement.

"I'm sorry," she gasped, at last. "Please continue, Professor."

"The School has need of your assistance, students," Ardith said, pacing back and forth in the small space like a strutting rooster. "The containment vessels are currently filled with waste aspects. We need to transfer those aspects into transport vessels so they can be disposed of properly. This is not pleasant work, but it will give you all practical experience in handling dangerous aspects."

"Now we're garbage men," I muttered, setting Rachel off into another burst of choking laughter. She elbowed me in the ribs as Ardith glared at her.

The professor was clearly unamused with Rachel's laughter, and he pointed one slender finger at her over the heads of our classmates.

"Since it appears that Ms. Lu cannot control herself, she will be our first volunteer," he said. "Headmistress Cruzal, please step over here, beside me, and we will begin."

With his boss out of the way, Ardith raised his hands toward the opposite wall of the hallway. Thin threads of jinsei sprang from his fingertips to the faint outline of a design inscribed into the stone. Silver light poured through the complicated pattern, eliminating edges that had been weathered and rounded by the centuries. Despite its great age, the scrivening etched into the wall had no missing links or loops and appeared as sound and strong as the day it'd been created.

A few moments after Professor Ardith activated the scrivening, the intricate design faded away to reveal an open archway into a silo-like chamber. I saw a cluster of tall, thin cylinders through the opening, and caught a glimpse of the much larger room past them. It was impossible to say for certain how many aspects those vessels could contain. If I had to guess, I would have said they held several million aspects.

"Ms. Lu," Ardith said, "please step into the chamber. The silver vessels are for containment, the copper vessels behind them are for transport. You will find a small spigot at the bottom of each containment unit, and a focusing funnel at the top of each transport unit. Your task is to transfer the waste aspects from the spigot to the funnel. I suggest you open the spigot very slowly and very carefully. You may begin when you are ready."

"Hey," I said and caught Rachel's arm. "Just crack the spigot a tiny bit. Cycle your breathing, transfer the waste aspects through your aura, then purge them into the funnel. Don't try to rush."

"Thanks for the advice," Rachel said and squeezed my hand. Then she stepped away from me and marched into the garbage dump.

Ardith's eyes flicked from me to Rachel, and his lips twisted into a smarmy smirk. Of all our professors, he was the one who wore his clan allegiance on his sleeve the most clearly. He didn't think anyone but his beloved Resplendent Suns were capable of performing even the simplest of actions, despite the fact that I'd shown repeatedly that there wasn't anyone in the School better at handling aspects and raw jinsei than I was. Even without my core, the experience I'd gained working with Hahen put me far, far ahead of any other students in my class.

"Let's get closer," I said to Clem and pulled her toward the other side of the hallway, where we could get a better look at Rachel's progress.

"I don't like this," my friend whispered. "It's dangerous."

"I agree," I said. "Ardith's being a very special kind of jerk today."

"Cruzal should know better," Clem muttered. And then we were too close to the teachers to speak and had to worm our way through the other students to get a front-row seat to Rachel's attempt.

She'd already cracked the spigot open by the time we could see her, and her aura contained the first waste aspects that had leaked out of the containment vessel. Her face was wrinkled into a disgusted frown at the stink and slimy feel of the rot aspects she'd already processed. She wasn't used to handling waste like this, and the handful of disgusting green motes clogging her aura must have tasted like a hearty gulp from a gallon jug of spoiled milk.

With one shaking hand, she closed the spigot and cycled deep, cleansing breaths through her core. The air in the waste unit was far from pure and clean, but it was a far cry better than the disgusting mess in Rachel's aura. As we watched, she fashioned one of her serpents and guided it toward the funnel. With each breath she took after that, the rot aspects flowed out of her aura and into the transport vessel. It was a gross, annoying job, and I was impressed at how well Rachel had handled herself.

She'd lost some aspects by not using a serpent to gather them from the spigot, but she'd still done very well.

Much better than I had my first time in Hahen's laboratory, as a matter of fact.

"I suppose that's acceptable for a Disciple," Professor Ardith said. "When you've cleansed your aura, you may exit the chamber and our next volunteer can continue the process. Perhaps we'll finish the transfer by sometime next year."

"Considering her background, she's done very well," Headmistress Cruzal said. The words set my teeth on edge, and I opened my mouth to say something.

Only to be stopped by Clem's sudden stomp on my toes.

"Don't get yourself in trouble," Clem said. "Rachel can handle herself."

While my friend's words were true, that didn't make it any easier for me to swallow my anger. I knew what it was like to be treated like dirt. Clem didn't. Still, it wouldn't do any of us any good for me to start a fight with the headmistress. So far, she liked me. If I upset that apple cart, there was no telling what kind of trouble I might get myself into. Assassins were enough for me to deal with at the moment.

Rachel finally shambled out of the chamber, her eyes wide, her forehead dotted with beads of perspiration. She blew strands of her bangs out of her eyes with an exasperated breath and bowed to Professor Ardith.

"Thank you for the instruction, honored Professor," she said. "It was most enlightening."

"Yes," Ardith agreed. "I'm sure it was. Since your friends also can't quit talking during a demonstration, Ms. Hark will be our next volunteer."

Clem frowned at the professor's words, and I braced myself for an angry retort. Instead, the adjudicator's daughter nodded, bit her lip, and marched into the chamber. She stiffened her spine and took up a position midway between the spigot and the funnel. She cycled her breathing, filling her aura with aspects from her surroundings and her own unique aspects. From the latter, she fashioned her serpents, and they rose from her palms like a pair of ivory cobras.

Clem guided her right hand's serpent toward the spigot and her left toward the funnel. I recognized what she was trying to do and wondered if she could pull it off. Pulling the rot aspects in through one serpent and pushing them out through the other was a tricky maneuver for someone without the benefits of a core like mine, and I'd never seen my friend do anything remotely like this before.

Ardith must've really ticked her off.

Clem took another deep breath, and at the same instant used her serpent to crack the spigot on the containment vessel. The glowing tentacle of her essence swooped down to plug the spigot so the aspects couldn't escape into the air. She then inserted the other tentacle into the funnel, closed her eyes, and began her meditation technique.

With every cycle of breath, Clem absorbed more and more rot aspects into her aura. I was no expert on waste management, so I wasn't sure why the School had so many garbage aspects around. Maybe they were reclaiming the jinsei and storing the waste aspects, like I'd done for Tycho.

Whatever the case, the containment vessel had far more rot aspects than Clem had anticipated. Her aura filled with them, and she struggled to push the toxic gunk up through her other serpent and into the funnel. She was overwhelmed and needed help.

I took a step forward, only to be hauled up short by Ardith's barked command.

"Stop." He stepped forward, put a hand on my shoulder, and glanced into the room where Clem struggled valiantly to do as she'd been asked. "She's fine. Certainly the daughter of someone so powerful as Adjudicator Hark won't have any trouble with a little job like this."

"It's poisoning her," I said. "Let me close the spigot so she can process the aspects."

"It's an important lesson to learn," Ardith said, his voice low. "She thought she was more capable than she was. It's a mistake she won't make again."

I glanced toward the headmistress, who was busy discussing some unimportant bit of school business with one of my fellow students. I started to raise my hand, and Ardith snatched it out of the air and forced it back down to my side.

"Don't embarrass your friend," he said. "Or me."

Clem's aura had taken on the the foul, sickly green of stagnant swamp water. Her head lolled on her neck, and the only thing that held her upright was the connection she'd forged between the vessels. I held my breath and counted, slowly, trying to calm myself, hoping that Clem would recover.

And then I saw what I'd feared.

The rot aspects were trying to push their way into her jinsei channels. The same thing had happened to me, only with fire aspects, when I was working with Hahen. Those had done significant damage, but I'd healed. Rot aspects, though, could destroy flesh. Clem could be crippled.

I moved toward the door again, and Ardith grabbed my arm. His eyes flashed with cold anger at my defiance. For the briefest flicker of a moment, I thought he'd strike me.

A heavy pressure built behind my eyes, and the dark urge wanted this confrontation. If Professor Ardith attacked me, he'd be dead before he knew the mistake he'd made. It'd be Singapore all over again. Only this time it wasn't a nobody from the camps who'd be dead, but a teacher at the most prestigious Empyreal school in the world. There'd be questions I couldn't answer, and then they'd put me under a microscope until they figured out what I'd done.

What I was.

"Headmistress Cruzal," I called out, my eyes fixed on Ardith's, "there's a problem in the waste unit."

"Mr. Warin," the headmistress responded with an annoyed sigh, "this is not your test. Please allow Ms. Hark to finish what she has begun."

"My apologies, honored Headmistress." I slipped my arm out of Ardith's fingers and bowed low to Cruzal even though I didn't feel like showing deference to the headmistress. I felt like punching her in the throat for standing in my way. "Ms. Hark was not aware of the multitude of aspects contained in the vessel. She needs a moment to recover, before the rot infests her jinsei channels and she's injured. I'm certain her mother would be grateful to know that you allowed a fellow student to step in to assist her in this way."

Cruzal eyed me with shrewd appraisal. A faint smile twisted the corner of her mouth, and she reached out to pat me on the shoulder.

"Yes," she said, glancing past me at Ardith. "I'm sure her mother wouldn't want anyone to suggest that Professor Ardith hadn't adequately warned Ms. Hark of the dangers of the assignment. Your assistance is most appreciated, Mr. Warin. You truly are the School's champion."

Ardith glared daggers at me as I stood up straight and headed in to help my friend.

It would be a simple matter to strip the aspects out of Clem's aura. My Thief's Shield would do it in the blink of an eye. But I knew that Ardith was watching me, and Headmistress Cruzal might be as well. I'd have to be very careful to keep the two of them from discovering what I really was.

I reached down and grabbed the spigot with my right hand, activating the Thief's Shield technique at the same instant. I twisted the valve clockwise, stopping the flow of aspects, and let my aura overlap Clem's.

"Jace?" she asked, her eyes more than a little foggy and disoriented. "What's going on?"

"I've got you," I whispered. "Keep cycling your breath. You're okay."

I'd never done this before, and I wasn't even sure it would work. I stepped behind Clem, supporting her with a hand under each of her arms. Then I formed a serpent and entwined it with hers. To most Empyreals, it would look like a single serpent, and I hoped it would be enough to fool my instructors.

The second problem I had, though, was hiding the aspects I leeched away from Clem. If they showed up in my aura, Ardith would instantly know something was up. That would not only embarrass Clem, but it might give the professor and headmistress more information about my abilities than I wanted them to have. Ardith was already angry, I didn't need him looking for more reasons to cause me problems.

The only way to hide what I was doing was to not hold the aspects in my aura at all. I had to pull them out of Clem and immediately push them through my serpent and into the funnel. I'd never done anything like that and wasn't even sure it was possible. I took a deep breath and gave it my best shot.

My Eclipse nature didn't make things easy on me. It was greedy and wanted to take more than just the aspects out of Clem's aura. I struggled to contain its hunger and wrestled with my own serpent to keep it from plunging into my friend's core and draining her jinsei. As overwhelmed as she was, Clem wouldn't stand a chance against that attack. She'd be a husk in seconds.

"Hold on," I whispered to Clem. "Try not to act surprised."

I took a deep breath and cycled my breath as rapidly as I could. Aspects flooded from Clem's aura into mine, absorbed by the Thief's Shield technique. I stifled a groan and forced the rot aspects away from my core, through my aura, and into my serpent faster than anyone could possibly see. The disgusting mess left a foul taste in my mouth and a dark shadow across my thoughts, and then it was gone, safely contained in the transport vessel.

I stepped away from Clem, who only had a few motes remaining in her aura. She glanced back at me, mouthed her thanks, then focused all of her attention on purging the last of the toxic mess from her aura. She'd recover, but she'd have a heck of a headache and it'd be days before she could smell anything but the stink of warm sewage.

I slipped out of the room and past Ardith's angry gaze and Cruzal's appraising look.

"You handled Ardith and the headmistress very smoothly," Rachel said as I returned to her side. "Will Clem be okay?"

"She'll be fine," I said. "Just bit off a little more than she could chew."

"Seems like that happens around you quite a bit," Rachel said with a wink. "What did you do?"

"It's just a stupid thing I learned working in Tycho's lab." That was far from the truth. What I'd done in there should have been impossible. I'd never heard of anyone who could pull aspects out of the air and channel them directly through their serpent without passing them through their core or aura. "I don't want to make a big deal about it. Clem's probably going to be embarrassed as it is."

And she was, which worked out to my benefit. For once, Clem took the first explanation I offered and didn't chase after me for more details.

Thank the Flame for small miracles, I guess.

# ⊂HE SLIP

OTHER THAN CLEM'S NEAR MISS WITH THE garbage disposal, classes went by without any notable incidents. I kept showing up and tried to pay attention. While my clan could, and no doubt would, help cover up any failings in my grades, I didn't want that. To master the dark urges of my Eclipse nature, I needed to learn as much as I possibly could.

Which was easier said than done, when I spent every day nervous there'd be another attempt on my life. It wasn't so much that I was scared of the assassins, as I didn't want anyone else to get caught in the crossfire.

If something happened to any of my friends because I'd become the top target for a heretic hit team, I wouldn't be able to live with myself.

It didn't help matters that the Portal Defense Force had tightened their security around the School for reasons entirely unrelated to the attack on me. As far as I knew, none of the School's authorities or staff had any idea there'd been an assassination attempt on school grounds. The PDF were concerned about heightened risks of terrorist attacks following a series of minor, but still worrying, incidents in the overcities. Someone had been breaking into government buildings and spray-painting "Free the Slave" on the monuments to the Empyrean Flame.

It was obvious to me that this was the work of the heretics, but the PDF was positive it was related to Grayson Bishop's trial.

"Why would anyone take Bishop's side?" Rachel asked my friends and me at dinner one night. "He was caught red-handed dealing with the Locust Court. I'm surprised they bothered with a trial."

"Of course there'll be a trial," Clem said. Her mother was an adjudicator, and her whole family firmly believed in the rule of Imperial Law. "Even with ironclad proof, the code of Empyrean Law demands that we conduct an investigation and give the accused a chance to defend themselves against the crimes they're charged with. I know it seems unlikely, but there's always a possibility that Grayson didn't actually do any of the things he's been accused of."

That drew a lot of raised eyebrows from the rest of the table. It was one thing to defend the system, it was entirely another to pretend like we hadn't caught Grayson's Locust Court emissary red-handed. Tycho had even presented Bishop's journal at trial, confirming what I'd already known. There wasn't much wiggle room there.

"It will all be over in a few months," I said and scooped up a spoonful of the best chili I'd ever had. It was spicy, with just a hint of chocolate sweetness and the faint bitter bite of coffee. The meat was tender with the right amount of chew to it, and I'd already finished one bowl topped with diced onions, sour cream, and sharp cheddar cheese. The second helping tasted every bit as good as the first had. "One way or another."

"Let's hope so," Eric said. "My clan is just about sick of this case. We're ready for it to be over. Most of us just want to get past it so we can repair the damage all this has caused."

I felt bad for my friend. Grayson was a member of his clan and had been one of the world's five sacred sages. He brought prestige and honor to the Resplendent Suns, and his fall from grace had plunged Eric's clan into turmoil over whether to support their former elder or condemn him before the trial.

We kicked the subject around for a while longer, then let it go. There was nothing any of us could do about the case, and arguing about it would just end with hurt feelings. As always, we drifted away after dinner, heading off to do homework or study for the next day's classes. The School of Swords and Serpents was one of the most challenging environments I'd ever experienced. Between the physical demands of martial arts training for four hours every morning, the mental demands of our academics, and the fact that every time I touched an inscriber I broke something, I ended every day more than ready to hit my bed.

These days, though, I didn't get the bed.

Hagar did.

I'd been relegated to the couch in the sitting room, which was comfortable, if a little short for my long legs. I'd floated the idea of trading places every other night, but Hagar wasn't having any of that. As my handler, she thought she had seniority, and she abused it at every turn. She got the bed, used up all the hot water before I could take my showers, and had even rearranged the furniture according to some plan that made no sense to me.

Which is why most nights, I went to the small library rooms to research more about my Eclipse core. Since my advancement, its hunger had changed. It was easier for me to control now, but it was also greedier. Every time I was even the slightest bit irritated or annoyed, my core wanted me to remove the source of that annoyance immediately if not sooner. I was also getting more paranoid, though it was open to debate whether that was from my Eclipse nature or from the recent assassination attempt.

The small research cells worked on demand. If you concentrated on the type of book you needed, it would replace one of the books already on the shelves. It took me a while to get the hang of it, but soon I learned how to summon books on important moments in Empyreal History, including the Utter War.

The irritating part of researching an event that no one wanted to talk about was that whoever had written these history books had gone to great pains to remove any mention of the events that surrounded the war with the Locust Court. There were lots of cryptic passages regarding a great weapon that was unleashed to protect the world against the hungry spirits. Some historians even referred to that weapon as the last defense of the Empyrean Flame. But they never said what the weapon was or how it defeated the Locust Court.

I knew those cryptic hints were about the Eclipse Warriors. I just didn't know how to dig any deeper to find out the truth about them. It was driving me crazy.

The closest I got during my research came in a book about military units in the Portal Defense Force. Those were the frontline troops in the first phase of the Utter War, and they were the last ones still stationed in the Far Horizon when the war ended. Most of the information about those units was boring, though I did learn that students from the School of Swords and

Serpents were impressed into service after the Empyreals suffered tremendous casualties in the war's opening stages. Abi's unit, the Scholar's Brigade, still had many of the same commanders that had served during the war. They must have been powerful Empyreals to resist the effects of aging for so long, or they'd been blessed by the Flame with extended lifespans. Maybe they'd be able to answer some of my questions.

I considered asking him for an introduction, then discarded the idea. Abi would want to know why I was looking into this, and if he caught me in a lie, our friendship would be on the rocks again. It wasn't worth the risk just to hear an adult lie to me.

The most intriguing tidbit was hidden amongst all the boring lists of names and ranks in that same essay. There'd been a unit known as the Lost. They'd apparently been distinguished in service and had been instrumental in turning the tide against the hungry spirits during the war's final stages. Despite that, they warranted only a single paragraph of description, which ended with the strangest euphemism for death I'd ever read.

*The Lost left the Far Horizon for stranger places and were never seen again.*

I let those words roll around in my head, hoping that'd jog something loose. That sentence didn't line up with what I knew about the Eclipse Warriors, who'd all been executed by the Empyreals who'd created them. Maybe the Lost had made a break for it when they found out the fate of their Earthbound counterparts. That would have been enough to convince me to run away, too. Only, there wasn't anything beyond the Far Horizon except dead worlds and hungry spirits. Running into that would only have been a slower and more painful death for the Eclipse Warriors.

I was just about to request a book on Empyreal cosmology when a hand fell on my shoulder.

My Eclipse nature instantly activated the Borrowed Core technique to harvest beast aspects from the rats that scuttled along the ceiling above me. It forged a single serpent and lashed out at whoever had been foolish enough to touch me.

Aspects of fear and confusion flooded into my aura, strengthening my serpent. Before I even knew what was happening, the construct had wrenched the hand away from my body and slammed its owner against the wall of the library cell.

"Jace!" Rachel shouted. "What are you doing?"

The sound of her voice shattered the spell of violence around my darker nature, and the urge retreated. My heart froze, and I prayed my Eclipse nature hadn't hurt my girlfriend.

Rachel's robes were in disarray, one sleeve torn almost completely off. She cradled her right hand against her chest, and a livid purple bruise had already started to rise against her skin. Tears streamed down her cheeks, and her lips trembled.

I reached out for her, but Rachel pulled back.

"I'm sorry," I said, ashamed of what had happened.

"Your eyes," Rachel whispered, her voice low and wavering. "What are you?"

The words stung more than a slap. I blinked hard, willing the darkness of my Eclipse nature to leave me. The look of terror on Rachel's face was like a knife through my heart, and I knew she'd seen the truth about me in that moment.

Even if Rachel didn't understand the change that had overtaken me, she knew it was horrible.

"Rachel," I said, "it's me, Jace. You just surprised me, that's all. My new technique—"

"That was more than a new technique," she whispered.

"Please," I begged. "Let me explain."

The terror in Rachel's eyes convinced me to tell her everything, even if that was a death sentence for me. If I couldn't control myself, if I hurt those closest to me, then maybe I didn't deserve to live.

Rachel wasn't in the mood to listen to anything I had to say. She bit her lip and backed away from me, her eyes locked on mine as if she were afraid I'd attack her again if she dared to look away. When she reached the door, she bolted out of the library cell.

I followed my girlfriend. I had to talk to her. I needed to make her understand.

I nearly collided with Clem, who was heading into my cell as I was rushing out.

"Jace?" Clem stopped me with a hand on my chest. She looked down the hall at Rachel's fleeing form. "What happened?"

"I don't know," I said, raking my fingers through my hair.

"Oh, Jace," she said. "I'll talk to her. She looked really upset."

"No," I started, then stopped at the quizzical look on Clem's face.

"She's my friend, too," she said. "Even if I wish things might have worked out differently. Let me help you both."

The hurt in Clem's eyes cut me deeper than a fusion blade. I wasn't sure what it meant, but I knew I couldn't stop her. I watched, frustrated and uncertain, as the two most important women still in my life walked away from me.

# THE HIT

AS GOOD AS THE FIRST HALF OF MY SECOND YEAR at the School of Swords and Serpents had been, the second half was shaping up to be a complete disaster. After what had happened in the library cell, Rachel avoided me like the plague. Clem didn't exactly take my former girlfriend's side, but she did tell me to give her some space.

"I don't know what happened in there, but she's scared," Clem said, her eyes searching my face for some clue that would shed light on the mystery. She hated not knowing things, and this thing in particular bothered her. "If you won't talk to me about it, either, there's not much I can do to help. Just give her some time. She'll come around."

Rachel was still avoiding me when the winter chill had given way to spring's warm breezes. She'd gotten very good at being where I wasn't, even going so far as to transfer out of the Intermediate Scrivening class. When I did catch sight of her in the halls, she ducked her head and took off like a shot.

I tried to reach her through Rafael, but that was exactly the wrong thing to do. Whatever grudging respect he'd had for me after our duel had burned away. He was furious that I'd scared his sister, and I didn't blame him.

"Leave her alone," he told me flatly. "If you keep after her, we'll cross swords again. And this time, Song won't be there to keep score."

My Eclipse nature bristled at the threat, and I turned away before Rafael saw the darkness flow into my eyes. As nice as it would have been to stomp him flat for standing in my way, that would only prove his sister was right.

I was a monster.

The tension from living with Hagar and having hidden security teams patrolling my quarters at all hours of the day and night certainly made matters worse. I couldn't concentrate on my schoolwork. My Intermediate Scrivening mark had fallen to a C-, and Professor Shan made it clear that if I didn't turn things around before the end of the year I might have to repeat the course.

The thought of repeating a class I'd already suffered through once made me so miserable I was almost relieved when Hagar dropped a bomb on me on a cloudy Tuesday in the last week of May.

"We know who's coming for you," my handler said. "It's very exciting."

"What are you talking about?" I wasn't in the mood for word games. "Spit it out."

"The assassin who'll try to kill you next. It's Preethi Adjadumlun." Hagar followed me into the kitchen. "They call her the Death Weaver."

"And that name should mean something to me?" The elders had replaced my coffee set with a much nicer one that made me nervous to use. I carefully placed it on the counter.

"She's a very high-priced murderer for hire," Hagar said matter-of-factly. "She'll be here tonight."

"I see," I said. "I assume I won't be here when she arrives. Claude and Brand will deal with it?"

"Oh, no." Hagar wiggled her eyebrows. "There's a security team here, and we've set some traps in preparation. Unfortunately, the elders can't be here because they've been called to Kyoto."

"Kyoto?" It hit me. "Grayson's trial. I'd almost totally forgotten."

"You have a lot to think about, with your girl troubles and assassins and whatnot," Hagar said with a grin. "But don't worry about it. Our best guys are here, and the Death Weaver relies on surprise to get the job done. Thanks to our intelligence teams, we have the advantage there. She won't last thirty seconds."

"What if she needs less than thirty seconds to kill me?" I asked.

The truth was, I didn't know how I felt about another killer showing up. My core had gotten stronger day by day, even after I'd advanced. My senses had grown so sharp it was almost impossible to sneak up on me now. Anyone approaching from behind roused my Eclipse nature from its slumber, ready to fight. That wasn't so convenient at school, but it would certainly come in handy with a mysterious killer on her way. Maybe I could beat the assassin.

But that might not save anyone who got in her way. Hagar was a pain, but I'd feel terrible if something happened to her during the attempt on my life. I didn't know the guards—they'd made it a point to avoid me while they patrolled the grounds to keep their professional distance. I assumed, though, that they had families and friends who would miss them if an assassin snuffed their lives out. Their lives were on my shoulders, too.

"It's going to be fine, Jace," Hagar said. "Preethi always strikes at night, so we've got an hour or two. Come upstairs. I want to show you what we've got."

I followed Hagar up to my bedroom, where she pointed out the scrivened circles around each of the windows. They radiated a subdued golden glow to my enhanced sight, and what I could understand of their sigils told me they'd alert us to any intruders who broke the glass. The circles also had a nifty set of aggressive countermeasures that I couldn't interpret.

"Don't stand too close to those," Hagar cautioned. "You can't set them off, but their offensive capabilities have a blast radius."

"Blast radius?" I didn't like the sound of that. "Don't destroy my bedroom or blow the roof off the cottage, all right?"

"No promises." Hagar winked and crossed to the closet. She opened it to reveal that all my clothes had been removed. The small space now held a wiry man dressed in black, an ugly gun holstered on the webbed harness that crossed his chest. "This is Henry. He's here to make sure nothing happens to you."

I waved to the man, and he closed the closet doors.

"Friendly guy," I said.

"He's not paid to be your friend. There are three more guards around the perimeter, and two more on standby." Hagar nodded to the stairs. "Let's get some coffee, then we can hunker down and see what happens."

I tried to prepare our drinks, but Hagar pushed me aside.

"Let's not break another set," she said. "Your hands are shaking. It's probably the adrenaline. Take a seat. I'll make the coffee."

"How can you be so calm?" I asked. She was right, my hands were shaking. Part of it was adrenaline, but the rest was raw fear pushing its way past my confidence. The idea that someone had been paid to kill me preyed on my thoughts. Even with guards all over the cottage, there was still a chance the Death Weaver would find her target. In the heat of combat, almost anything could happen. For that matter, in these close quarters, friendly fire was almost as much of a danger as the enemy. Even if the assassin didn't kill me, there was a very, very good chance someone would be badly injured or killed during her attack. I didn't know how to process the idea of other people putting their lives on the line to save mine.

"This isn't my first rodeo," Hagar said with a grin. "I've been working with the elders for years. This isn't even close to the weirdest or most dangerous thing I've ever seen."

Once again, I was reminded of how not everything I saw was what it seemed. Rachel and Rafael being related had been completely unexpected. Last year I'd considered Hagar to be one of my worst enemies. This year, she was one of the few people I could trust, and she'd had an exciting few years as an Empyreal secret agent. It was a lot to take in. I sat in silence and pondered the potential secret lives of my friends.

Eric was a member of the Resplendent Suns, a clan that still hadn't publically denounced Grayson Bishop's compact with the Locust Court.

Abi was a cadet in the Portal Defense Force, and he was just full of classified secrets he'd learned from that job.

And Clem...

She was Adjudicator Hark's daughter. If any of my friends was a secret agent, it was her.

"You're thinking too hard." Hagar placed a mug of coffee in front of me. She fetched the cream and sugar that we'd both ignore, dropped them on the table, then retrieved her own cup from the counter. "I know this is all strange and scary, but you'll get used to it. One day, people will know what we've done. When this is all over, we'll be heroes."

I didn't say it, but we both knew she was sugarcoating things. We might be dead by the time the fight with the heretics was over. Their attacks were getting more dangerous. Graffiti was out of fashion, and firebombs had taken its place. And now they were hiring assassins to take out Empyreal agents.

To take *me* out.

"I don't want to be a hero," I admitted. "I thought I did, but I'm not so sure anymore."

Hagar chuckled. "No real hero wants to be one." She sipped her coffee and looked out the window next to the kitchen table with a wistful sigh.

"Do you even know what the heretics want?" I asked. "I know they hate the Grand Design, but that hardly seems worth all this trouble."

"They want to tear it all down," Hagar said. "The whole Empyreal Society. Clans, elders, the Flame, all of it."

That idea filled me with a cold dread. The idea of maniacs who wanted to destroy everything the

Empyreals had built over the millennia of their existence was horrifying. I couldn't imagine how deranged someone would have to be to even attempt such a thing.

"But why?" I asked.

"The Grand Design is bigger than mortals can understand. It's like this coffee." Hagar dropped a dollop of cream into her coffee and stirred her finger through the cloud it formed on the surface. "What we see is just the shallows. If we try to dig too deep into it, we get burned. Some people don't like that. The idea that there's an invisible hand that keeps them on a path they didn't pick for themselves makes them furious."

I wanted to chase after that philosophical question, but Hagar suddenly tilted her head to one side. She pressed her fingers against her temple, and I noticed she had an eye-snapper connected.

"Stay calm," she said. "The scouts reported an ether blip. Someone's opened a portal here. Don't run. Take one more drink of your coffee, put it in the sink, and then walk upstairs. Imagine you have to use the bedroom for something boring. Don't look like that. Be normal."

"What are you going to do?" I asked, doing my best to mask my concern over the fact that there was a stone-cold killer minutes away from her target.

Me.

"She's not after me, Jace," Hagar assured me. "I'll be fine right where I am."

I hid my displeasure behind a drink from my mug. The coffee was warm and velvety on my tongue, and I enjoyed it like it was the last drink I'd ever have.

Because it just might be.

I put the cup in the sink, rinsed it with a little water, then headed upstairs at a leisurely pace. I even faked a yawn.

But every step seemed more difficult than the last. As I climbed up the steps, I leaned on the banister for support. Someone was coming to kill me, and I was walking straight into their line of fire. That was much harder to do than anyone could imagine.

"Don't let anything happen to me, Henry," I whispered as I entered my bedroom. There was no answer from the closet, and I hoped that meant my temporary bodyguard was just being extra cautious not to tip our hand.

I forced myself to take a seat at my desk and opened my computer. The quantic laptop was an impressive piece of tech, though I wasn't as fascinated by it as Eric was. I held my hands above its keys, careful not to make contact with the laptop. The last thing I wanted to do was make myself blind and deaf by connecting to it.

After what felt like hours of pretending to type some homework, I was sure we'd fallen for a false alarm. I felt terrible for Henry stuck in the closet, cramped from standing still until his feet swelled inside his boots. He had to be hurting no matter how much of a professional he was. Maybe I could go down and get him something to eat. Slide it under the door.

I stood up from my desk to do just that, stretched my arms overhead, and headed for the stairs.

That's when everything went to pieces.

Lines of black jinsei shot through the air outside the cottage's rear window. They converged on a central point and wove a web of dark lines that pulsed with movement and deception aspects. There was no more than a single heartbeat between the instant the first line had appeared and the last one forged the final connection.

The web unfolded in a flash of black light, and a woman clad in a tight-fitting black bodysuit burst through the darkness at the heart of the jinsei web. She wielded a short jinsei blade in each hand and hurtled toward my window so fast she was little more than a blur of motion.

"Incoming!" I shouted. It was the first and only warning I could think to shout, and I hoped it didn't confuse anyone.

My fusion blade appeared in my hand, and I dropped back into a defensive stance, blade raised horizontally across my body. My Eclipse nature greedily sucked up aspects as I cycled my breath. My adept-level core merged with my aura and nascent serpents, uniting all three parts of my being so they could work together in perfect unsion. It would only take a few seconds for me to gather enough energy for the Thief's Shield.

I didn't get the time I needed.

The Death Weaver burst through the window at astonishing speed. She was incredibly fast, but the scrivened circle that guarded my window was even faster. A siren wailed, and a tremendous flash of white light washed through my bedroom.

I was blinded for a moment and prayed the assassin was crippled as well. If she recovered from the scrivening first, I was a sitting duck.

"Burn you!" The woman cried out in obvious agony. When my vision cleared, I saw why.

The trap had knocked her flat on her face. Three rings of red jinsei encircled her shoulders, waist, and ankles. They'd pinned her arms to her sides, and smoke drifted away from the points where the rings touched her.

Before I could move, Henry burst from the closet and pounced on the assassin. He landed with his knee in her back and rammed the muzzle of his pistol into the back of her head. The big, ugly weapon forced her face into the carpet, and she went instantly still.

I couldn't blame her. The weapon looked big enough to turn her skull into a messy red stain on my floor.

"Clear!" Henry shouted.

"Clear at the back!" a man called from outside the rear window.

"Clear front," another guard shouted.

"The portal's closed," Hagar called as she poked her head up from the stairway. "No more hostiles detected. Good work, everyone."

Henry stood and dragged the Death Weaver onto her feet. She staggered and winced as the jinsei rings bit into her. The barrel of the pistol against the back of her skull couldn't have felt nice, either.

"They know it's you, Jace Warin," the assassin spat at me. "I won't be the last one to take the offer. Your luck will run out, eventually."

"Shut your mouth," Henry said.

"Wait." I raised a hand. "Who knows what about me?"

The Death Weaver glared at me, eyes burning with hatred.

"You called them," she said. "You'll pay for that."

Hagar appeared at the top of the stairs, and she and Henry both looked at me quizzically.

I shrugged. I had no idea what this woman was talking about. She sounded insane.

"Now what do we do with her?" I asked.

"We'll secure her, then arrange for transport to a holding facility," Henry said. "She's worth a pretty penny to the authorities, so after we've finished with her, the elders will turn her over for the reward."

The Death Weaver opened her mouth to say something, and her face exploded in a fountain of blood. She stood for a moment, then her knees buckled, and she crumpled to the floor. Henry was already on the ground behind her, a fist-sized hole through the center of his head. I saw the red-stained wooden floor through the space where his face should have been.

The guards downstairs shouted in alarm, and Hagar screamed a warning. It was all just noise to me. A warbling hum surrounded me, and my Eclipse nature bayed like a wolf answering a distant howl. Something tugged at my core, and I had a sudden urge to kneel.

What the hell was going on?

There was a blur at the stairway, and Hagar shouted in surprise. Her red Mohawk vanished, hidden behind a strange blurry smear across my vision. Blood blossomed in the space where my handler had been standing, and she tumbled down the stairs to the cottage's first floor.

I wanted to rush to Hagar's side and make sure she wasn't hurt.

Instead, I stood frozen in place, silent as the grave.

A tall, thin woman with a face as pale as a full moon stepped through the blur that had taken Hagar down. Her hair was as utterly colorless as her face, every strand as smooth and glossy as wet paint. She wore a tight gray T-shirt and matching shorts that hardly covered enough to be decent. She had no shoes, no jewelry, no weapon.

Her fingers dripped red as she stalked across the floor toward me. Her eyes were empty black voids, utterly at odds with the faint warm smile on her lips.

"Come with me, Brother," she said. "You're free now."

# THE PRISONER

THE WOMAN TILTED HER HEAD FROM SIDE TO SIDE as she approached me, as if I wasn't at all what she'd expected to see. Her black eyes burrowed into mine and her brows bunched up with concern.

"Are you all right?" she asked.

Something about this woman called to me in a way I didn't understand. My Eclipse nature wasn't sure whether it wanted to kill her or kiss her. There was something so familiar and yet so completely alien about the woman who'd just killed two, maybe three, people.

"What did you do?" I asked, peering past her at the dead bodies on the floor.

"Come with me." She extended her bloodstained right hand to me as if it was a foregone conclusion that I'd take it. "We can talk about this away from your captors. They will send more jailers. We should be gone before then."

"I'm not going anywhere with you," I barked. I still couldn't move, but I didn't want her to know that. "I don't know you. You killed the members of my clan. You killed my friend."

The pale woman frowned deeply, and wrinkles blacker than night creased her brow. She took my limp hand, her fingers still warm and sticky with the blood of her victims. She gasped when her skin touched mine.

Something flashed in my skull. A fragment of thought that flickered through my mind so quickly I couldn't capture it. My core roared, suddenly frantic. I wasn't sure if it was terrified or furious.

Maybe both.

"Don't fight it," she whispered. "You will only hurt yourself."

"What are you doing to me?" I shouted. "Let go!"

"We've waited so long for you." Her grip tightened around my hand. I couldn't have pulled free without breaking at least a few fingers. "Come with me and everything will be made clear to you."

"Who are you?" I asked again.

"Lost," she said, her voice a faint whisper. "We have returned to take what is owed us. You will have the reward you so richly deserve for the invaluable part you have played."

The Lost. My mind reeled at that name.

"You're one of the Eclipse Warriors who ran from the Far Horizon at the end of the Utter War." Saying it aloud didn't make it seem any less insane.

"That is one name that they used for us," she confirmed. "For the ones who escaped their betrayal. It's a pity for them, really. Now that you've shown us the way back, they'll pay for what they did. They'll all pay."

Her fingers tightened around mine as she spoke. Her words took on a hard, brutal edge. I didn't need any visions to read her intent as clear as day.

Revenge.

"You can't fight them all," I said. "Even as strong as you are, you can't win that battle."

Her smile widened into a feral snarl.

"We can," she said. "Because of you. When you realized your birthright, you opened the doorway for us to return. You shone a light into our dark exile, and we followed it to you. But you also did something much more important."

"I didn't do anything," I protested. This was not what I'd wanted. I'd only tried to heal my core.

To become whole.

"Oh, but you did." She stroked my cheek with her bloody fingers. "And, in doing so, you have gathered our enemies together for us. For the first time since the great war, our foes are all in the same place."

The trial in Kyoto.

All five of the sacred sages would be there, four of them to judge, one of them to be judged for his crimes. The elders of every clan would be there, too, as witnesses to this dark moment in history.

The Lost couldn't destroy all of Imperial Society. But, thanks to me, they wouldn't have to.

They'd cut the head off the Empyrean Flame's forces in one dire swoop.

"You can't do this," I said. "There has to be another way."

"Don't fight us," she pleaded. "We want to bring you into our fold so you may rule the world as one of us. When we finish with those who betrayed us, the rest will fall in line. We will break the clans and shatter the society they have created. We will claim our rightful place as the masters of this world. And then, when we have replenished our numbers, we will finish what we started. We will destroy the Locust Court. We will scourge the worlds beyond the Far. We will ensure that what happened to us never happens to anyone else, ever again. This is the beginning of the end for the old world, and the end of the beginning for a new one."

My Eclipse nature responded to her words with a horrifying thrill of exultation. That's what it wanted. To conquer our enemies. To destroy our foes. To crush any who would stand before us. To annihilate any possibility of a threat for all time.

For the first time in my life, I felt like I truly understood another person and they understood me.

And it terrified me.

"You can't," I said. "I can't let you."

"Enough," she snarled. "Return with me, now, or be destroyed. The opportunity to sow the seeds of our dominion and reap the harvest of our revenge will not be squandered."

"I was afraid you'd say that." I dropped my voice to a near whisper. I closed my fingers tighter around hers. "I guess we're fighting."

In the split second before the Lost could react, I triggered the Thief's Shield technique that I'd started to fuel when the Death Weaver struck. Strange aspects I couldn't identify poured out of her aura and lodged in mine. The raw, wild jinsei in her core transferred to mine in a heady rush, and I pushed the feral sacred energy deep into the channels in my arms and legs.

The Lost triggered an aura technique that pushed back against the Thief's Shield before I could drain the rest of her strength. My technique sputtered and died, and my enhanced senses showed me she'd erected a powerful defense around her core. If I wanted any more of her jinsei, I'd have to rip that down, first.

Whatever spell the woman had cast over me was shattered into a thousand crystalline shards. My Eclipse nature threw off the enchantment she'd woven around it and screamed for her blood. She'd said she was going to kill me. That was all it took for my dark urge to remember whose team it was on.

I threw a wild, hooking punch that caught the woman in the side of the neck, snapping her head hard to one side. I yanked the hand I was holding toward me and drove my knee up into her abdomen with all the strength I'd stolen from her core. The blow lifted the Lost off her feet and drove the air from her lungs in a single barking yelp.

The pale woman landed hard, then reared back and slammed the top of her skull into my chin and rocked me back onto my heels. She grabbed my thumb with her free hand and wrenched my grip away from her fingers. Her other hand chopped down into the juncture of my neck and shoulder.

Pain exploded from the impact, and my left arm went numb as the jangled nerves refused to carry messages from my brain. I twisted to avoid another chop that would've taken out my right arm, stomped down hard on the woman's leading foot, and threw my weight into her chest.

The unexpected maneuver knocked her off balance, and she stumbled to the edge of the bed. Her knees buckled when they smashed into the obstruction, and she collapsed onto the bed. With a surprised shout, she threw her hands up to defend herself from my follow-through attacks.

I followed up with an ax kick that crashed down on the woman's right thigh. The blow smashed the jinsei from the channels in her stark-white leg, and she howled in pain. With a shout of raw rage, I leaped into the air and channeled jinsei into my right arm and hand. There was no way she'd be able to avoid the amplified attack I drove straight into her core.

The Lost didn't even try to defend herself.

Jinsei exploded from my fist like a spear at the precise moment my knuckles slammed into the woman's solar plexus. The blast of spiritual energy shredded the cage the Lost had built around her core, revealing it to the Thief's Shield.

"It's over," I said as my technique stole her jinsei.

"It is over," she agreed.

With a start I realized how I'd been tricked. Her core latched onto the channels in my arm and reversed the flow of jinsei. The prey had become the predator.

"You can't do this," I shouted.

I'd struggled so hard to get this far. Now, when everything was finally falling into place, she was here to ruin everything. My Eclipse nature raged against the pain as she ruthlessly drained my jinsei. She was too experienced in this art, too powerful for me to save myself.

"I can, and I will," she said. "You are a pup. A brave, fierce pup, but just a pup. I am a wolf. Only one of us leaves here today."

My core was powerful enough to slow her leech-like draining, but strength faded from my muscles by the second, and my legs gave out. I slithered off the end of the bed and onto the floor next to Henry's corpse. My dead weight pulled the Lost down with me.

She hardly noticed when she hit the wooden floor. Her eyes were half-lidded, lost in bliss as she fed on me like a tick on a hound's throat. A faint smile played across her lips. She was enjoying this, reveling in my final moments.

I tried to summon my spirits, but as fast as I could gather aspects, the Lost consumed them. I raked my fingers across the floor, searching for the fusion blade I'd dropped in the fray. My groping hand found something hard and closed around it.

"No." The Lost bolted upright, but she was slow to shake off the feeding stupor. For a split second, she was too sluggish to stop me.

I raised Henry's pistol and rammed it into her chest. I squeezed the trigger and prayed that the safety wasn't on.

The weapon roared, and the Lost shrieked.

I pulled the trigger, again and again, until it clicked impotently in my fist.

"You could have had the world," the Lost gasped, blood bubbling on her lips.

Her eyes faded from black to blue, the vivid iris surrounded by bloodshot white. Her mouth fell open.

A final bloody breath escaped the Lost, and her core faded away.

# THE REVELATION

THE LOST'S BODY SEEMED SMALLER CURLED UP on the floor. It was hard to believe the slight woman had killed my clan's guards. And yet, the proof was all around me. Henry's cratered head had leaked a pool of blood that mingled with the Death Weaver's crimson drool.

Hagar had fallen—

I ran down the stairs and found my friend slumped against the wall at the bottom of the steps. Her eyes were badly bruised and closed tight. A crimson thread spilled from her split lips down the center of her chin, and another red trail oozed from her left ear and down the side of her neck. I dropped to my knees next to Hagar and grabbed her wrist.

"Come on," I whispered urgently. "You're tougher than this."

My fingertips found a pulse. The beats were weak and thready, but it was there. Flickers of jinsei lit up her core with fitful flashes. She wouldn't last much longer. I scooped Hagar over my shoulder, surprised at how little she weighed.

I ran to the front door, where I found one of the clan guards splattered across the front porch. It looked like someone had dragged a heavy hook through his stomach and unspooled his organs around him. I

267

remembered the Lost's bloodied fingers, and their sticky touch against my skin.

My footsteps echoed from the wooden bridge, a rapid hammering that sent birds flying from the trees and fish diving deeper beneath the water's surface. I sprinted down the path and threw my door open. I willed the School to get me to the infirmary in the fastest possible way.

My mind raced as I rushed Hagar to the help she needed. There were so many things I needed to do.

For starters, someone had to warn Kyoto that trouble was coming. The clans and sages would certainly have their own protection, and Kyoto's regional defense force would definitely have a presence at the trial. But I had no idea how many of the Lost were coming, or what they had planned. A single Eclipse Warrior had gotten the drop on us and carved her way through trained bodyguards like they were nothing.

What if a dozen Lost fighters dropped in on the trial?

What if there were a hundred?

Less than a minute after I'd left my quarters, the School had me in front of a door with a red cross on it. I hammered at the glass and shouted for help. Hagar didn't have time for me to be polite about this.

"What in the world?" someone called from inside. Shuffling footsteps hurried to the door, and a burly nurse with an angry expression ripped it open. For a moment, she stared at me, confused and upset. Then she saw Hagar over my shoulder, and her demeanor changed to a cool, professional calm. "Inside. Now."

I hustled Hagar over to the examination table in the middle of the room and laid her down on the strip of paper that ran down its center.

"What happened?" the nurse asked. "Are you all right?"

"I'm fine," I confirmed. "This blood's not mine. She fell down the stairs and hit the wall."

"Have a seat over there," the nurse said. "I'll see to her."

"I can't stay," I said.

"I have to fill out a report," the nurse called out as she started her examination, but I was already gone. I didn't have time for paperwork.

I didn't have time for anything.

The instant I left the infirmary I raced to the administrative office. Someone could call Kyoto. They could warn the courthouse an attack was coming. And then…

And then what?

No one would believe me, for starters. They'd probably think it was some prank or some protest trick to stir up trouble around the trial. If I was lucky, the administration would ignore me. If I was unlucky, I'd wind up in a holding cell until the disaster hit.

Then they'd haul me up on charges for knowing about the attack.

I froze in the hallway, a terrible plan rising through my confusion.

I didn't care how risky it was. I had to do something. No matter what happened, Kyoto would know something serious was happening. It was worth the risk.

I fixed my destination in mind and raced through the School. The halls warped and bent around me faster and faster to keep up with my sprint. Five minutes later,

I burst through an intersection, took a hard left, and almost crashed into Abi.

"I need to use the portal." I grabbed my friend by the shoulders. "I have to get to Kyoto."

Abi stiffened under my hands. His eyes scanned my face, and his lips pursed into a narrow line across his face.

"Are you insane?" he asked. "I'm part of the Portal Defense Force. I'm here to defend the network *against* people using it without authorization."

"Abi, listen to me." I held his gaze. "Something very bad is about to happen in Kyoto. I'm the only one who can stop it."

Abi brushed my hands from his shoulders. "What is going on? We can call my commander. You're a student, not a superhero. We will let the professionals handle the trouble, whatever it is."

This was exactly why I hadn't gone to the administration.

"Abi, please," I begged. "You have to trust me. People will die if I don't get to Kyoto."

"My friend," Abi said, his eyes flitting nervously from side to side as if looking for backup that wasn't coming, "don't try to force my hand on this. I have a sworn duty."

"Abi," I urged, "Eclipse Warriors will attack Kyoto. They'll kill Grayson and the other sages at his trial. That's the truth. Do you think your captain will believe that?"

My friend's eyes narrowed with skepticism. He let out a frustrated breath, crossed his arms over his chest, and shook his head.

"There are no more Eclipse Warriors," Abi said. "They all died out during the war. Why do you believe this madness?"

My stomach tightened into a painful knot. Abi had swallowed the official Empyreal story hook, line, and sinker. He believed the Eclipse Warriors were long gone. Everyone did.

"Because one of them tried to kill me." I raised my bloody fingers to the stain on my cheek. "Hagar's in the infirmary. There are dead guards in my quarters. I know what's happening because the Eclipse Warrior told me before I killed her."

It was Abi's turn to grab my shoulders. He held onto me, tight, and leaned forward until our faces were only inches apart. His eyes were wide and bright against his dark skin.

"There is something wrong with you, Jace," he said. "I've known it since our first day back at school. Whatever it is has eaten you up inside. You have to stop this before you get hurt or you hurt someone else. Now, go. Come back to me when you have the truth on your lips. Not before."

I didn't have many good options here. Abi was no match for me in a fight, even if I didn't have my Eclipse Warrior abilities. My adept core was a whole level above his initiate core, so it would be like fighting a child, with the bonus that I might accidentally kill my friend if I lost control of my Eclipse nature.

There also wasn't any guarantee that taking Abi down would get me what I wanted. I didn't know how to pilot the portal. I'd need him or another guard like him to do that. If I knocked Abi out and had to hunt down another guard, I'd be right back where I was right now.

I had to convince Abi that I was telling the truth.

"You have to let me through," I said. "If we've ever been friends, Abi, if you've ever believed me about anything, you have to believe me about this. If I don't use that portal, a lot of very important people will die. The world will be thrown into chaos. And what happens after that will be much, much worse than any of you can imagine."

"Jace," Abi said sternly, "this has gone on long enough. I'm calling my commander." He turned his head toward the lapel of his robe and reached toward his belt for something.

I activated the Stolen Aura technique. Desperation and adrenaline pushed the technique to new heights.

The stone floor beneath my feet cracked and splintered when I stole its strength aspects. My aura flared and expanded in a dark cloud. It encompassed a nearby potted plant, which withered, blackened, then crumbled to dust. The overhead lights, powered by jinsei and light aspects, dimmed, guttered, and died as I stole their power.

Abi took a labored breath, his eyes fluttering.

My Eclipse nature wanted his aspects. Strength, life, honor. It wanted them all.

"Enough," Abi said. "Stop."

I let the technique go and my aura returned to its natural size. It was crowded with aspects that demanded to be used, and my core boiled with stolen jinsei. My vision was smeared with dark streaks that showed me the dead spots I'd created. The pressure behind my eyes told me I'd donned the visage of the Eclipse Warrior in all its horror.

"Do you believe me now?" I asked Abi, holding his gaze with my black, bottomless eyes.

Abi shook his head. I couldn't tell if he was denying me or if he was trying to clear his thoughts. Either way, I didn't have time to wait for him.

"Look at me," I commanded.

He looked at me with real fear in his eyes. There was a flash of anger there, too, replaced almost as quickly as it appeared by a deep, abiding sorrow. For a moment, I thought he was going to turn away from me. But he clenched his fists, steeled himself, then reached out and put one hand on my shoulder.

"Your eyes," he said. "They're as black as midnight."

"I know," I said. "It's what happens when I let go of it. When I lose control or have to push myself. It's who I am. It's what I am. An Eclipse Warrior."

"You can't say that," Abi insisted. "They'll kill you, Jace. They'll think you're a monster."

"Maybe I am." I looked around at the damage I'd caused, the dead lights, the dusted plant, the broken floor, my friend's still-labored breathing. "But I'm the only one who can stop even worse monsters from turning the world upside down. You have to believe me."

"Perhaps you are," he admitted. "I'm sorry, Jace. I had no idea. I would never have made you reveal this, not to me, not to anyone."

"I don't blame you, Abi," I said, my voice choked with emotion. "But I can't hide it anymore. That's what's caused all this trouble. No one wants to talk about what happened after the war. No one wants to admit what the clans did was wrong. Let me fix this."

"I hope this ends the way you see it, my friend," Abi said slowly. "There'll be repercussions for what I do now. But I trust you. So, go, save the world."

# ᴄHE ᴀRRIᴠᴀL

"I AM NOT AN EXPERT," ABI WARNED ME. "I can only pilot the portal to an area where there is an anchor. Kyoto is unfamiliar to me, but I will try to get you as close to the central courthouse as possible. No guarantees, though."

"You're the only shot I've got." I gave Abi a one-armed hug. "You'll do fine."

Abi turned his attention to the console in front of the portal. His fingers flew over the keyboard. His eyes scanned a screen I couldn't see, flitting from point to point as if tracing a route on a roadmap.

"Godspeed, my friend," he said, and pressed a button with a dramatic final gesture.

Golden light flowed over the gateway like warm honey. Its outline sharpened and something moved in its center. I wouldn't know what lay on the other side until I crossed through. It didn't really matter, though. My fate was in Abi's hand, and I'd have to play whatever cards it dealt me.

I stepped across the threshold of the hole in space, and my stomach churned as the world turned itself inside out. For the briefest moment, I had one foot back in the School and the other on the cool white tiles of a spartan, efficient building in the Kyoto overcity.

Surprised shouts erupted at my sudden appearance, and the portal closed behind me with a sharp, electric snap. Abi had been wrong about his accuracy. He hadn't put me down near the courthouse, he'd put me inside it. Given the high-profile case taking place there that day, there were plenty of security guards and media nearby to be alarmed at my abrupt entrance.

The more quickwitted reporters amongst the crowd snapped pictures of me with cameras they produced as if by magic. Their slower peers jumped and shouted in alarm.

The guards on duty had an altogether different reaction.

One of them drew his sidearm and shouted at me in a language I assumed was Japanese. The weapon was centered on my chest. A little more pressure on the trigger, and I was a dead man.

And so was everyone else in this building. I was the only hope any of them had of surviving what was on its way.

"English!" I shouted. "I only speak English."

The reporters and civilians moved away from me at top speed, leaving me alone on the ground floor just past a security checkpoint. A set of stairs led up to the next floor ahead of me, and elevators flanked either side of the lobby. There were two guards on the steps, five guards at the security checkpoint, and one guard near each bank of elevators. All of them had their weapons trained on me.

"Adjudicator Hark." I said the only important name that might be the least bit friendly to me and raised my hands over my head. Getting punched full of bullet holes seemed like a bad idea. An idea occurred to me. "I need to talk to Adjudicator Hark."

Even if they didn't speak English, I hoped that name would get their attention. Clem's mom was the ruling authority who'd sentenced Grayson Bishop. She wasn't overseeing his trial here, that fell to the five sacred sages, but she would definitely be on hand.

The guards on the stairs ahead of me glanced at one another. One of them tilted his head to the side and said something into the boxy microphone attached to his shoulder. His eyes and gun stayed focused on me as he spoke. A few moments later, his radio crackled a response that I didn't understand. I hoped that meant someone I could talk to was on their way.

All of those guns aimed at my chest made it hard to concentrate. My Eclipse nature did not approve of the many, many threats surrounding us. It wanted me to lash out and end them, immediately. After all the craziness in my cottage, it was very, very difficult to bring the dark urge to heel.

A tall man in the white and red robes of the Resplendent Suns clan appeared at the head of the stairs. He held his fusion blade, a slender scimitar of golden flame, in his right hand. His serpents twined around him in spirals of blazing light, ready to strike or defend at a thought. He passed between the guards and stopped at the bottom of the staircase. The weight of his attention pressed against my aura, an insistent force that demanded my attention.

"Who are you and what are you doing here?" he barked at me, surprised that my veil rebuffed his attempts to read me.

"I need to speak to Adjudicator Hark," I said. My supernatural sight showed me the man's core was only slightly more powerful than mine. That would've put him at the disciple rank, one level above me. He would probably beat me in a fair fight. I wouldn't let it come to that. "There's an attack coming on this building."

The weight of the Empyreal's attention bore down on me, oozing through my aura to wrap around my core. He tried again, and failed, to penetrate my veil.

My Eclipse nature didn't like being poked and prodded. The familiar pressure built behind my eyes. I was seconds from losing control and lashing out.

"Get on the ground," the man growled as my eyes shifted to black. He shouted something in Japanese, and the guards around me tensed. "If you move, they'll kill you."

"You don't understand," I said. "There are Eclipse Warriors coming here, right now. I'm the only one who can stop them."

"On the ground!" The Empyreal advanced on me, his blade raised and ready to strike. The guards on the stairs adjusted their positions to keep their firing lanes wide open.

I had no way to know how much time remained before the Lost attacked. It could be minutes. Or hours. Or seconds. The only way I could be sure I'd be ready to fight them was if I was in the hearing room. Easier said than done.

Deciding that survival was better than instant death, I followed the man's orders. I lowered myself to my knees, then lay prone, facedown, hands stretched out above my head, palms flat on the stone floor.

"These men will restrain you now," the man said. "If you resist, I will kill you."

"I understand," I said. "Just listen. Warn the sages in the Bishop case. An attack—"

"The most powerful members of Empyreal society are in that room," my captor said. "You're what, an adept? There's nothing that you can do that they can't do better. If a threat appears, they will dispatch it."

A strange chill washed over my skin. A low, throbbing hum intruded on my thoughts. I'd felt this before, at the cottage.

"They don't know what they're dealing with," I said. "The Eclipse Warriors are too strong. Without me, the sages are all dead."

"I fought in the Utter War," the man said. "But you're no Eclipse Warrior."

Two guards grabbed my arms and dragged them behind me. One of them fastened a handcuff around my right wrist. The cold metal's grip infuriated my Eclipse nature. Dark memories of a past I'd never experienced flashed like lightning through my mind. A cold, clear rage sliced through me like a knife. First, they'd manacle me.

Then they'd drag me to the pit.

And burn me.

The humming intensified, and pulses of cold wind ruffled my robes. My ears popped as the air pressure changed. The guards jumped back from me, and the Resplendent Sun shouted something I didn't understand.

"Whatever you're doing, stop it!" The heat of his fusion blade warmed the back of my neck.

"I'm not doing this," I said. "It's them! You have to let me up. I have to stop them."

The Sun said nothing, and in that moment I knew he'd decided to kill me.

My aura was still packed with aspects I'd stolen from the School. If I didn't use them, my life was over. It was now or never.

My Eclipse nature tried to break free of my control, but I held it in check even as I used its unique power. These guards didn't deserve to die. I only needed to get past them.

My serpents whipped out of my core and wound tightly around the Sun's burning fusion blade. There was a moment of searing pain as the fiery weapon burned into the tendrils of jinsei connected to my core. My instinct was to pull the serpents away from the pain, but I rejected that and maintained my steely grip on the Sun's blade.

The Resplendent Sun reacted with shocking speed despite his surprise. He yanked back hard on his fusion blade to tear it free of my serpents' grip. It was a smart move on his part, because he'd rightly guessed most of the pressure for my serpents would be pushing up against the weapon to keep it from slicing my head off.

What he hadn't anticipated was that I didn't need to pry the blade out of his grip to make it useless.

My serpents stripped the fire aspects from the weapon and reduced it to a pale shadow of itself in the space between heartbeats. They took its jinsei next, and the blade vanished entirely.

With the threat of immediate extermination out of the way, I rolled hard to the left and bounced up to my feet. The guards were trained Empyreals, but they were only initiates. To them, this fight had been nothing more than a blur of motion. Their weak cores weren't strong enough to keep up with what was happening.

I used that to my advantage and lashed out at the two men who'd tried to manacle me. My serpents whipped through their auras and instantly drained most of their aspects and jinsei. I stepped past the stunned Resplendent Sun and drained the two guards behind him on the stairs in the same motion.

With their auras empty, the guards slumped to the floor. I'd held the dark urge at bay just enough to spare their lives. I wasn't sure how much longer I could fight it. My willpower was running low.

"Stop or they'll shoot!" the Resplendent Sun shouted from behind me.

Naturally, I didn't stop. I pushed jinsei out of my core and into my channels to climb the stairs at top speed. I wove a serpentine pattern to the second floor, and the guards' shots missed me and chipped stone from the steps.

The humming had grown to an almost deafening droning by the time I'd climbed the stairs. Dust devils tore through the building's hallways, and spirals of tortured air pulled at my robes and hair. Whatever the Lost were up to was extraordinarily powerful.

I ignored the elevators because I knew the guards would kill them as soon as they recovered. Instead, I charged through the nearest exit door and into the stairwell. I raced up the narrow concrete steps, around and around the square silo at the heart of the courthouse. I passed each floor in the space of a heartbeat and made it to the sixth level before a door above me burst open.

Guards spilled into the stairwell with their weapons raised. They wore plated body armor and carried much bigger, much scarier sidearms than the lobby crew. They completely blocked my path with a barrier of bodies and guns. Their eyes were hard and cold under the brims of their riot helmets.

The guys downstairs had been grunts. These were the elites, ready and willing to kill me.

There was no way to pass them on the stairs without catching enough lead to sink a ship, even with my enhanced speed. Instead, I leaped into the open space at the heart of the stairwell. Guns roared behind me, sending a storm of bullets after me.

My jinsei-enhanced leap carried me to the next landing, and I kicked off the railing there to propel myself up and onto the floor above.

Bullets slammed into the concrete steps instead of me. The guards shouted in surprise and alarm when they realized I'd escaped without so much as a scrape.

I didn't stop to gloat. These guys were pros, and I doubted my trick would work a second time. If I wanted to live, I needed to stay ahead of them.

I made it to the tenth floor without another attack, the guards chasing after me. They might close the gap by the time I reached my target, but by then they'd have other things to worry about.

The droning had become an endless groan that raked icy fingers across my nerves. There was something terribly wrong about that sound. Madness echoed in its eerie harmonies. Death lurked in the melodies that wound higher and higher.

My stomach churned as the noise built. More frighteningly, my Eclipse nature seemed to like the cacophony.

I wondered if that meant the Lost were close.

I crashed through a door and burst onto the eleventh floor. The power was there, nearby. It pulled at my core like a lodestone to iron filings. I followed it, activating the Borrowed Core technique as I ran. I lashed connections to any living creature I could find. Rats, cockroaches, tiny snakes coiled around warm pipes.

Other cores flickered at the edges of my awareness, and my Borrowed Core flinched away from them before they could make a connection. I recognized those hideous targets and my mouth went dry.

The Locust Court was here.

The Lost hadn't just attacked the leaders of Empyreal society. They'd betrayed them in the most devastating way possible. They'd allied themselves with humanity's deadliest enemies and unleashed the hungry spirits on the world.

I crashed through a pair of double doors and into the courtroom where Bishop was on trial. The chamber was in utter disarray. Hot, red blood stained the walls in streaks that glistened in the reflected light from burning orange circles in the ceiling. Darkness oozed through those portals and filled the room with shadows that made it difficult to understand what was happening.

The dead, dying, and wounded were scattered around the courtroom like broken dolls. Most of those who'd come as officials or witnesses to the trial were down and motionless. I spotted guard uniforms among the fallen and caught a glimpse of Grayson Bishop's ashen face in the witness stand. He was slumped in a chair behind a wooden rail, and I couldn't tell if he was alive or dead. Elder Hirani was on the floor a few feet in front of where Grayson sat, her hair splayed out around her head, a puddle of blood oozing from a wound in her belly. Her core still glowed, though her eyes were closed and the jinsei channels in her body were nearly empty.

The chairs in the jury box were filled with broken bodies that my mind refused to catalog. The audience seating was even worse. The majority of the portals had opened above that section of the courtroom, and those sitting there had been caught completely unaware. Their bodies had been torn to shreds, the pieces tossed around like hurricane debris.

The only survivors had gathered in the courtroom's far corner, to the right of the wide, empty judges' bench. Tycho Reyes and the three sacred sages still on their feet had triggered defensive techniques to shelter themselves and a handful of other Empyreals who'd managed to survive the first wave of madness. Sanrin was with them, slumped in the corner, eyes fluttering as he tried to hang onto consciousness. A ragged gash across his face and a puncture wound on the left side of his chest leaked far too much blood. He wouldn't last long.

A swarm of Locust Court spirits surrounded the survivors and hammered at their defenses with glowing fists of pure jinsei. Already, the shields raised by the sages were flickering. It wouldn't be long before they collapsed and the spirits had their way with the Empyrean Flame's most powerful servants.

I despised Tycho for the way he'd used me, but I wouldn't let anyone, not even him, die by the Locusts.

My Eclipse nature surged within me, and I embraced it. These were the enemies I'd been born to fight.

And I would destroy them.

# THE ASSAULT

'D EXPECTED MY ECLIPSE NATURE TO RAGE AT the sight of dozens of Locust Court spirits. Instead, it became a still, icy presence that surrounded my core like a protective mother bear sheltering a cub. It was strangely comforting in the way it numbed me to the horrors and let me focus on the killing that needed to be done.

The hungry spirits were too intent on reaching the prey right under their noses to notice my arrival. Their single-minded lust to devour the living gave me a few moments to assess the situation and prepare myself for battle, and I took advantage of every second.

I threw bonds from the Borrowed Core technique far and wide, harnessing the courthouse's many unseen inhabitants. We cycled our breaths together, filling my core with jinsei and my aura with aspects.

I summoned my fusion blade, called forth my serpents, and let out a long, slow breath.

It was time.

I crammed jinsei into my channels and hurled myself at the back of the Locust Court horde. My weapon rose and fell in brutal butchery. Its blade carved through screaming spirits, ripping their corrupted jinsei bodies to shreds and casting them aside in swathes of gore. My serpents speared the creatures' cores with deadly accuracy and drained their jinsei in one greedy gulp after another.

For the first time since that fateful day in Singapore, I unleashed my Eclipse nature. My foes were not humans. They weren't even beasts. They were evil incarnate, hungry spirits who plotted and schemed beyond the Far Horizon, their leaders bent on devouring all of humanity to fuel their wanton lust for conquest.

I was an Eclipse Warrior, and these fearsome beasts would know fear this day.

My onslaught annihilated a dozen of the Locust Court before they recognized they were under attack. The creatures withered and burst apart in blooms of gray threads as I drained their jinsei. Without sacred energy, the spirits were truly nothing.

"Mr. Warin." Tycho called out to me in a surprisingly calm voice. "How good of you to join us. I hope you brought more reinforcements."

"No such luck," I shouted over the yowling of the furious spirits, slicing a cluster of them into jinsei-spurting chunks with my fusion blade. My serpents speared another pair who'd charged from my side and drained them away into gray threads. "I'm all you're getting."

"That's a pity." Despite his calm demeanor, Tycho's face bore signs of stress. Deep shadows under his eyes showed the strain of this encounter clearly. As strong as the sages were, the surprise attack by the Court had pushed them to their limits. "We tried to summon aid when the assault began, but our attackers were clever enough to block any communications in or out of the area. We will have to make the best of it."

The powerful Empyreals redoubled their efforts and pushed the shield they'd raised back onto their attackers. The defensive technique's surface flared with sparks of jinsei that lashed out to gouge chunks of crystallized jinsei from the creatures' twisted forms. The stink of ozone flooded the courtroom, and the foul creatures shrieked and recoiled from their prey.

Trapped between my wailing fusion blade and the aggressive defense mounted by the sages, the monsters split into two groups. The smaller part of the horde kept up the pressure on Tycho's team. The others fanned out around me, searching for a blind spot. Those behind me darted in to swipe at my back with claws and stingers, then fell back out of sword's reach when I spun to face them. It was a classic wolf pack attack that would wear me down if I didn't end this fight in a big hurry.

Pure offense had worked while I had the element of surprise and the spirits had their attention split. Now that most of them had focused on me, I switched to a defensive stance and activated the Thief's Shield technique. That irritated my Eclipse nature, which wanted me to keep slashing and draining my enemies to feed it, and I struggled to control its dark urge. The Shield would still steal aspects and jinsei from anything that touched me, though much slower than I could manage with my serpents, and it would weaken their attacks against me. That was my best chance of survival, and I took it.

Minutes passed in a delicate dance that required me to constantly adjust my stance and position in the circle of spirits. I hardened my aura with aspects I stole from the creatures and relied on the Thief's Shield to ward off the worst of the attacks my enemies launched from my blind side. That tactic allowed me to push my attack against the spirits, killing several of them and weakening their circle. It also cost me a dozen minor injuries to my back and legs.

In the midst of the battle, something grazed my core. It was a gentle touch, gone almost before I registered it. My brow furrowed at the distraction. I didn't have time to worry about something so minor when I was surrounded by hungry spirits.

The spirits became cannier as the fight wore on. They faded away from my assaults and surged in to claw and bite in concentrated attacks that penetrated the Thief's Shield. The painful injuries they inflicted slowed my reactions and forced me to spend precious jinsei to stop the bleeding and restore my flagging strength. A trio of the foul creatures slammed into my left leg, howling with glee when their concerted effort staggered me.

"You need to fight," I shouted to Tycho. That last attack had nearly brought me to my knees. "I can't kill them all on my own!"

"We're trying," the sage called back. "We were ambushed, and they drained the jinsei from several of us. The hungry spirits are consuming the sacred energy from the area faster than we can cycle it into our cores."

Oh. That sucked.

I hadn't noticed the drain because I'd stolen power back from the Locust Court killers through my serpents and with my Thief's Shield. While the monsters' attacks had physically weakened me, they'd bolstered my stores of aspects and jinsei.

I'd have to carry the weight of the fight.

That called for a new strategy. The Thief's Shield was a powerful defense that stole from the spirits when they attacked. The sacred energy and aspects I gained from it let me fill my jinsei channels to harden my body against damage and accelerate my reflexes, and the aspects further reinforced my aura to strengthen the technique. Unfortunately, my enemies had figured out they could overwhelm the Shield with brute force.

I changed tactics, dropping back into a defensive posture, my fusion blade held before me. A series of wide sweeps cleared a gap in the circle of spirits, and I darted through it to put my back against a wall. My new position traded mobility for a narrower battle front. The spirits had to come at me head-on, now, and that meant they'd have to get past my weapon to do any damage.

The Locust Court proved too smart to fall for that. They pulled back into a cordon of teeth and claws, then raised their heads and howled a repetitive series of alien syllables. The sound tore at my ears and nerves, and even my Eclipse nature recoiled at the horrifying cry.

At first, I thought it was some sort of assault. Then the orange borders around the portal grew brighter and widened.

They weren't attacking. They'd called for reinforcements.

Locust Court monsters poured through the portals into the courtroom. Their chitinous forms crashed into dead bodies and splintered furniture in a cacophonous hailstorm. They howled eagerly, ready to rip and rend.

"Jace," Tycho called, his voice weak and ragged, barely audible over the battle cries of our enemies, "there are too many. They're draining our jinsei faster than we can replenish it. Get out of here."

"Too late," I shouted back.

The wall of spirits around me had doubled, then tripled in strength. There was nowhere for me to run even if I wanted to. This was my last stand.

Last stand…

I remembered one of the stories I'd read about the Utter War. How a single Eclipse Warrior had held off unit after unit of Locust Court killers to save a retreating force of Resplendent Sun shock troopers. How had they done it?

A spirit leaped at my head, jaws wide and claws stretched out to flay my skull open, and I slashed its head off its shoulders. A cloud of jinsei blinded me for a moment, and two more of the creatures took advantage, rushing my flanks. The one on my right screamed when I cut its arm off, and it staggered away with sacred energy spurting from the wound. The one on my left, though, got past my blade and punched through the Thief's Shield to open a shallow gash across my ribs.

The pain drove me back to the wall behind me, my hand clutched over the injury. It burned like fire. My Eclipse nature urged me to tear and shred. Nothing would have made me happier, but all I could think of was healing the pain with a flow of jinsei through my channels.

The spirits smelled weakness and moved in. Their mere presence drained the jinsei from the air and pulled threads of it loose from my core. There were too many. I needed more sacred energy to fight them. I activated my Borrowed Core technique to connect to more creatures, and a cascade of thoughts clicked into place.

That technique bound itself to cores, not creatures.

If I wasn't careful, I could drain the cores I connected to.

I understood how that Eclipse Warrior had held off the Locust Court.

The technique didn't want to do what I needed, and it took me precious seconds to force it to make the first connection.

The monsters had evolved to become the most efficient and ruthless devourers of jinsei in the many worlds. Their cores were perfect at taking jinsei into themselves, wasting not a drop of the precious energy.

They had no defense as a thread of sacred energy from my core slid into the closest Locust Court spirit. The Borrowed Core connection snapped into place.

The spirit was mine.

The monsters screeched when my sacred energy touched them, furious at the unaccustomed violation. Ten of the creatures were mine, then twenty, thirty. My breath became a whirling blur of power through our united cores. Jinsei filled me to bursting, and aspects of hunger and horror clotted in my aura. And when I thought I'd reached my limit, my advanced adept core proved me wrong.

I bound forty, then fifty of the spirits to my core.

Every breath I took drained more of my foes. The first batch vanished in puffs of gray dust, and I lashed fifty more to my technique. My core swelled and stretched to accommodate the sacred energy I'd stolen.

The spirits panicked and howled for more of their brothers and sisters to come aid them. There was no answer.

Realizing what they faced, the monsters screamed and scrambled away from me. I consumed more and more of them, until my aura couldn't hold any more aspects, and the power I stole leaked away and evaporated into nothingness. My Eclipse nature gloated over the destruction, encouraging me to kill more, to take them all. For once, I didn't fight it.

The sages let their barrier fall and greedily cycled the jinsei that had returned to the room as I mopped up the battle's remnants. The weight of the powerful Empyreals' attention crashed against my aura, then slipped away like a wave pounding against a beach. Their curiosity slowly turned to fear and confusion, and I wondered if any of them really understood what, exactly, I was.

And what they'd do about it once they did.

The last of the spirits screeched and came apart. I'd done it. I'd destroyed the spirits and saved the survivors of the initial assault.

The dark urge I'd unleashed, though, was still inside me. It wanted more. The death and hunger aspects and jinsei I'd stolen didn't satisfy it. Those had only whetted its appetite. It needed to consume the bubbling vibrancy of life.

This was what the Empyreals feared. A hunger that couldn't be stopped. A threat that made the Locust Court look like nothing more than a passing annoyance. The dark urge told me I could kill everyone in the room. I could devour the elders and the sages. All I had to do was let it go. It would do the rest.

"Mr. Warin," Tycho said, his voice tinged with the faintest threads of concern, "thank you for what you did here. Are you quite all right?"

My teeth ached with the need to bite and tear. The Empyreals before me would fill me with power. Maybe enough to advance my core to the disciple level. Or further. It would be so easy...

"No," I whispered. "That isn't happening."

It took a monumental effort of will to shut down the feral greed for life that flowed from the dark urge in a heady stream. I clenched my fists, gritted my teeth, and begged the Empyrean Flame for the self-control to beat this thing inside me. Finally, I trusted myself to speak.

"I'm fine," I said. "I just need a few minutes."

I turned away from the sages, my eyes locked on the far wall of the courtroom. The patterns of blood there seemed to shift and writhe, though I knew that was impossible. It was just my supernatural senses showing me the churning currents of jinsei that teemed within the red splatters. They were merely echoes of life, the remnants of the people they'd spilled from.

Emergency personnel and guards burst into the courtroom behind me. They went to work with quiet efficiency, searching the fallen to separate those who could be helped from those who were far beyond the reach of technological or mystical medicine. Guards shouted over the clatter of their beeping and flashing equipment, and the confusing flood of Japanese made it hard for me to concentrate on keeping my Eclipse nature at bay.

"Leave him be. He saved us," Tycho said, and then let fly a string of syllables in a language the guards could understand. For once, I was grateful to have him speak for me.

Despite the tragedy that had occurred, a sense of relief flooded the room. There'd been an attack, but now it was over. The bad guys had been driven back, and the good guys could start putting the pieces of their worlds back together. It wouldn't be easy, and the survivors would remember what had happened here for a very long time. For the moment, though, we were safe.

So why couldn't I relax?

I pushed back against my Eclipse nature. Its hungry demands had distracted me from the real danger.

The droning hum I'd heard during my mad rush to the courtroom hadn't stopped.

It was growing stronger.

"Do you hear that?" I asked no one in particular.

I turned to face the disaster. Emergency medical technicians and jinsei artists loaded the fallen onto gurneys or into body bags. The courthouse guards stood around, looking ineffectual now that there was no immediate danger to deal with.

"Hear what?" Tycho asked from his position near the witness stand. It looked like Grayson wasn't dead, which was a relief. I wanted to see him punished for what he'd done.

"That humming noise," I said, distracted by the sensation of someone peering at my core. It was a soft touch, but annoying. "You can't hear it?"

"No," Tycho said warily.

Orange light poured into the courtroom accompanied by an earsplitting shriek. A blast of freezing wind poured over my back and whipped my hair around my head. My Eclipse nature howled, a joyous sound of recognition.

Oh, no.

Something heavy whipped past me and smashed into the wood next to me. Splinters of wood flew in every direction, and I threw an arm up to protect my eyes from the shrapnel.

"You fool," a voice snarled behind me. "How could you betray us?"

The room erupted in confusion. The civilians screamed in panic and horror. The sages shouted to one another in a cacophony of languages I didn't understand. I wasn't sure if they'd gathered their strength enough after the spirit ambush to be of any use against this new threat.

How could we have been so stupid?

# THE LOST

MY SERPENTS BURST FROM MY CORE TO DEFLECT an attack my Eclipse nature detected, and I spun to face my attacker, fusion blade still in my hand.

He was tall and thin, completely naked save for wisps of sacred energy that encircled his body in hazy clouds. His eyes were the same black voids as mine. Like the woman who'd killed the Death Weaver and Henry in my cottage, he was completely bald, and his white scalp gleamed in the orange light from the portal he'd opened in the courtroom. The air cracked and hissed around him as he pulled streams of jinsei into his aura.

"I didn't betray you," I said. "But I can't let you destroy those who did."

"Let me?" The man laughed, a sound as sharp and jagged as breaking glass. "We've planned this since before the Empyreals turned on us. You can no more stop what is coming than you could halt a tidal wave approaching a distant shore."

Even if he was right, that didn't mean I wouldn't try.

My aura was still filled with the aspects I'd stolen from the Locust Court. I fed them into my serpents, amplifying them again and again as I surged across the courtroom. I leaped into the air, clearing the fallen seats, and raised my long-hilted blade above my head to split my foe in half. The jinsei I'd shoved into my channels moved me faster than humanly possible. The world blurred around me as I sped toward my target like a bladed missile.

The Lost slipped out of my path with surprising ease, and his aura flared out toward me as I landed next to him.

My Eclipse core yowled and drove jinsei into my legs. Its raw survival instinct sent me hurtling away from the aura before it could drain me dry. The dark urge made it clear that any contact with the Lost's aura would leave me an empty husk. As powerful as I was, this man was far stronger.

The Lost hadn't expected me to evade his aura, and his moment of surprise gave me time to act. I thrust my blade toward his exposed left side, burning more of my jinsei to speed and strengthen my attack. The weapon's tip tore through my enemy's alabaster skin, revealing a strip of striated muscle that glistened like wet ivory.

My foe spun away from the attack at a blinding speed. An arc of straw-colored blood hung in the air behind him for a moment like a string of gemstones from a broken necklace. He lashed out with one hand and caught my blade before I could recoil. A wave of cold rushed up the blade toward me. The Lost smiled a shark's grin. The instant that cold touched my flesh, I was a dead man. He'd devour my core. He was sure he'd won.

And, if I'd been anyone else, he would have.

I banished the blade, and my enemy's technique snapped closed around nothing.

The Lost staggered back, stunned by his failed technique.

"The final assault is coming even now." He stepped to one side, and we circled one another warily. "You showed us the way. Your light is what guided us through the darkness. Don't stand in our way now. Accept what you are. Stand beside us, and rule over these lesser creatures."

He swept a hand toward the sages, who had gathered in a defensive ring around Grayson Bishop. The ex-headmaster was conscious, though he looked too weak to do anything but watch in horror as the scene unfolded before him. The other sages weren't handling this much better. They hadn't even raised a defense, and their cores flickered within them like dying embers.

The Lost was ripping jinsei out of everything and everyone nearby, except for me. The civilians had collapsed to their knees, their eyes fluttering as they struggled to escape from his dread grasp.

If I didn't do something soon, they'd all die.

"You know this isn't right," I said and summoned my blade once more. The hunger and terror aspects I'd stolen from the Locust Court clung to its surface in a mottled black pattern that writhed like drops of ink on a turbulent stream. "What they did to you was wrong. But destroying everything that you once defended won't fix that. It will only make us all vulnerable to the next attack."

"Attack of what?" the Lost asked with a smile. "The Locust Court is no threat to those like us, Jace. Do you think the hungry spirits would have served as our vanguard if we were still enemies?"

Images danced unbidden in my thoughts. I didn't know where they came from, but I knew they were true.

Pale men and women wandering through a night-black wilderness, hungry and empty, desperate, willing to do anything to survive.

The Lost had struck a deal with the Locust Court. In return for safety in the worlds beyond the Far Horizon, the exiled Eclipse Warriors would show humanity's ancient enemies how to find us again.

When I'd become an Eclipse Warrior, it had been a flare in the darkness. They'd followed the light back to Earth.

"No," I said. "They'll betray you. They'll turn on all of us."

"We've already been betrayed once," my opponent said. "We were more careful this time. We've made arrangements that ensure we will not suffer the same fate again. The Court will serve us here, and we will aid them in their battles beyond the Far Horizon. Time has grown short, Jace. You must choose. Join your people, now, or die in this futile attempt to save a world that has been doomed for longer than any of us have been alive."

I hung my head. It all seemed so pointless. I'd struggled and stolen and fought and suffered to finally be accepted into Empyreal society. And now that I finally had what I wanted, it was all going to be washed away.

Unless I joined the Lost.

Or beat them.

I whipped my arm forward, burning the last of my jinsei for one last attack. My fusion blade screeched through the air as it traveled toward the Eclipse Warrior. The black patterns on its surface blazed with an unnatural light, and the sharpened blade gleamed like a flash of sunlight in the desert.

The Lost was too slow to avoid this attack. The perfectly thrown weapon was on a direct course with his throat. It would punch through his neck and shatter his spine at the base of his skull. The pale fighter would die, and we could close the portal he'd opened. Whatever horrors were coming, I'd work with the sages to stop them.

I'd won.

Again.

Something brushed my core, twice, in quick succession. It distracted me enough that I missed what happened next.

There was a blur of motion and a metallic clang reverberated through the courtroom. My fusion blade vibrated where it had impaled itself in the wall, deflected by the Eclipse Warrior's lightning-fast parry.

"I am sorry, Jace." He looked at the wound my blade had opened in his arm as if surprised he felt anything at all. "If you had accepted your role, this would not have to happen."

The Lost glided toward me. His hand descended, pointed fingers glowing like white stars of annihilation headed straight for my heart. The man's dark eyes were narrowed, and I sensed an abiding sorrow deep within him.

He didn't want to kill me.

But his nature wouldn't allow anything, anyone, to stand in his way.

A sound like a ripping sheet of paper roared through the air between us. The Lost's arm plunged into nothingness, just before his fingers would've pierced my heart. His momentum carried him forward, and half his body vanished into the narrow portal that had opened between us. He glared at me from above its edge and tried to recoil his arm.

The gateway snapped shut with an electric hiss.

The Lost screamed and fell away from me. His right arm and half his chest were gone, the flesh scooped away to reveal the gleaming white loops and whorls of his innards. The man sagged to his knees, blood spurting from open arteries and drooling from dissected veins.

Abi, Clem, Eric, and Rachel stared at me through a portal just beyond where my foe had fallen. The hole in space showed me the pilot's station Abi was supposed to be guarding. He carefully lifted his hands away from the control panel, then rushed through the portal with the rest of my friends right behind him.

"I'm really glad that worked," Abi said, his eyes wide with shock.

"You shouldn't be here," I said. "None of you should be."

"You're welcome," Eric said. "Next time we'll wait for the bad guy to kill you before we take him out."

"Are you okay?" Clem and Rachel asked at the same time.

"I will be." I was angry at my friends for putting their lives in danger, but I was grateful for what they'd done. As soon as I finished this, I'd figure out some way to show them that.

But, first, I had to deal with the Lost.

I summoned my fusion blade again.

"Why?" he gasped through the blood that bubbled from his lips. "You were meant for so much more. You could have led the next generation, Jace. Why would you throw all that away?"

"You can't fix anything by burning it to the ground," I said with a shake of my head. "I couldn't step aside and let that happen."

"Killing me hasn't stopped anything," the Lost gasped. Pale, almost colorless, blood oozed from his terrible wound. "The hungry spirit horde is coming. It will pour across this world in a flood of death. If we are not here to control it, there won't be anything left when the waters recede."

"I'll stop it." My blade plunged through the center of the man's forehead.

Satisfied he was dead, I put my foot on his chest and pushed his body off my weapon.

The Eclipse Warrior collapsed to the floor, his mutilated body curling into itself.

I turned my back on my fallen enemy and strode toward the portal he'd created. Blackness boiled beyond its orange ring, the dark cold of the Far Horizon just inches away.

This is where I should've had something heroic to say. Some last words to bolster my friends' spirits and let everyone know I'd be back right after I saved the day.

But there weren't any words, and no guarantee any of us would ever see each other again. I had to stop the Locust Court, but I didn't know how. Stepping into the Far Horizon might very well be a hopeless battle.

But it was my battle.

I'd summoned the Lost back to Earth. This was my mess to clean up.

I rolled my neck on my shoulders, and it crackled like a string of firecrackers. Then I hefted my blade and followed in the footsteps of mankind's greatest creation and most horrible enemy.

# THE HOST

THE FAR HORIZON WAS A BUFFER BETWEEN EARTH and everything else that was out there in the universe. Some said it was created by the Empyrean Flame by burning away the worlds that ventured too close to its territory. Others believed the dead space around Earth was proof that humans were the only non-spirit culture in all the universe. I didn't know who was right, and it didn't matter at the moment. The dead black plane of glossy stone and gray ash was just another obstacle in my way.

"What can we do?" Clem asked from the other side of the portal, her voice frantic. "I won't leave you alone."

I took in as much of the scene as I could stand. Hundreds, maybe thousands, of portals hung in the darkness, their orange frames lit by the cityscapes within. I recognized Dallas, Paris, and Rio de Janeiro, and I glimpsed what might have been New York. Every one of those portals was an attack point for the Locust Court. If I didn't stop the attack, the hungry spirits would pour across the Far Horizon and strip those cities to their metal bones by morning.

Far across the black emptiness, an arch of violet fire faced the smaller portals. I saw a strange and twisting landscape on its far side, a place of chaos and constant change. Hills crumbled into valleys and were washed away by turbulent rivers of lava, which spread into wide, deep lakes before vanishing into whirlpools rimed with frost.

In the distance, an army of crystalline figures swarmed through the nightmare landscape. They glittered like sharpened blades under a shifting sun, drawing closer to the portal every moment.

Closer, but they hadn't arrived.

There was still a chance to stop them.

"Abi, you have to to tell your commander we need to close a portal," I called back to my friends. "A big one. I'll try to hold them off, but I don't know how long I can last."

"I'll tell them," he said, his eyes searching my face. "How will we find it?"

"How did you know where to open the portal that cut the Lost in half?" I asked.

"Rachel and Clem," he admitted. "They thought of you, and we used that as an anchor to find you. Once we'd opened the portal to your location, I opened a second portal to deal with the Lost. The offset was tricky, and I wasn't sure it would work. Thank the Flame that it did."

"Thank you for taking the chance. I don't think I'd be here if you hadn't. If Rachel and Clem can find me, they can find the gate," I said. "Because I'll be standing in it."

"We can't close it with you inside," he said. "It will kill you."

"Just do it," I said. "It's the only way. There's an army of hungry spirits from the Locust Court headed this way. If they get through that portal, they'll kill us all, anyway."

"We can close this portal," he protested. "That will keep them on the other side of the Far Horizon."

"No," I said. "There are hundreds of portals already opened. Trust me, Abi. This is the only way. Get your people and seal the gate as fast as you can. You have to do this."

My friend's eyes were wet with unshed tears. He reached out, one hand coming through the portal. I clasped it in mine, and he pulled me close to throw an arm around my shoulders.

"I do not want things to end like this," he whispered. "But I will tell you, Jace, that I finally sense the peace within your grasp. Whatever tormented you before, today is the day you can reconcile with it."

"We'll see," I said.

I wasn't sure Abi was right. I certainly didn't feel at peace with the monster still raging in my head and a terrible hunger squeezing my stomach in a black fist. Even if I pulled this off, I was a monster. The sages had seen that, and they would make me pay. Dying a hero seemed far preferable to facing that punishment and disgrace again.

I left my friends behind and sped across the Far Horizon at the speed of thought. Distance there was an illusion, a conceptual space that I found I could discard. One moment I was far from the enemy gate. The next I stood before it.

The world of the hungry spirits was a horrifying place. It broke itself down and built itself up following rules I didn't understand. How the spirits could survive there was a mystery to me. I wasn't sure I could do the same.

*Let's find out*, I thought. Other Eclipse Warriors had done it.

My fusion blade hummed in my hand, a comforting presence, and my aura throbbed with power. My Eclipse nature was ready to devour everything in sight.

It was time to give it that chance.

I took a deep breath, cycled the strange alien air of the Far Horizon through my core, and stepped through the gate into the world of the Locust Court.

The shift was disorienting and yanked my stomach up into my throat. There was solid ground beneath my feet, but everything else changed faster than I could comprehend. Forests bloomed and then collapsed into ash. Thickets of blackberries burst from the ground in coiled, thorny brambles, only to fade away when I got close to them.

There was something familiar about this place. Not the chaos or instability, but the way it seemed to respect the edges of my presence.

"It's like the School," I muttered.

I concentrated on the horde and willed the shifting terrain to take me to them. It wasn't easy, but the place slowly, painfully, bent to my will. The ground remained solid beneath my soles, and a stretch of ground ten feet ahead of me remained stable and clear of obstructions. That was the most I could do. If my core had still been at the initiate level, I likely wouldn't have been able to even manage that.

I pushed ahead on a collision course with the invading army. The path ahead of me was straight and true, but what burst from the ground on either side and behind me was another matter entirely. Ravens the size of grown men erupted from patches of moldy ground.

Droplets of rain fell from a black sky and cried like children when they splashed into the dirt.

"No," I said. "None of this is real."

I was an Eclipse Warrior. I'd been built to defeat this madness, and that is what I was going to do. There was nothing to be gained by chasing after the invaders, when I could make them come to me.

I stopped moving and sculpted my surroundings into a steep-walled ravine that funneled from its wide mouth to a narrow exit behind me. I stood in that gap, blade ready, determined to stop the horde from passing through to reach the portal. It took me what seemed like an hour to complete the task, and I finished not a moment too soon.

The Locust Court poured into the ravine's mouth in a boiling tide. Unlike the animalistic creatures I'd battled in the courtroom, these seemed more advanced. They wore crystalline armor covered in hooked spines and wielded jagged weapons that danced with sparks of jinsei. Aspects of violence and destruction, chaos and death, churned in the spirits' auras as they bore down on me in a crazed flood.

This was it.

My last stand.

My mind hung in a cold, dark space far removed from the fear that coursed through my veins or the hunger that poured from my Eclipse nature in an endless torrent. The grim calculus was obvious. There were too many enemies coming for me, and eventually they would wear me down and rip me limb from limb.

If I couldn't win, then I'd make the monsters pay for killing me. I'd hold them until Abi and the Portal Defense Force could seal the gate between worlds.

I could do that.

That was enough.

I sank into my Eclipse Warrior nature. I felt the hunger bubble up within me like poison gas. I didn't fight it or try to control it. This was what I was meant to do. It was the reason I'd been born, and I finally understood that. My core, aura, and blade were all in perfect unison. I was as ready as I'd ever be.

The first wave of hungry spirits slammed into me, and the Thief's Shield technique devoured them. The shattered armor tumbled away from the wisps of their bodies and crashed into their allies. The next rank stepped up and I sheared through their chitinous blades with my fusion blade.

My Eclipse nature transformed me into a tornado of destruction. My weapon carved through spirit bodies, while my Shield technique consumed their sacred energy and twisted their aspects to harden my aura. In this strange and alien world, I'd become more than I'd ever thought possible.

It was a terrible thing to behold.

My blade killed spirits on contact. It devoured their jinsei and stole their aspects. No sooner did an enemy come near me than it was consumed and its remains cast aside.

I was an untouchable god of death.

That power, though, had a price. The unrestrained dark urge consumed any spirit who touched my aura or was touched by my blade. It fed a constant stream of jinsei into my core, pushing it to its limits. The pain from an overfull core threatened to overwhelm me, and I pushed as much of it as I could into my body's channels. I became stronger and faster than ever before.

Much stronger and faster than my body could stand. My channels were overloading, and the jinsei they couldn't contain burned through my flesh like acid. That damage couldn't be healed by jinsei, and as the battle wore on, it would only become more serious.

But I couldn't stop. While I was up and fighting, the spirits wouldn't get past me. They couldn't reach Earth.

That was all that mattered.

I felt a gentle touch across the throbbing ache of my core and recognized the tingling sensation from the moments before Abi and the others had arrived. It must have been Clem and Rachel helping anchor the portal to my core. That meant Abi had gotten through to his people. They knew where I was. They'd find the gate. If I kept fighting and held the gap for just a bit longer, they could close the gateway forever.

Then, I wouldn't have to fight anymore.

The fight melted into a timeless slough of burst bodies and jinsei. Time had no meaning in the heart of darkness, and survival was the only thing that mattered. My channels burned, so overloaded with sacred energy they glowed through my skin.

And, then, the spirits retreated. They pulled back from the fray and set up a perimeter around me.

I had no idea what they were up to, but I knew it wouldn't be good.

# THE TRUTH

THE LOCUST COURT HAD GIVEN UP ON GETTING past my choke point and had called in the big guns.

The army of spirits split down the middle to reveal a group of the Lost. The pale figures advanced toward me with determined strides, their black eyes fixed on mine with a hypnotic intensity. Their hands were wreathed in black fire and the ground smoked where their feet touched it.

"You cannot stop this," their leader said. She was more muscular and taller than the rest, her physical presence the most imposing of all the Lost I'd seen so far. "We are the inevitable price of betrayal, and the Empyreals must pay what is owed."

I wasn't in the mood to start this song and dance again. In the next few minutes, the portal between this world and the Far Horizon would close forever. Spending eternity debating what I could or could not do wasn't my idea of fun.

"I've already been over this," I shot back. "Whatever you're selling, I'm not buying."

"I can take you to your mother," the tall woman said. "Right now. You can make sure she's safe while we deal with the betrayers."

The offer hit me like a bucket of ice water.

"You don't know where she is." It was a trick. There was no way it could be true. The Lost hadn't even been on Earth before I was born. They'd been here, trapped on the wrong side of the Far Horizon.

"We do," she said. "Eve and I were friends, Jace. Long before you were born. I was called Larissa then. Now I am simply First among the Lost. Come with me, and your mother will be happy to tell you the truth."

It couldn't be true.

Niddhogg had told me the Utter War had ended a hundred years ago. That would make my mother much, much older than she looked. I couldn't see how that was even possible. Only the most advanced practitioners could slow their aging and extend their lives for centuries.

Memories of my mother's strength flashed through my thoughts like blasts of lightning. She'd taught me to fight despite my broken core. She'd healed my shattered hand at the tournament. She'd somehow designed the Machina…

The truth crashed through my thoughts like a wrecking ball. The pieces of the jigsaw puzzle that was my life clicked together to form a picture that made me want to run screaming into the darkness.

"No." The tip of my fusion blade drooped to the ground. The more I understood about the world, the more I hated it.

"You see it now," the woman said, her voice low and calm.

The Lost in my cottage had insisted I'd guided them back when I'd healed my core and become the first of a new generation of Eclipse Warriors. If that was true, then they'd planned for that to happen.

Somehow, the Lost had crippled me before I was born. They'd forced me into the misery I'd suffered. That's why my core was veiled. They didn't want anyone to know what I was.

"Tycho did this," I snarled. He was the veil's creator. Zephyr had told me as much.

"He helped, but he was not the architect of this plan," First said dismissively. "His veil hid you, and the others, from discovery. And, of course, he pushed you harder than the rest. Perhaps that is why you were the first to manifest."

The first...

There were other people out there, kids like me with broken cores and ruined lives. And none of them had gotten as far as me. Their lives must be horror shows.

"The Empyreals killed your people," I said. "But what you did to me was worse. You stole my life and gave me pain. You turned me into a slave before I was even born."

"Pain is the crucible of greatness," First said with a dismissive wave of her hand. "You are better for what you have experienced. And, now, you will be a king. A truly perfect fighter with the power of an Eclipse Warrior and the soul of a pure Empyreal. We will, of course, have to cull the others, but that is a detail you will not have to concern yourself with."

"You're lying," I shouted at her. My mother would never have agreed to this insanity. She wouldn't have let her own child be turned into a monster. She was kind and good. She'd sheltered me through my life, she'd taught me how to fight. "I'm not like you."

"I know what you are," First insisted. "When your mother's husband told us of our betrayal, I knew what had to be done."

The spirits started restlessly behind the warriors, and the woman's companions watched her with nervous eyes. It was clear they didn't want her to tell me this part of the story, and even clearer that she didn't care. She wanted me to join her, and this was her chance to convince me that I should.

"There was no way to save all of our people," First continued. "They'd already rounded up most of us. The only ones who survived the first wave were stationed beyond the Far Horizon. The Lost."

A trace of sorrow flickered across the woman's face.

"The Lost knew we wouldn't be safe on Earth," she said. "We fled deeper into the world of the Locust Court. We learned how to survive here, how to control our environment well enough to avoid our enemies. It was a terrible life."

"Then why did you keep fighting?" I asked.

"Because someone had to keep the foolish Empyreals safe, Jace. We had to hold back the darkness."

"But you've brought that darkness back," I shouted. "You went to all this trouble, only to destroy what you swore to save."

I had to keep her talking. Soon, the Portal Defense Force would close this gate, and then none of this would matter. We'd be sealed up on this side of the portal, and Earth would be safe.

Unless someone else manifested.

My thoughts raced. I had to get word back to the others that Tycho had to be questioned. He could have a list of the other children with hollow cores. They had to be found, rounded up before they could manifest, because…

313

That was the kind of thinking that had started all this. I shuddered and hung my head. I didn't know how I'd gotten here or what I was supposed to do next. If the Empyrean Flame had put me on the board to do something, it should have told me what that something was.

"I never wanted any of this," I said. "I didn't want to be an Eclipse Warrior. I just wanted to be normal."

"Oh, Jace," she said. "You were never meant to be normal. Your mother will be so proud when she sees what she and I created."

"You're lying," I spat. "My mother didn't make me like this."

"This is precisely what your mother wanted," the woman said. "She's the one who reverse engineered the Eclipse Theory, Jace. Her husband sacrificed his core so her child could be made."

Memories from the *Manual* flooded my thoughts. The New Moon clan, the first Eclipse Warriors, were created through a mystical union of a Resplendent Sun and a Thunder's Children. Two cores made into one.

"He went through the gate alone," I said. "That's what was wrong with me. I only had half of his core."

"Yes," First agreed. "Now you see. He hated the Empyreals for what they'd done, Jace. He sacrificed himself so you could be made. He gave up his life in service to our vengeance. It took so very long for our plan to come to fruition. Your mother spent so many years hiding to conceal her agelessness while she searched for the answer to save us and a suitable host to bring you into being. You have no idea how hard she fought for all of this. For you."

My mind ached, and my heart shattered. All the pain, all the suffering I'd gone through, just to bring these monsters back to destroy the world? I couldn't accept that.

"That isn't what I am," I roared. "I'm more than a tool."

"Of course you are," First said, her voice soft and strangely comforting. "You are our champion, the first of your kind. You are more powerful than you know. You have only to believe in your true self."

Zephyr's words came back to me.

Be true to yourself.

Rachel had asked me which Jace was the real one.

I understood what I had to do.

Since I'd healed my core, I'd thought of the dark urge, my Eclipse nature, as something outside of me. It had been a force that pushed me to do things I hated. It wanted me to become a monster.

I'd fought it every step of the way. That had been my mistake.

"I'm sorry," I said, honestly. "I wish this could've ended a different way."

My core ached from the abuse I'd heaped on it. I'd cycled more jinsei through it in one day than I had in a year. It was ragged and beaten, and I was about to beat it even harder.

Everything I'd learned since returning from the Five Dragons Challenge clawed up from my memories.

Song's enhanced meditation techniques.

The true power of the Borrowed Core.

The unity of core, aura, and blade.

What I really was.

"You don't understand what you're doing." First stared at me with awe in her eyes. "You can't—"

315

"I will," I said.

I cycled my breath one last time.

Jinsei flooded me. It carried dark aspects along with it that I didn't bother to purge. There was no need. My core was my aura was my blade was my body. The separations I'd been taught were lies that meant nothing to me. I was not an Empyreal or an Eclipse Warrior. I was both, and neither.

I was different.

My Eclipse nature shrieked as it merged with my thoughts, where it belonged. It had never been a separate thing. Its darkness was mine, and I had to accept that truth to reach my full potential.

The Lost rushed toward me when they saw what was coming. They'd imagined I was the start of a new phase for them.

Instead, I was their end.

The beginning of a new age.

"Stop him!" First shrieked.

My aura blazed like a dark sun. For one perfect moment, I saw the Eclipse Warrior half of my soul and the Locust Court half. They fit together, but they were still two pieces only pretending to be whole.

"It's over." I raised my hand and willed the halves to fuse in perfect harmony.

The veil around my core shattered.

And I was born anew.

My ties to the Lost and the hungry spirits empowered me in ways they could never have anticipated. Here, in a world made of nothing but jinsei and tortured, shifting aspects, I was more powerful than all of them combined. The sacred energy flooded into my core, pushing it to its limits and beyond.

And the spirits of the Locust Court unraveled as I consumed their power.

The Lost screamed and fell to their knees as I drained their cores.

And then, when I thought I couldn't absorb any more jinsei, my core advanced in a burst of ecstatic agony.

But even a disciple core couldn't hold all the spiritual power I'd have to drain to kill my enemies.

Fortunately, I now knew I didn't have to.

The Borrowed Core technique speared into Lost and hungry spirits alike. I drained them in an instant and let the jinsei flow into my core and back out again. I no longer had to cycle power. I was an open conduit, and it flowed through me like a raging river. My enemies fell, their bodies disintegrating as I drained their life away. I'd never have been able to do that on Earth, where the laws of reality were stronger and more difficult to bend. There, though, beyond the Far Horizon in a world of madness, my power was absolute.

The air was hazy with the sacred energy that poured out of me. It shimmered like a mirage and burned away like morning mist. My enemies vanished with it until only one remained.

First lay on the ground, her body twisted in on itself. She raised one hand toward me, eyes pleading.

"You don't know what you've done," she whispered. "I loved you, Jace. You were mine before you were born. Tell Eve your mother sends her love."

"You're not my mother."

"Something's coming." First's voice had faded away to almost nothing. "Something worse. Watch the Design, Jace. Watch—"

First's fingernails peeled back and floated away, feathers on the wind. Her skin unraveled down the length of her arm in alabaster ribbons. Blood spilled from her wound, then transformed into black sand that vanished before it hit the ground.

I sagged to my knees and let the tears come.

# THE PLAN

T HE PORTAL DEFENSE FORCE DRAGGED ME OUT of the Locust Court's dying kingdom before it could completely come apart. My friends must have sent them to find me.

I wasn't sure I wanted to be found, but it was easier to go along with them than to fight.

I was so tired.

"Hands up," one of them barked. He held a strange gun with glowing crystals rotating around its barrel. At least it wasn't aimed at me. "Raise your hands. We have to be sure."

I was far too tired and shellshocked to do anything other than what I was told. I held my hands in the air and waited while a pair of white-uniformed guardians seized my arms and wrenched them behind me. I didn't even fight when they slapped handcuffs on me.

It would be stupid to blame them for their caution. There'd been a horrible attack on the five sacred sages, not to mention the clan elders who'd come to view the trial. For all they knew, I was one of the terrorists.

While they secured me, their companions aligned a strange machine with the gate. It reminded me of a telescope, though its long barrel was composed entirely of copper, and it sat atop an enormous faceted gemstone that glowed with jinsei.

"Prepared to fire," a woman next to the device said. "In three…"

I let the guardians guide me away from the portal. It was a relief to let someone else help support me, for once.

"Two."

The PDF troopers marched me toward another portal and into the courtroom. The bodies were gone, though bloodstains and scraps of gore had yet to be cleaned up. I wondered how many had died, how many of the elders we'd lost.

"One."

I glanced over my shoulder as the telescope did its work. A cone of light erupted from the end nearest the portal. A grinding thrumming noise echoed across the Far Horizon as the cone settled over the edges of the gate and slowly, so slowly, pulled them together. And then, there was a faint pop, and the gateway was gone.

"We won't see them again," one of the guards said to me.

"Thank the Flame for that," I sighed.

"Jace?" Abi and my friends had been gathered around Tycho on the same side of the room, talking amongst themselves. "It's him! They found him!"

"This is your friend?" the guard asked. "We found him near the portal. We thought he was one of them."

"No!" Abi shouted. "He needs a medic!"

Eric, Clem, and Rachel rushed to Abi's side as he took me from the other guardians. Their eyes were filled with concern, and they handled me like I was made of glass. I must've looked even worse than I felt.

"Let me get his hands," the guard said, and fumbled with the manacles.

I didn't care what they did to me. I just wanted to lie down.

For, like, a year.

"This way," Rachel said. "There are EMTs."

"I'm fine," I protested, even though I knew I wasn't.

"You're not fine," Clem said. "Let them do their job."

The medical professionals swarmed me the instant I stepped out of the courtroom. Someone pushed a gurney over, and they hoisted me off my feet and laid me down. Someone shoved a stethoscope against my chest, someone else probed my core with a penetrating gaze. Voices shouted medical statuses back and forth.

None of it made any sense.

I was drifting. That was good.

That was fine.

"We'll be there when you wake up," Rachel promised.

My eyes fluttered closed, and I went away for a while.

When I came back, the sun stung my eyes, and I blinked away tears as I shielded my face with my left arm. Which, it turned out, was wrapped in bandages. An IV needle jutted from the back of my hand. Somehow that hurt more than the other aches and pains from every other quarter of my body.

"That was something else, Mr. Warin," Elder Sanrin said. "You've certainly kicked the hornet's nest this time."

"Water," I croaked. My throat felt as dry as desert sand.

"Of course." The elder scooped a pitcher off the nightstand next to my head, poured a small glass, tore a straw from its paper wrapper, and plunked it into the drink. "Just a small sip."

I wanted to gulp the water down all in one go. But when he placed the straw against my lips, it was all I could do to suck in the tiniest of drinks before the effort exhausted me.

"Better," I said, my voice no longer quite so raspy. "How long has it been?"

"Three weeks," Sanrin said. "The school year is almost over, I'm afraid."

"Figures," I said. I'd probably have to repeat Intermediate Scrivening.

Crap.

Sanrin pulled a chair across the room to sit next to my bed. He leaned back, steepled his fingers, and watched me in silence.

"I'm not sure what to do with you, now," he said. "Claude and Brand think we should kill you."

"That's comforting," I said. "Maybe they're right."

I'd defeated the Lost, sealed the portal to the land of the Locust Court, and wiped out legions of hungry spirits. That didn't mean I was safe for anyone to be around.

"Hirani disagrees," Sanrin said. "I do, too, for that matter. It's a split decision, now that we only have four elders."

I winced at that. Elder Ariana hadn't exactly endeared herself to me during our first meeting, but the news of her death still stung. That thought reminded me we weren't out of the woods, yet. First had warned me something else was coming. Something to do with the Empyrean Flame's Grand Design.

"Is it safe to talk here?" I asked Sanrin. "There's something you need to know."

Elder Sanrin flicked his fingers, and a script around the room's ceiling ignited in a burst of jinsei.

"It is, now," he said.

"When I was on the other side, with the Locust Court," I said, "the Lost's leader told me something else is coming. Something big."

"Did they give you any other information?" Sanrin asked, his eyes burrowing into mine.

"I don't know," I said, dejected. "She said to watch the Design, whatever that means."

Sanrin looked down at his steepled fingers for a long moment. As powerful as he was, he seemed smaller to me. His shoulders were slumped, and his head was bowed in concentration. He looked old, tired.

"We'll figure it out," he said at last. "There's still the matter of the heretics to deal with."

"I'm ready," I said. I was dangerous, to myself and others, but this was a lifeline for me. I could do real work for the Shadow Phoenixes.

"I'm not so sure we should do that," Sanrin said. "You're not the same as you were before you went into that portal, Jace."

"I'm stronger," I said. "I'm whole, for the first time. You have no idea what I can do."

"I do not." The Elder leaned forward. "Do you?"

"Not exactly," I admitted.

"And you can't hide what you've become any longer," he said.

"The veil's broken."

"Yes," Sanrin said. "You won't be able to hide from the core detectors. And, let me say, you are quite unique."

"Kind of makes it hard to be a secret agent," I sighed.

Sanrin chuckled and patted my shoulder. He leaned back in his chair and put his feet up on the edge of my bed. When he pinched the bridge of his nose, he reminded me of my mother after a particularly hard day of work. Worn thin by her labor, so exhausted all she wanted to do was lie back and sleep. And knowing it wasn't yet time to rest.

"No, you're fairly distinctive with that core," he said. "And those eyes. Contacts might do something for them, though I'm not sure that's terribly feasible as a long-term solution. You're a rather remarkable person these days, Jace."

The thought of being stuck with those black eyes for the rest of my life was far from thrilling.

I wrestled with telling Sanrin the whole story, though. I didn't know everything about the contingency plan the New Moon sympathizers had put in place. If I was wrong, I'd look awfully foolish.

But, if I was right, we could save a lot of kids from feeling miserable and growing up confused. We might even be able to stop the Lost from coming back.

"I'm not unique," I said. "I think there are others like me."

That got Sanrin's attention. He pursed his lips and stroked his beard.

"That is an interesting piece of news," he said at last. "Care to elaborate?"

"The Eclipse Warriors," I started. "Not all the Empyreals agreed that they should be murdered."

"It was a very contentious decision," the elder said. "The five sages and the Council of Dragons eventually decided they were too dangerous to keep around. I imagine from your earlier statement that you agree with that sentiment."

"Yes," I said. "And no. I mean, the Eclipse Warriors are incredibly dangerous. The things they can do are straight out of a nightmare. But if there's something dangerous headed our way, couldn't we use more people like me?"

"That is a question that borders on the heretical, young man," Sanrin said. "The Empyrean Flame agreed with the destruction of our weapon at the end of the Utter War. Why would it have done that if we would need them in the future?"

"I don't know," I said. "But we still need to find anyone else like me. The Lost, if there are any of them left, can use them to return. Like they did with me."

Sanrin and I chewed on the problem until he leaned forward with his head in his hands.

"I'm too tired to make sense of this," Sanrin said. "If there are others like you, how would we find them?"

"I think I know someone who could help," I said.

# THE FAREWELL

THERE WERE STILL A FEW DAYS OF SCHOOL LEFT when the doctors got tired of my whining and released me from the Shadow Phoenix hospital. Other than a headache that seemed destined to stick around for a while, I'd mostly recovered. I had some wicked new scars on my arms from my fights with assassins and the Lost and an ugly patch of discolored skin on my stomach that no amount of jinsei had been able to fix. None of the doctors knew what had caused that damage, and I wasn't going to tell them the truth.

That was the mark I'd earned when I fused my core. I was sort of glad it was still there. It reminded me that I was more than I thought I'd ever be. And of the price I'd paid for that power.

"Look who it is," Clem said as I joined them in the breakfast line. "If it isn't the hero of Kyoto."

"As if." I chuckled. "The freak of Kyoto is more like it."

Abi glanced at me, then shook his head. He put one arm around my shoulder and pulled me close to his side.

"All heroes change," he said. "They are marked by their experiences. You are no different, my friend. You've seen things most cannot even imagine. Your eyes will now tell that tale for you, so you will not have to speak of it."

That was a surprisingly profound way to look at things, and it wasn't what I'd expected from Abi. I'd worried he'd be afraid of me, afraid of the darkness that had taken root inside me. He wouldn't be the only one.

Stories about the Eclipse Warrior terrorist attack had spread to the news like wildfire while I was laid up in my clan's secret hospital. I'd spent a lot of time worrying about what people would think when they saw my eyes after that. Even without the attack, all-black eyes were pretty freaky.

"Thanks," I said. "I just wish it wasn't quite so scary."

"Who would be scared of you?" Eric said with a smirk. "You're a big old teddy bear."

"This teddy bear's got fangs and claws," Hagar said from behind us. "I wouldn't want to be on his bad side."

My handler looked like she'd been through the ringer. One side of her head was bandaged beneath the shock of red hair that ran down the center of her skull. Both of her eyes were ringed by shadowy bruises, and she was still on crutches.

"You look like you recovered all right," I said and made some space for her in the line. "Let's get you some breakfast."

"Sounds like a plan," she said. "I'm so hungry I could eat a whole pig."

"You'll fit right in here, then," Clem said with a grin.

She and I worked together to get Hagar a heaping tray of bacon and sausage, a trio of fried eggs, and what looked like half a loaf of heavily buttered toast. I carried the warden's tray back to our table, and the five of us all sat down together.

"Sounds like Grayson's going to recover," Eric said. "The spirits almost got him, but I guess sages are tougher than they look."

"He might have survived, but I wonder if he really wanted to," Clem said. "From what I read he'll be laid up for months. The Locust Court did a real number on him. Siegfried didn't fare much better. Both the Suns and the Titans will be without their sages for a while, now."

"I'm just glad we all made it," I said. "You guys really shouldn't have come to Kyoto, you know."

"It's a good thing we did," Abi said. "Otherwise, you wouldn't have been around to save the world."

That was true, though I didn't like to admit it.

"You cut it awfully close," I said. "But, thank you. I really couldn't have done it without you guys."

"We know," Clem said with a grin. "If it hadn't been for me and Rachel, Abi would never have found you."

"So, what did Eric do?" I said, nudging my friend with an elbow.

"Look good for the cameras," he said. "Somebody had to talk to the press, and it sure couldn't have been any of you three."

Abi and Clem glanced at one another, then stared at Eric with openmouthed surprise.

"What's wrong with how I look?" Clem said.

"Other than the fact that you're the color of cotton candy?" Eric shot back. "And Abi's so serious he'd depress everyone. They needed a pretty face, like mine, to lighten the mood. Keep people from freaking out."

The rest of breakfast passed easily, and I felt my mood lifting. Hagar was the first to leave the table, and Eric offered to help her with her tray. Abi left not long after, saying he had to report for Portal Defense Force duty. That left Clem and me alone, and we fidgeted with our food in the awkward silence.

"I was really scared," Clem confided in me. "When Abi came and found us after you'd gone to Kyoto, I didn't know what would happen. I didn't know what I'd do if…"

She let the words trail off and stared down at her plate. Her hands trembled on the table.

"I'm sorry I put you through that," I said. "There wasn't time to think. I was the only one who could stop them."

"I know," Clem said, her voice strained. She sniffed, then lowered her utensils to the table.

"I didn't want any of you to get hurt," I said. It was my turn for my throat to tighten. "That was my fight, not yours."

"You should've," Clem started, then shook her head. She looked up at me, her cheeks streaked with tears. "You could have told me. About what was happening to you."

"I had to keep it a secret," I said, my voice low. "No one knew. Not even my clan elders. Hahen warned me that if anyone found out, it would be the end for me and everyone else who knew about my secret."

Clem chewed at the inside of her lip. A single tear rolled down her face and splashed onto the edge of her plate.

"I wouldn't have told anyone," she said. "I would've helped you. Somehow."

"Clem," I said, trying to placate her, "it's not that easy. People died to keep me safe. The Eclipse Warriors didn't care about anyone around me. If you'd known, they might have killed you. And I—no. I couldn't live with that."

"Me, either," Clem said, forcing a smile. She reached across the table, took my hand, and squeezed my fingers tight. "We made it, though. But if you ever lie to me again, you won't."

I laughed.

"I won't," I said. "No more secrets. No more lies."

"Good," she said. She took her hand back and sawed off a big bite of pancake with her fork.

"Hey, guys," Rachel said as she slipped in next to Clem. "You look terrible, Jace."

"You don't like it?" I asked. "I thought black eyes was the hot new style these days."

"Hardly," Clem said. "Let me give you guys some space."

"No," Rachel said, her hand closed over Clem's. "Don't go. I want you to hear this, too."

"Okay," Clem agreed. She took another bite of her pancakes to hide her embarrassment, then glanced away.

"I'm leaving the School," Rachel said.

"No," I said. "You worked so hard to get here. If it's because of me I'll—"

"Not everything's about you," Rachel said with a snort. "Though this kind of actually is."

Clem raised an eyebrow in my direction, then nudged Rachel with an elbow.

"Don't keep us in suspense here. What happened?"

"I got a job offer," Rachel said. "Working with kids in the undercities. There's a new outreach program the Shadow Phoenix clan put together. The School of Swords and Serpents will have annexes all over the world to help find promising new students. Elder Sanrin said someone recommended me as an ambassador. So, technically, I guess I'm still going to school here, just not here here."

"That's clear as mud," I said.

"Don't pretend you weren't the one who suggested me to your clan elders," Rachel said with a grin. "Not that I'm not happy to do it. It'll give kids a chance to get a good education without getting their butts beat in the Five Dragons Challenge."

"If somebody had practiced their martial arts, their fight might have gone differently," I said.

"I think we both know that's probably not true," Rachel said. "Somebody had advantages the rest of us didn't."

Her words stung more than I knew she intended, and I struggled to keep the pain off my face. No one knew everything I'd been through, not even my closest friends.

"Point taken," I said. "When do you leave?"

"After the last day of classes," Rachel said. "I'll be porting over to Dallas for three months. Then London. I'm not sure what's after that."

Rachel looked at me, a faint, sad smile on her lips. She started to say something, stopped, and found something interesting on the back of her thumbnail. After a few seconds of awkward silence, she reached over and held my hand. Gingerly, as if she were afraid touching me might hurt.

"I just wanted to thank you for this," she said to me. "It really is perfect for me. I'll finally have a chance to be myself and show other kids there's a better way. They can be themselves and still make it."

"I don't know what you're talking about." I feigned ignorance. "But congratulations again."

"Yeah," Rachel said. She stood, leaned across the table, and gave me a quick peck on the cheek. "Take care of yourself, Jace."

She left us without another word, and I felt a searing jolt of loss. I wished things could have gone differently. I wished I hadn't lost control in the library and nearly killed Rachel. But, without those experiences, I wouldn't have been able to make the right choice at the end of the day. Whether she knew it or not, Rachel had helped me save the world.

"She'll never get over you," Clem said quietly.

"I think she already has," I corrected. "I think she's been over me for a while."

"About the library?"

"I scared her half to death," I said. "I lost control. There's no telling what might've happened."

"You scared her?" Clem scoffed. "That's not why she ran."

"She told you about that?" It was bad enough that I'd scared Rachel. It was infinitely worse that Clem knew the gory details.

"We were friends. I mean, we still are," Clem said. "She scared herself, Jace."

"That doesn't make any sense. She didn't do anything," I said.

"When you went all Eclipse Warrior on her, that was scary," she said. "But what scared Rachel wasn't that you slipped. It was that she liked the darkness she saw in you."

"That's not—"

"It is," Clem confirmed. "You should remember that the next time you decide to hide yourself from your friends. You're not as scary as you think you are."

Clem leaned forward and brushed my lips with hers. Then she picked up her tray and walked away.

# THE NEWS

THE *MANUAL OF THE NEW MOON* WAS MISSING from my desk. I'd tucked it into the top drawer after I'd gotten out of the hospital and forgot about it until the last day of school. It just didn't seem all that important anymore. I wasn't really one of them, and my history wasn't the same as theirs.

I was rooting around for it in the closet when I heard footsteps on the stairs.

"Who's there?" I called. The last person who'd arrived in my cottage without knocking was an assassin.

"Elder Hirani," a melodious voice answered. "I hope I'm not disturbing you."

"Not at all, honored Elder," I said. "I was looking for something. Gathering up my stuff to move back into the regular dorms."

"Ah," Hirani said. "Your time as the School champion has come to an end. How did they pick one this year?"

"The headmistress did it based on grades," I said. "Not a terribly popular opinion, especially since it had nothing to do with fighting ability. The Five Dragons Challenge is going to be very interesting this year."

"Anyone you know?" she asked.

"Nope," I said. "A fourth year, I guess. Should be a bigger batch of new initiates next year, though."

Eclipse Core: School of Swords and Serpents

We both had a laugh at that, and Hirani's voice sent shivers down my spine. She possessed an ageless, effortless beauty that was enthralling. Spending time with her made me feel warm and giddy.

Also nervous. She was, after all, one of my clan's four elders.

"I have news for you," she said. "Let's have some coffee, and we can talk about it."

"My mother?" My heart leaped into my throat.

"Coffee," Hirani said. "Then talk."

I followed the elder downstairs and sat at the kitchen table while she busied herself with the coffee set. After filling the pot with water and setting it on to boil, she glanced in my direction.

"Does it always take this long?" she asked, deadly serious. "It feels like it's taking a very long time for this water to get hot."

"Well, yes," I said. "It's not a quick process."

"Oh, for Flame's sake." She snapped her fingers and a pair of mugs filled with steaming coffee appeared on the table in front of me. "Don't tell Sanrin. He hates that trick."

"How did you do that?" I'd never seen anyone make something out of nothing. As far as I knew it violated all kinds of metaphysical laws.

"Somewhere in France, there is a very angry couple who want to know why their French press was not delivered to their room." Hirani's smile reminded me of a cat's feral grin. "Like I said, don't tell."

I hid my urgency to continue our conversation behind a sip of coffee from the mug. It really was delicious.

"You were saying you had news," I prodded.

"Yes." Hirani's brows furrowed. She put her coffee on the table and reached out to squeeze my hands. "We've found your mother."

"When do I get to see her?" It had been more than a year since I'd heard my mother's voice. The thought of seeing her again brought a lump to my throat.

"It's not that easy." The elder leaned so close to me I could smell the coffee on her breath. "She was in the data you pulled from the heretics. She's with them, Jace."

"No way." I shook my head. Despite the nonsense that First had told me about my mother and the Eclipse Theory, I didn't believe she was a mad scientist. It was just one more way the Lost had tried to turn me. "My mother would never side with those lunatics."

"The intel is solid, Jace." Hirani shook her head. "I'm sorry. We're not sure why she went over. Our hookups say it was last year sometime—"

"It's my fault," I said. "I crossed Tycho, and he threatened my family. I warned her, and she ran."

"When?" Hirani's eyes were calm and comforting. Staring into them eased the knot of tension that had taken root in my gut.

"It was before the holidays." I remembered that day like it was yesterday. How angry I'd been. How stupid.

"Then it wasn't your fault." Hirani let out a sigh of relief. "She joined the Machina Project in October. Not long after you started class here."

A chill settled over me. My mother, who First claimed had been instrumental in the New Moon resurgence plan. My mother, who was a better fighter than she had any right to be. My mother, a camper who knew at least two of the sacred sages on a first-name basis.

"What do we do now?" I asked, knuckles whitening around my coffee mug.

"She's important to them," Hirani said. "They'll have her under close guard. She's brilliant. The Machina you stole was her work."

"What do we do now?" I asked again. I had to know.

"We have to stop the project," Hirani said as gently as possible. "The Machina were built to interfere with the Grand Design. They warp jinsei and distort probabilities. The models they have now are unpredictable and as dangerous to them as to their enemies, but they're getting close to a breakthrough. We can't let that happen."

"You'll kill her." The words tasted like acid on my tongue.

Hirani took my mug and placed it gently on the table. She pulled me into a hug and held me tight.

"No, no, no," she whispered. "We'll save her, Jace. And you'll help us do it."

"When?" My eyes burned and my throat was clogged with emotion. I hadn't ever really known my mother, and that hurt.

"Soon." Hirani kissed the top of my head. A surge of warmth and calm passed through me, and she held me back at arm's length. "We'll get her out of there, Jace. I promise you that. And you'll be there when it happens."

I don't know how long we stayed like that, and I wished it could have gone on forever. Despite Hirani's incredible power and status, she had a comforting aura that made it easier for me to relax. I'd realized the only time I truly felt safe was with her.

"I have to go," she whispered and stroked my hair. "But I have one more piece of news for you. Go to the stacks. An old friend is waiting for you."

# THE MENTOR

SOMEONE HAD REPLACED THE BAR MY ECLIPSE nature had shattered. The stout wooden beam stood beside the door to the stacks like a silent sentinel. The sight of it raised my hackles and triggered my Borrowed Core technique. I cycled my breathing and filled my aura with bestial aspects before I pulled the door open and crossed its threshold. If there was any trouble waiting on the other side, I'd be able to summon my serpents and attack in the blink of an eye.

"Hello?" I called when no one tried to kill me. The stacks were still empty, the dust on the floor disturbed only by my footsteps from earlier in the year. "Who's here?"

"An old friend," a familiar voice called from deeper in the chamber. A silver ball of jinsei appeared in the air.

Tycho Reyes stood on the far side of the room, one hand raised defensively. He looked much worse than he had the last time I'd seen him. Bandages covered the left side of his face, including a bloody bit of gauze over his eye. His robes were very plain, adorned only by scorch marks and what could have been bloodstains. He looked more like a homeless beggar than one of the five sacred sages.

"You're no friend of mine," I spat. Despite his ragged appearance, I couldn't find any shreds of kindness for Tycho in my heart. He'd conspired to ruin my life and destroy the world. He could burn for all I cared. "How did you convince Elder Hirani to get your message to me?"

"He didn't," Hahen said as he appeared from the shadows. "I did. You need to hear this, Jace."

The rat spirit and Tycho advanced toward me, stirring up dust, which billowed up around them like thunderclouds. Tycho's core was dim, as if badly injured, and the weight of his attention was no greater than a feather against my aura. I doubted he was capable of an attack in his current condition.

"That's close enough," I called when they were a few yards away. I didn't see any reason to take chances. "Say whatever you have to say and leave me alone."

"If being alone is what you want, then I'm sad to say you will be very disappointed in your future," Tycho said with a chuckle that quickly turned into a ragged cough. "You undid the work of a very many powerful people, Jace, and not all of them will forgive as quickly as I have."

"Maybe powerful people should ask people for help instead of trying to force us onto the paths they want for us," I said. "You've got five minutes, and then I'm heading back to the School. I'm sure there are a lot of people who'd like to talk to you here."

"I'm sure you're right," Tycho said. "Thanks to Sanrin—"

"Elder Sanrin," I corrected.

"Yes, him," Tycho continued, "I'm a fugitive. As you can see from my current condition, that status has not treated me kindly."

"They should have killed you." I shrugged. "You conspired to bring the Lost back to destroy the world."

"Not destroy it," Tycho sighed. "Save it. The Grand Design is flawed, Jace. It will create ripples in the ether, and those will grow to waves, and they will come crashing back on us. But we can still stop that. If you listen to me—"

"No," I snapped. "Not another word out of you. You used me, and it almost ruined my life. You made yourself rich off my pain, and you nearly got me and everyone else killed with your plans. I'm done listening to you. Whatever you've got to say will be weighed by the adjudicators when they catch you."

Tycho glared at me. For a moment, I wondered if he'd attack me. Then he looked away and sighed.

"Foolish boy," he said. "I made you a king, and you threw away the crown. Very well, if you refuse to listen, I cannot afford to waste any more time on you. Come, Hahen—"

"No," I snarled. "He's not your slave anymore. He stays here."

Tycho's left hand flashed out, and a coil of jinsei looped around Hahen's throat. The rat spirit squeaked in surprise and his feet left the floor as the sage hauled him into the air by his neck.

"Enough." My serpents appeared and flashed through the air faster than I could see. The tendrils of beast-aspected jinsei seized Hahen's noose and drained it away to nothing in the space of a heartbeat. I caught the rat spirit in the coils of my serpent and gently lowered him to the ground.

"How dare you." Tycho advanced toward me, his hands raised.

"I'll kill you," I said. My serpents coiled in the air above me, their heads weaving, ready to strike.

"Such promise, squandered," Tycho said. He raised his hands and stepped back. "I am too weak to deal with you at the moment, boy. But there will come a time when you will pay for this pathetic victory."

"Get out," I said. I wasn't sure I could kill Tycho and didn't want to risk my life in a fight against a sage. Even weakened as he was, Tycho had centuries of experience and tricks up his sleeve.

"As you wish." Tycho bowed and stepped into the shadows.

"Thank you." Hahen rubbed his throat. "You've made a powerful enemy this day, Jace. That you did it on my behalf puts me deeply into your debt."

"No," I said. "You owe me nothing, honored Spirit. You are my friend, even if my choices disappointed you. And I don't tally my friend's debts."

"That is a refreshing change." The rat spirit chuckled. "Then allow me to continue your training. The world is in danger, and it needs you. Now more than ever."

# THE REVIVAL

WHEN THE LAST DAY OF THE SCHOOL YEAR arrived, I still wasn't sure what I would do over the summer. I didn't have any home to go back to, and spending three months in this old building with no one but the staff and Hahen to keep me company wasn't my idea of fun. I could meditate, sure, cycle my jinsei and try to push my core from disciple to artist. Very few people, not even graduates of the School of Swords and Serpents, made it to that level. The majority spent their lives as adepts, much more powerful than your average person, but a far, far cry from the strength of the sages.

But a whole summer of that? When I was about to turn sixteen?

No, that didn't sound like any fun at all.

To distract myself from that bleak prospect, I rounded up my friends and dragged them out to the beach for one last afternoon of fun. We played volleyball, chased each other through the surf, and cooked hot dogs we'd stolen from the kitchen over a driftwood fire. When the sun was low on the horizon, I called them all over to me.

"What is it?" Clem asked as they gathered.

"I've been working on something," I said. Hahen had opened my eyes to new ways of using my abilities.

343

"A new technique. One that builds off what I've learned since Kyoto."

"Look at Mr. Disciple over here," Eric said. "Showing off."

I pointed at a patch of strange crystallized sand and blackened grass.

"I did this when I came back to school at the beginning of the year," I said. "Stripped the aspects and jinsei out of the earth. I nearly lost control."

"You're killing me with the suspense," Clem said. "What is it you want to show us?"

"This," I said.

I closed my eyes and took a deep breath, and a rush of jinsei poured into my core. It brought with it the natural aspects of my surroundings: growth, life, plants, beast, and vitality. There were more, but those five were the most important aspects, and the most dominant. Taking them in this way wasn't the same as when I stripped them with Borrowed Core. It was like the difference between ripping leaves off a tree and picking up those that had already fallen to the ground.

I let out a long, slow breath and pushed the aspects out of my aura toward the blighted patch at my feet.

It was slow at first. I was doing the exact opposite of what my Eclipse core had specialized in, and the effort of creation was far greater than the effort of destruction. Beads of sweat burst from my forehead as I pushed against the fabric of reality. The world didn't like having its authority challenged.

And I didn't care.

One aspect at a time, I put the jigsaw puzzle back together. The world slowed to a crawl as I forced the aspects to fit where they'd once belonged. And then...

"By the Flame," Clem whispered.

The black was gone. The grass was lush and green and six inches taller than it had been. There was no sign of sand or dead earth anywhere around us.

"How?" Abi asked, his voice thick with emotion.

"The Eclipse core could drain jinsei from the environment or people," I explained. "It's so powerful it shreds the aspects from wherever it gets the jinsei. That's why they were so powerful against the Locust Court. They not only drained the power out of the spirits' cores, they destroyed the aspects that made up their bodies."

"That explains how you killed the grass in the first place, not how you fixed it," Clem said.

"It's like cycling." I took a deep breath of jinsei-laden air. "You pull the energy in, but the aspects get stuck in your aura until you can cleanse them. You exhale, and those aspects go back out into the world, leaving your core with clean, pure jinsei. The only difference is, I can move a lot of aspects out of my aura at the same time. And I can tell them where to go."

"That's incredible," Eric said, his voice low and shaky. "You just... I can't believe this. That grass was dead. And now it's alive. I'd say it was impossible if I hadn't seen it for myself."

"You have to tell someone about this, Jace," Abi said. "What will you do with such a power?"

I considered the question for a moment. I'd started my life as a camper with a broken core, the lowest among the low. I'd fought so hard to make my way into the School, only to be treated like dirt. And, now, I'd saved everyone and become a hero.

There was really only one thing left for me to do.

"Change the world," I said quietly.

Gage Lee

# BOOKS, MAILING LIST, AND REVIEWS

If you enjoyed reading about Jace and the rest of the gang in *Eclipse Core* and want to stay in the loop about the latest book releases, awesome promotional deals, and upcoming book giveaways be sure to subscribe to our email list at:

**www.ShadowAlleyPress.com**

Word-of-mouth and book reviews are crazy helpful for the success of any writer. If you *really* enjoyed reading *Eclipse Core*, please consider leaving a short, honest review—just a couple of lines about your overall reading experience. Thank you in advance!

# ABOUT THE AUTHOR

Gage Lee is a long-time fan of wuxia, cultivation, fantasy, and science fiction stories. The School of Swords and Serpents combines all his favorite genres, along with a healthy helping of seasoning from his years as an avid gamer. To follow his exploits, and get a sneak peek of what's coming down the authorial pipeline, visit www.gagelee.com.

# BOOKS BY SHADOW ALLEY PRESS

If you enjoyed *Eclipse Core*, you might also enjoy other awesome stories from Shadow Alley Press, such as Viridian Gate Online, Rogue Dungeon, the Yancy Lazarus Series, or the Jubal Van Zandt Series. You can find all of our books listed at www.ShadowAlleyPress.com.

### James A. Hunter
Viridian Gate Online: Cataclysm (Book 1)
Viridian Gate Online: Crimson Alliance (Book 2)
Viridian Gate Online: The Jade Lord (Book 3)
Viridian Gate Online: The Imperial Legion (Book 4)
Viridian Gate Online: The Lich Priest (Book 5)
Viridian Gate Online: Doom Forge (Book 6)

⊥

Viridian Gate Online: The Artificer (Imperial Initiative)
Viridian Gate Online: Nomad Soul (Illusionist 1)
Viridian Gate Online: Dead Man's Tide (Illusionist 2)
Viridian Gate Online: Inquisitor's Foil (Illusionist 3)
Viridian Gate Online: Firebrand (Firebrand 1)

Gage Lee

Viridian Gate Online: Embers of Rebellion (Firebrand 2)
Viridian Gate Online: Path of the Blood Phoenix (Firebrand 3)
Viridian Gate Online: Vindication (The Alchemic Weaponeer 1)
Viridian Gate Online: Absolution (The Alchemic Weaponeer 2)

Rogue Dungeon (Book 1)
Rogue Dungeon: Civil War (Book 2)
Rogue Dungeon: Troll Nation (Book 3)

Strange Magic: Yancy Lazarus Episode One
Cold Heatred: Yancy Lazarus Episode Two
Flashback: Siren Song (Episode 2.5)
Wendigo Rising: Yancy Lazarus Episode Three
Flashback: The Morrigan (Episode 3.5)
Savage Prophet: Yancy Lazarus Episode Four
Brimstone Blues: Yancy Lazarus Episode Five

MudMan: A Lazarus World Novel

Two Faced: Legend of the Treesinger (Book 1)
Soul Game: Legend of the Treesinger (Book 2)

**eden Hudson**

Eclipse Core: School of Swords and Serpents

Revenge of the Bloodslinger: A Jubal Van Zandt Novel
Beautiful Corpse: A Jubal Van Zandt Novel
Soul Jar: A Jubal Van Zandt Novel
Garden of Time: A Jubal Van Zandt Novel
Wasteside: A Jubal Van Zandt Novel

Darkening Skies (Path of the Thunderbird 1)
Stone Soul (Path of the Thunderbird 2)
Demon Beast (Path of the Thunderbird 3)

**Gage Lee**

Hollow Core (School of Swords and Serpents Book 1)
Eclipse Core (School of Swords and Serpents Book 2)

**Aaron Ritchey**

Armageddon Girls (The Juniper Wars 1)
Machine-Gun Girls (The Juniper Wars 2)
Inferno Girls (The Juniper Wars 3)
Storm Girls (The Juniper Wars 4)

Sages of the Underpass (Battle Artists Book 1)

# BOOKS FROM BLACK FORGE

Looking for valiant heroes and dangerous women?
Check out the adventure stories from Black Forge, such
as War God's Mantle, American Dragons, Dungeon
Bringer, Witch King, or Full Frontal Galaxy. You can
find all of our books listed at
www.BlackForgeBooks.com.

**Aaron Crash**

War God's Mantle: Ascension (Book 1)
War God's Mantle: Descent (Book 2)
War God's Mantle: Underworld (Book 3)

American Dragons: Denver Fury (Book 1)
American Dragons: Cheyenne Magic (Book 2)
American Dragons: Montana Firestorm (Book 3)
American Dragons: Texas Showdown (Book 4)
American Dragons: California Imperium (Book 5)
American Dragons: Dodge City Knights (Book 6)
American Dragons: Leadville Crucible (Book 7)
American Dragons: Alaska Kingdom (Book 8)

Eclipse Core: School of Swords and Serpents

American Dragons: Alamosa Arena (Book 9)

⏚

Robot Bangarang (Full Frontal Galaxy Book 1)
Space Dragon Boogaloo (Full Frontal Galaxy Book 2)

## Nick Harrow

Dungeon Bringer 1
Dungeon Bringer 2
Dungeon Bringer 3

⏚

Witch King 1
Witch King 2
Witch King 3

Made in United States
Troutdale, OR
12/08/2024